ROGUE

ROGUE

FREDERICK RAMSAY

W☉RLDWIDE®

TORONTO • NEW YORK • LONDON
AMSTERDAM • PARIS • SYDNEY • HAMBURG
STOCKHOLM • ATHENS • TOKYO • MILAN
MADRID • WARSAW • BUDAPEST • AUCKLAND

Recycling programs for this product may not exist in your area.

Rogue

A Worldwide Mystery/May 2018

First published by Poisoned Pen Press

ISBN-13: 978-1-335-50656-6

Copyright © 2011 by Frederick Ramsay

Printed in U.S.A.

To the Rev. Philip Burwell Roulette.
He will deny it, but he was the first of The Six.

INTRODUCTION

As always, I wish to thank the staff at Poisoned Pen Press for their patience and flexibility in making this book a reality. I would name them all, but fear I will forget one or two and/or get them out of sequence and, well, you can see how it might go. I do need to thank Barbara Peters and Annette Rogers, whose scolding, suggestions, and occasional application of pruning shears helped turn this into a readable and, I hope, enjoyable book. Also a quick thanks to Glenda Sibley for her attention to detail, and to my wife Susan who, in spite of being immersed in studying Hebrew, still found time to occasionally pat me on the head and give me an "atta boy" when I needed one.

Research into the activity on the cerebral cortex in patients with insulted or injured brains is fascinating and complex, as well as confusing. That people in comatose states occasionally hear and attempt to respond to verbal stimuli from the world outside their perceptive capabilities has been well documented. It is less certain whether those responses are in the form of linear thinking, or dreams, or something else entirely. But it is clear that voices are sometimes heard and at least some, perhaps all, of the content of the speech, recalled. In any case, do not expect authoritative, exact, or even insightful science from this fiction writer. It's a story.

Finally, one comment and one caveat.

In certain parts of the Mid-Atlantic States, an apparatus designed to cut grass and fitted with a motor of some sort, is often referred to as a power mower. The caveat: As Spencer Tracy said to Katherine Hepburn on the roof of an anonymous building in New York in the movie, *Desk Set*, "Never assume."

And on those obscure notes, I hope you will enjoy the folks in Picketsville as they sort themselves out during an election year, contemplate an atypical series of murders, and worry over the health of one of their own. And while you're at it, soak up the spectacular colors that the hardwood forests of the Shenandoah Valley of Virginia provide every fall.

Frederick Ramsay, 2011

rogue (rōg)
    Noun: A wandering beggar or tramp; a vagabond, a rascal; a scoundrel, a fun-loving, mischievous person; a lion, elephant, or other animal that wanders apart from the herd and is fierce and wild; an individual varying markedly from the standard; a police officer or other authority operating outside his jurisdiction.

ONE

COLD RAIN PELTED the windows as the first of October's storms powered across the nation's capitol, leaving fallen tree limbs and electrical outages in its wake. Inside, away from the cold and wind, the room brightened periodically as lightning struck somewhere, close or far. The rumble of thunder followed at varying intervals, its volume muted by triple glazing. Inside, except for the lightning flashes, the hospital room remained dark and eerily quiet. In this antiseptic cave, only the soft rhythmic beeping from the monitor in the corner, the wheeze and gurgle from the ventilator, and an irregular, soft clack from the IV regulator broke the near silence. Soft light illuminated a single bed and its occupant. With her shattered left leg elevated, her mouth obscured by the ventilator, a neck brace, and her head swathed in bandages, Ruth Harris would be recognizable only by those who knew her well enough to recognize her eyes.

But they were closed.

Charlie Garland shuffled his feet and did his best to ignore the pervading odor of disinfectant. He disliked hospitals and everything they represented—pain, fear, and death. He had but rarely visited one during a happy occasion, the birth of a child, the recovery from a serious illness. As a bachelor with no immediate family, those moments did not often fall to him. But this night he was oblivious to the sounds in the room and those outside. His concerns were focused on his friends: the deathly pale woman in the bed and a perfectly healthy Ike Schwartz.

Ike stood at the foot of the bed, as if carved from gray New England granite, eyes red-rimmed, weary, and fixed on Ruth. Charlie shifted his gaze away from the green lines that snaked hypnotically across the monitor's screen and directed it toward Ike. He reached out and touched his raincoat sleeve, still damp after four hours indoors.

"Ike? You should get some rest. There is nothing more we can do here tonight. You need sleep."

Ike did not move or speak. Charlie didn't really expect that he would. He could only imagine the pain Ike felt. Five years previously, Eloise, Ike's wife of a hundred days, had died in his arms, a victim of an errant assassin's bullet. It had taken him three years to begin to put that behind him. The woman who now lay deathly still in the bed had been in large part responsible for his recovery, for his reentry into life, as it were. Charlie feared this could end as very bad déjà vu.

"She can't die, Charlie," Ike said, his voice husky, uncertain.

"No, Ike, she can't."

They spoke as if somehow they could, by sheer exercise of their will, assume control of the physiological events taking place in Ruth's broken body. Charlie realized that, indeed, if he could, he would. The IV drip clacked as if to disabuse him of this presumption.

It is bad enough to lose one person you love to mindless violence, but two? Ike, he feared, may have had enough. And Ike said it, she can't die. God only knows what Ike must be thinking.

"Ike, we should go."

Again, Ike did not move.

A tired looking nurse wearing rumpled purple scrubs and sporting a disordered blonde-going-to-gray pony-tail slipped into the room.

"Gentlemen, I have to ask you to leave. I have to change some dressings and check the patient's cathe-ter." She paused and peered at Ike. "It is past two a.m. and time to shut this down for now. You can come back in the morning."

Ike did not budge.

"We have your contact information, sir. I promise I will call you if there is any change in Ms. Harris' con-dition." She spoke in a voice worn smooth from saying those words many, perhaps too many times. "Now you really must leave."

"Ike," Charlie took him by the arm and turned him so that he faced away from the bed, "Ike, we have to go. Let me buy you a cup of coffee and then we'll eat some-thing, rest up and be back first thing in the morning."

"She can't die, Charlie."

"No, Ike, she can't and she won't. Come on. Nurse…" Charlie squinted in the dim light to read the nurse's name tag, "…Nurse Annie Struthers will call you if there's any change."

The nurse graced him with a ghost of a smile and nodded, then stepped to the bed. She reached for the draw drapes and proceeded to close them, blocking their view. That seemed to break the spell that had Ike frozen in place. He nodded and allowed Charlie to lead him out into the hall and to the elevators.

"Coffee and breakfast," Charlie said.

"Okay, but first we go to the precinct station and ask for a copy of the accident report. If Ruth lost control of the car, I want to know where, when, and how. She had a lead foot, Charlie, but she drove like she might have taught Driver's Ed. Accidents did not happen to her."

"Okay, accident report, then food, then sleep."

THE BEEFY DESK sergeant seemed singularly unresponsive to Ike's request.

"Who are you, and why should I give you a copy of an accident report? It's official police business. You a lawyer or something?"

Charlie saw the muscles in Ike's jaw flicker and hoped he wouldn't pop off to this thick Metro cop. He wouldn't blame him—enough was enough. Ike's jaw muscles flexed and then relaxed.

"As it happens I am, but that is not why I'm asking. It concerns my fiancée. I want to know what happened."

"You think that's going to work? Look, trust us to do our job, okay? And if you're thinking about lawsuits, you'll have to go through channels to get the report."

Ike drew in a breath and let it out slowly. One… two…three…four… "Okay, Sarge, how about you give it to me as an act of professional courtesy." Ike slid his badge across the scarred desk surface.

The cop peered myopically at it and smirked. "Wee-hah, a sheriff. Where's your posse, Sheriff? Listen, this ain't the Wild West, Bunky. Go through channels."

Charlie had, in the not too distant past, witnessed his friend at work in the field. So, before Ike could reach across the desk and land the punch that he knew could cause some serious dental mayhem, he stepped between both men and dropped his CIA ID on the table next to Ike's badge.

"How about we try this," he said. "You make a copy of that report right now, this minute, or I make a call. I do that and this house goes into twenty-four/seven lockdown until our friends from the Hoover Building discover which of your compadres is leaking information to a local terrorist cell about the routes the president's car takes."

"What the hell. You can't do that. There's nobody in this precinct that has any access to that kind of information."

"There, you see? The very fact you know that convinces me that there really is a leak. Now, do I make the call to the FBI, or do you surrender a copy of the accident report to my friend here?"

"Son of a—"

"Tsk, none of that, now, Sergeant. Think of yourself as a dedicated advocate of the Freedom of Information Act who was happy to accommodate Sheriff Schwartz. Who knows, someday he may pull your chestnuts out of the fire and you will be happy he is a friend of yours."

"Yeah, and I'm Matthew McConaughey." Moments later the Sergeant handed Ike the report. "Okay, on your way, Cowboy."

Ike skimmed the report and fixed the cop with a look that could etch glass.

"What kind of bullshit is this? There are no witness statements. No site analysis—skid marks, speed estimates. Who ran up this piece of crap?"

"Look buddy, we had a slick street, the car was wrapped around a utility pole, it's raining cats and dogs, and it's dark as an outhouse at midnight. What else is there to know? The driver lost control, the car skidded and slammed into the pole, end of story."

"If your guys were working for me, they'd be back out there at that accident scene and wouldn't come in again until they either caught pneumonia and died, or filed a complete report."

"Right. Happy trails, Sheer-if."

The two left and found an open Denny's. Charlie ate breakfast. One of life's absolutes—Denny's might be a major contributor to the nation's dangerously elevated cholesterol levels, but they knew how to do breakfast. Ike sipped his coffee and, when he'd sufficiently cooled down, began to read. At three thirty a.m. Ike slammed the report against the table, stood, and headed for the door.

"I need to see the car."

"Ike, it's too early, the facility where they towed the car will be locked up tight, and you haven't touched your food. Besides what can you see in the dark?"

"They screwed this up, Charlie. Come on. We'll find a way to take a peek."

"No we won't. Sit down. We'll eat, rest a bit, and when they open at eight, go visit your car."

Frustrated, Ike slumped back in the booth, his eye glued to the clock over the order pickup window while a perfectly good Grand Slam cooled and congealed before him.

TWO

CHARLIE COULD NOT hold Ike in place. The manager at Denny's had not minded them occupying a booth for nearly three hours. The place had remained nearly empty the whole time, so it wasn't needed. Charlie drank and regretted the endless cups of coffee he'd imbibed, which now had him simultaneously wired and suffering from a volcanic case of acid reflux. Ike spent the time reading and rereading the accident report silently and then aloud to Charlie.

"Do you hear it, Charlie?" he'd said. Charlie didn't. "Listen…" and Ike had read the paragraphs which described the rear passenger's side quarter panel and bumper to him again. He punctuated his sentences by thumping the table with the soft side of his fist. "See?"

Charlie nodded but he didn't see anything. Finally, with the sun up and streetlights extinguished, he'd yielded to Ike's impatience and they left for the tow yard. On their way, they stopped at a twenty-four-hour drugstore where Ike bought a box of latex gloves, a box of gallon-sized plastic freezer bags, a prepaid cell phone, and a cheap digital camera. Charlie knew better than to ask him why.

People who knew Ike, depending on whether they were among his admirers or detractors, believed that he moved through life as either paranoid, prescient, plain lucky, or a genius. He seemed to know in advance what he would probably find or need, or who might function in what unlikely roles. His only extant psychological profile, buried in one of Langley's alleged catacombs, rated him extremely high on the scale measuring intuition. When asked why he'd done this or that, Ike would only shrug. "Had a hunch," he'd say and that would cover it as far as he was concerned.

They arrived at Metro Towing and Salvage at seven forty-five. They met the owner at the yard's gate. Ike flashed his badge, which seemed sufficient to gain them entry. They found the crumpled mass of steel and glass that had once been Ike's Buick. He scanned the wreck as if he had a camera implanted in his head and every detail of the car need be recorded to be compared to other, older, perhaps happier, images of it. He circled the car three times. Then he repeated the process, this time with his drugstore camera. He donned the latex gloves and wrenched open one door. He sifted through the miscellany in the car, bagging some, tossing the rest.

"Okay, we're done here. I want to have this thing on a rollback and on the way to a forensic lab ASAP."

The yard owner shook his head. "Sorry, no can do, Bud. This here car sits where it's at because the cops had her towed in. They have to release it first."

"I'm a cop," Ike said, his gaze still fixed on the right rear panel of the car, "And I authorize its release."

"I'll still need the paperwork."

Ike wheeled back to the lot owner. "You know what? This car is moving today. Since I am the owner and I want it, you don't get a choice. Just tell me what the towing charge is and it's out of here."

"You wrecked this thing and lived?"

"No, someone else did. But that is not the point. It's

mine. Check the registration in the glove box and show me where to sign. I am also in possession of the accident report and it is clear that the cops are done with it." He shoved the report under the lot man's nose.

"Whoa. Take it easy." The lot man glanced at the report and Ike's badge again. He didn't appear too sure about what he should do. He squinted at the badge, threw his hands up, and sighed. "Okay, I guess. This won't get me in any trouble, will it? I should call the precinct. I'd hate to lose the business, you know? Times are tough. I depend on city towing to stay open."

"I promise there will be no backlash. Where can I hire a rollback?"

"I have a rollback. Where do you want it delivered?"

"Charlie, do you suppose I could borrow some of your people to go over this for me? There won't be much for them to do. I need some paint samples from the rear quarter panel, bumper, and passenger side door. I will retrieve the GPS tracking device from under the hood and put someone to work on decoding what happened to the car in its last minutes. Then we'll see what comes next."

Charlie noticed, but did not comment on the tracking device. More Ike.

"Sure, no problem. I'll have to tell a few lies. So what's new with that? If they pass muster, we also have people who can unravel your GPS data in a heartbeat." Charlie made two calls and then gave the lot man an address.

"It goes there? Who are you guys?"

"National security," Charlie whispered, "need to know, sorry."

"Right. My driver will be here in an hour. I'll get

him on it, mum's the word," the lot owner said, and laid a finger next to his nose.

"One more thing," Ike said. "Whatever you do, do not disturb the rear end or side of that car. It is evidence in a criminal investigation."

"Wow, okay. This is top secret, right?"

"You got it."

The yard man left to retrieve whatever forms he needed to effect the car's release.

"You think the locals will howl when they find out you grabbed your car?" Charlie sometimes felt he played Archie Goodwin to Ike's Nero Wolfe, but more often he felt like Watson to his Sherlock.

"Trust me, the Metro cops are done with this. You heard that side of beef at the desk. The report indicates they have already signed the release. We just don't have it in hand—minor detail."

"That's what I like about working with you, Ike. Things are what you need them to be."

"Don't mock me, Charlie. I'm not in the mood for banter this morning."

"No, of course not. I'm sorry. I am sure there will be ways to mollify the cops if that becomes necessary. But you are right, they are busy, uninterested in this case, and... You told the guy it is a criminal investigation. Is it?"

"It is now. This car has been smacked from behind."

"Ike, Ruth has had the car for a month. Someone could have banged into it at any time in the last four weeks."

"She would have said something."

"Then maybe last night."

"That is my point, Charlie. Someone hit it last night, in the rear and on the side. I aim to find out who and why."

"You're not buying accident?"

"Not until I have to."

"Okay, it's your call. What's next?"

"For you, make the calls to set up the car's arrival and inspection of the tracking device. It's on the firewall on the driver's side, by the way. Then go home and sleep. Take my car. It's an official police vehicle, so drive carefully."

"You'll need it, Ike. I'll take a cab."

"No, I insist. Look, after five years, I'm not sure I can find your place anymore. Then, you realize, I am running on adrenaline at the moment. I have a few things left that I must do, pronto. When the adrenaline rush finally wears off, I will crash. I don't want to be behind the wheel and have the metaphor become a reality. One smash-up this weekend is more than enough. Write your address on a piece of paper and stick it in my pocket. I'll see you in an hour or so."

"You're sure?"

"Sure."

Charlie did as he was asked, took Ike's keys, and drove away.

IKE WAITED FOR the lot owner to assemble the necessary papers. Then he reassured him once again that the release would cause no trouble, signed off on the car's removal, and thanked him. He retreated to the street, paused, and took a moment to study the report. He then flagged a cab and headed to the scene where Ruth had wrapped his Buick around the steel utility pole. He hoped the nervous energy that had sustained him for the last twenty-four hours would hold a bit longer. He needed to avoid being run over by rush hour traffic when he dodged in and out of cars and busses to take pictures of the accident scene, skid marks, and anything else the cops had missed.

Fortunately, the traffic on the street was not as heavy as he expected. He didn't know why. Mondays were usually busy everywhere. He did have a near miss when a woman holding a cell phone in one hand while she manipulated its keyboard, and sipping on a cup of coffee held in other, missed him by inches. She didn't see him before or after she whooshed by. Ike muttered an uncharitable and very sexist comment about females in general and texting while driving in particular. Had Ruth heard him, she would have been provoked to a classic response about his prehistoric ideas regarding the roles of the sexes. He smiled at the thought, but fleetingly.

Pictures taken, he paced the distances as best he could for the several skid marks. They were becoming less distinct as he did so. If he had waited until later, another hour or two, there would have been nothing for him to see, with the possible exception of some really nasty black tire marks where the car had jumped the curb before taking out the pole. He took another set of pictures there. His camera ran out of memory and he'd done what he could. He hailed a cab, handed Charlie's address to the driver, and fell asleep. He would remain that way until the driver shook him awake in the Virginia suburbs where Charlie had his townhouse.

THREE

IKE AWOKE GROGGY and unsure where he was or what time it might be. He rubbed his eyes and sat up. His skin felt gritty and his mouth like the entire Chinese army had marched across his tongue in their stocking feet. Then, as his mind cleared, the previous day's events surfaced and hit him like gale force winds straight off the arctic circle—not a good moment. He staggered to the bathroom and ran the shower. Charlie's plumbing had a slow recall for hot water. While he waited, he checked his cell phone. He had a dozen missed calls. It took effort but he managed to scroll though them, and clicked on the ones he thought he should listen to. Ruth's mother left a message; she was on her way to DC and would meet him at the hospital at three thirty.

Nurse Struthers had called to say there had been no change and Dr. Kravitz, the neurologist, wished to meet with him in the afternoon. If he had any further questions he should call the head nurse at the ICU. She was going off duty.

He looked at his watch. Two p.m. and an hour and a half before Eden Saint Clare arrived to assume a mother's prerogatives over her daughter's care.

Frank Sutherlin had called to extend his condolences and ask if there was anything he or any of the staff could do. His father had done the same, and then reminded Ike he had a speaking engagement at the Picketsville

Rotary and if he could possibly keep it he should. The election, he declared, might be a close one, and if Ike wanted to continue in the sheriff's job, he needed to be a presence.

Ike's decision to seek reelection as Sheriff of Picketsville was as much a matter of accepting the default settings on his mental computer as a considered one. It was just what he did, and he was good at it. The alternatives for the town were not good. And some—a little—of the mess he'd inherited when he first ran still needed attention. But at the moment, the election and everything it entailed seemed inconsequential, intrusive, almost disrespectful. Campaign now? He shook his head like a buffalo bothered by flies.

His only interest, his whole focus was directed toward finding what or who might have engineered Ruth's smash-up. One look at the car and his gut told him the accident had been rigged. He gritted his teeth. He needed to hold that thought, to keep the fire burning, or… He refused to entertain the idea Ruth might not survive—and intact. But the images of a broken Ruth would not leave him alone. They disrupted his train of thought like a colicky child at a family reunion. He could not will the images away.

He called Frank. Since his transfer from the Highway Patrol a year or so earlier, Frank Sutherlin had assumed the title of Acting Sheriff whenever Ike was not available. Of all Ike's deputies, Frank was the steadiest and most reliable, but not the most colorful or amusing. That honor fell to his younger brother, Billy. Frank answered on the second ring.

"Ike, we are devastated. What can we do?"

"For now, nothing, but thanks. I won't be available

for a while so you're in charge. Keep everybody on task and no worries. I can use a special favor from you, however."

"Anything."

"Your old outfit did a ton of automobile accident analyses, I imagine, and they're pretty good at it, right?"

"They are. You need me to call them about something?"

"More. In a few hours I will have a readout from the tracking device I installed in my car. It's the one Ruth was driving, and I will have photographs of the accident scene, the car, and measurements as well. All the stuff you normally collect in a fatal or near-fatal wreck." Ike paused and cleared his throat. How was he going to get through this? "That is as much as I could pick up on my own. The DC cops wrote the whole thing off as not requiring any but the most cursory attention. Oh, and I might have paint chips to analyze."

"I gather you don't think it was just an accident?"

"I don't, but my thinking and reality may not mesh. It's just that… Will you ask your friends to go through the data and reconstruct, or at least give me an idea what happened?"

"Sure. Just send everything you have to me as an e-mail attachment and I'm on it."

"Thanks. Okay, so for the time being, you're the boss. Anything happening?"

Ike didn't really care if Picketsville had a quiet weekend or was under siege by a brigade of North Korean ninja paratroopers, but he felt obliged to ask.

"Nothing important. Drunk and disorderly at the Roadhouse and a missing vehicle up at the university."

"Bikers back at the Roadhouse, I suppose. What about the vehicle?"

"It was reported missing Monday morning and then found parked in the wrong space an hour later. Some maintenance employee must have been in a hurry to go home or needed it for a little weekend moonlighting."

"Okay, I'll be back to you when I have the data. Thanks again."

Before he rang off, he gave Frank his new drugstore cell phone number and asked him to call him on it for the time being.

Water hot, he set the phones aside and stepped into the shower, which provided him a measure of therapy as well as cleanliness. Dressed, combed, and shaved, he made his way to the kitchen, where Charlie had left him a note. *Gone to work, call.* Ike finished with the remaining calls from his phone, ate an over-ripe banana, and left. He would find a drive-through Starbucks and purchase the first of the day's numerous cups of coffee. This one he supplemented with a scone, which he soon discovered was not designed to be eaten while driving. His lap disappeared in an avalanche of crumbs and blueberries. He didn't care.

He made it to the hospital with five minutes to spare and met Ruth's mother at the nurse's desk.

"Eden, I'm glad you could get here so quickly. Easy trip?"

"I have no idea. I just drove like hell non-stop and here I am. What can you tell me? The message you left was a little vague."

"Sorry. When I called I really didn't know anything. We're meeting the doctor in a few minutes. Then we'll both know."

"I want to see her."

"Of course. She is pretty banged up and in a coma so don't be shocked. You can talk to her but don't expect her to answer or even acknowledge you're there."

"Oh God, you may have to help me, Ike. I'm not good at this. First it was her father, now my baby."

My baby. Ruth's mother was barely twenty years older than she, and had recently spent considerable time and money on regimes, cosmetics, and some discreet bits of surgery intended to narrow that gap in terms of appearances. Give Eden Saint Clare an hour head start and soft lighting and she could pass for Ruth's blonde older sister.

"This way." They walked the length of the hallway and entered the ICU. Eden gasped when she saw her daughter, and collapsed in a chair.

"Oh my God, oh my God," she rasped. "Oh no, I can't be like this. Ruth needs me to be calm and collected, doesn't she?"

"She needs you to be here. She won't respond, but you should hold her hand and talk to her. I read somewhere that even when in a coma, people are sometimes aware of your presence and can often hear what you say." Ike swallowed back the bile that surged into his throat. He'd been here the night before, had seen this already, and yet the awfulness hit him as forcefully as before.

"You've talked to her?"

"Ah… Just a little last night. I had to stop. I didn't want…" Ike cleared his throat.

He stepped to one side of the bed and Eden to the other, and they each took a hand. Eden had to twist her wrist to adjust to the board that Ruth's arm had been strapped to.

"Honey, it's me. It's your mother. Can you hear me?

Oh dear, I'm sorry, I shouldn't be asking you questions, should I? Damn, I did it again. Sorry. I don't want to frustrate you if you can hear and aren't able to answer, so don't try. Here's Ike."

"I hope you're satisfied, Harris. I had a look at my beautiful silver Buick, and it is totaled. What did I tell you about driving and texting? Don't answer that. Just know I'm not finished with this, woman."

"Jesus, Ike, what are you doing?"

"I'm not sure, but… Ruth used to say I played her like the left side of an accordion."

"The what?"

"You know, an accordion has a keyboard on the right and all those buttons on the left. She claimed I deliberately pushed her buttons to get a rise out of her."

"Oh. And did she push your buttons, too?"

"She's more into throwing darts, I think."

"And did you both, push and throw…deliberately?"

"Not always. Sometimes, maybe, but…"

"It was just the way you two were."

"Yes…sometimes. It was rarely premeditated, like just now. Anyway, you asked what I was doing. If I know your daughter, and I think I do…don't I, Ruth? If there is an ounce of fight in her, she will not miss a chance to pull out of this if only long enough to give me hell. So, Ruth, you may expect a fair ration of political incorrectness and male chauvinism over the next few weeks. If you want it to stop, wake up and take a swipe at me."

It should have been funny. It would have been up to twenty-four hours ago, pushing her buttons, but not now.

"Ike, stop it. Don't listen to him, Honey, he's a monster. I don't know what you see in him, I truly don't."

Ike gave Eden a thumbs-up and a crooked smile. She

smiled back but with little enthusiasm. Shock therapy, if that was what this amounted to, did not resonate with her maternal instincts, such as they were.

A nurse entered and whispered that Doctor Kravitz would see them now.

"Be back in a jiff, Honey." Eden squeezed Ruth's hand and followed Ike into the corridor. "Okay, let's tackle the sawbones."

"He's a nice man, Eden. Don't be mean."

"How nice?"

"He's about your age and pretty good-looking, if you go for guys with stethoscopes in their pockets and ridiculously clean hands."

"You just described every doctor on the planet. Tell me about this one."

"You will see for yourself. That's him chatting up the nurse in the blue scrubs."

"Why do they wear those awful uniforms? They make them look dumpy and rumpled."

"Practical, I suppose. Now there is a cast of characters for your book that you say you might write someday, or not."

"Characters? Who, what?"

"Dumpy and Rumpled, the two dwarfs left out of the Snow White story for lack of room in the cottage. Think of it, a revisionist telling—"

"That's enough, Ike. I know you are sitting on a small volcano, and you think you need to be brave, not cry, all those idiotic guy things. I happen to know you have a history with this kind of stuff, so this can't be easy. And you think it's your job to divert me, but it isn't, so cut the crap."

"Okay, right, thanks. You're the mom. Let's hear what the doc has to say."

FOUR

IKE'S FATHER, the legendary Virginia politician, packed an almanac of useful advice tucked away in the recesses of his aging, but still alert brain. Were you in the process of selecting a barber, buying a house, choosing a wife? Abe had an aphorism for every occasion. "You can tell a good doc," he'd said years earlier on the occasion of Ike's departure for Harvard, "because he will always look tired." Dr. Barry Kravitz would have qualified as a good doctor by Abe Schwartz's standard. He did, indeed, appear to be very tired.

Ike introduced Eden to Doctor Kravitz. He shook her hand and then led them both to a break room and placed Styrofoam cups of truly wretched coffee before them. His, he drank. Ike and Eden thanked him and pushed their cups aside. He seemed not to notice.

"Okay," he said, and rubbed his eyes. "I filled Mr. Schwartz in on the early estimates last night. Or was that this morning?" He powered up an electronic device he held in his hand, tapped it several times with a black stylus and nodded. "Last night, nine thirty p.m., there it is."

"Excuse me," Eden's eyes were locked on the little handheld device. "Are all of my daughter's records in that little thing?"

"Yes Ma'am, they are."

"What happens if you lose it, or it is stolen, or stops working?"

"No problem, the information is password protected and encrypted. It automatically links to a mainframe server dedicated to our medical records and is stored there as quickly as it is entered here. The data can be retrieved and downloaded onto another compatible device at any time, provided you have access to it. So, no worries."

"I want one of those things."

"Yes? Well as I was saying, I have a better picture now. Your daughter, Mrs. Saint Clare, came here to our ER in pretty bad shape. Her system had completely shut down and we were not sure we would be able to save her."

"Oh, no. But you did."

Ike shifted in his chair. Even though he had not tasted it, the aroma of burnt coffee permeated the close, little room. "Doc, could you begin at the beginning, to remind me and, also, to fill in Mrs. Saint Clare on the details?"

Ike's head seemed as if it might explode. He needed to hear what Kravitz had to say, but wished it all to go away, wished he could wake up at the A-frame in the mountains in time to cook Ruth breakfast, to push some buttons.

"Yes, of course. As I have it—" he waved the stylus around like a conductor holding a miniature baton and tapped his electronic chart again "—your fiancée had an automobile accident. She apparently hit something—"

"A metal utility pole."

"Really? Well. She must have hit it pretty hard because her system went into shock. You were very lucky that didn't happen instantaneously. She took a lick on her head, probably against the door post, and concussed badly. People have died almost instantly from lesser trauma. She's very lucky."

"From where she is at the moment, she might debate that."

"No doubt she would. Okay, the car apparently didn't have side air bags. Too bad. Before the brain swelling resulting from the impact to her head completely shut down her system, the EMTs arrived. They saw she'd stopped breathing and bagged her."

"Did what to her? Bagged—like a body bag?" Eden had a vision of all the television cops she'd ever seen over the years zipping up black plastic bags over cold, grey faces. In her mind the face now belonged to her daughter.

"Oh no, sorry, I mean they fitted her with a manual ventilator. It has a bag on it that the technician compresses, which allows him to breathe for her."

"Him."

"Or her, yes."

"Sorry, you meant the person from the ambulance did the bagging."

"Yes. So then she was admitted to the ER and we discovered her to be unresponsive, BP dropping, thready pulse—"

"Thready what? Speak to me in mother-understandable language please, Doctor."

"Right. It's been a long night. Simple? She was slipping away. We put her on a ventilator so she could breathe, started an IV to raise her blood pressure, but then quickly realized she was bleeding internally and needed surgery. All we can do for the swelling in her cranium is give her an anti-inflammatory, blood thinners, keep her hydrated and quiet, and wait. If there is no reduction we'll tap some of the fluid out, but, like I said I'd rather wait. Well, long story short, she had a ruptured spleen, which we removed, a broken leg, which the orthopedist set, a small cranial fracture, a compression fracture at C4, three broken ribs, and bruising of most of her internal organs."

"Oh my God… What's a C4?"

"Sorry. It's one of the vertebrae in your neck."

"She has a broken neck?"

"Yes, but not serious. She'll need to wear a neck brace for a while until it heals."

Eden paled. Ike leaned forward to change the subject. "How long will she be unconscious, Doctor Kravitz?"

"I can't say for sure. In cases of brain insult…sorry, head trauma, we have no easy predictors. Much as I'd rather not, I have to tell you, worst case, she will continue downhill into a vegetative state. Best case, she'll pull out of her coma in a few days or a week or two."

"That's a pretty wide spread. What do you think?"

"Don't hold me to it, will you? I'd rather not ask you to fill out one of the hospital's waiver forms the Legal Department insists on." Kravitz paused, mopped his forehead with a tissue and sipped his coffee. "I'm guessing here, emphasis on guessing, that she'll come around in a week or ten days, maybe a little longer, say three weeks. There are no accurate predictors in cases like this. Some patients pop out in a few hours, some are down for months, even years. It all seems to depend on some sort of physiological clock we do not understand. If we did, we'd work with it. At any rate you should be aware that there are two main differences between a coma and a vegetative state. Vegetative patients will continue to go through their sleep–wake cycles. Those in comas don't. Also, a coma is always temporary, which means that if a patient never awakens, he or she will inevitably regress to a vegetative state and…death, but patients like your daughter do not stay

comatose forever. All of which may cause other difficulties for you in a day or two."

"Difficulties? What sort of difficulties?"

Kravitz shook his head, his expression like a basset
hound. "Bed allocation. Priorities and policies relevant
to long-term care. We can talk about that later. At any
rate, it could be months or years before she will remember what happened last night. Maybe never."

Ike's face clouded over. "You anticipated my next
question, Doc."

"Most people consider post-traumatic amnesia a
blessing."

"If it were just an accident, I would agree. But since
I don't think that's what happened, I would want it not
to be so."

The doctor and Eden started. "You think it wasn't
an accident?"

"Sorry, Eden, no I don't. Since she took the job with
the Department of Education, she has amassed a file as
thick as a phonebook filled with e-mails, phone messages, and letters from people whose views of her and
her work range from simply angry to overtly homicidal.
I read some of the e-mails and threats—not nice. She
dismissed them, but it would only take one nut with a
private agenda to do something idiotic. I don't want to,
but I believe one of them did."

"Oh, Ike, you can't be serious."

"Serious as a heart attack. Sorry, Doc, bad simile."

"Why did you ever let her take this job in Washington?"

"Let? Eden, you know as well as I do that Ruth asks
permission of no one. We talked about it. It was an offer,
as they say, she couldn't refuse."

"But she had a college to run, and you were supposed to get married and…"

Supposed to get married. Yes. Well, what were the chances now? Can't go through this again. Yes you can. God help me.

"I said we talked. We agreed with reluctance. Since the present administration leaves office in two years, it wouldn't be permanent. She saw it as an opportunity to become involved in things she cared about, and Picketsville isn't that far away. We commuted, as you know."

"Excuse me," Doctor Kravitz interrupted, "but you did say the Department of Education?"

"Yes. She was recruited by the secretary as an assistant secretary. Her job was to review the progress of Title Nine programs. I guess they hadn't had a thorough review in a while. After she arrived, she also assumed the chair of a committee set up to study school textbook standards."

"How is that connected to Title Nine?"

"It isn't. She took it because no one else would. She is that way. As you probably know, many state school boards have their own textbook screening committees and they, in turn, have notions about what constitutes correct and acceptable history and science. The concern the secretary had, and by indirection the president, centered on how new textbooks would mesh with the recently enacted National Curriculum Standards. Her committee was charged to look at that and perhaps recommend legislation to bring them into sync with the curriculum. That's when her Enemies List got started."

"Wow. Do you think she's still in danger? Do I need to contact Security?" The doctor seemed worried.

"I doubt it. If I'm right, that is, if the wreck was in

fact related to the job, then I think they will feel that they have sent their message. If and when she does go back to work, and that is not likely to be anytime soon, and if they need to, they will remind her of what happened. But I would guess her days as a federal bureaucrat are pretty much over. Meanwhile, the rest of her committee has been warned and, I assume, suitably intimidated."

"This is madness."

"No, this is the USA in the first decades of the twenty-first century."

The doctor shook his head. "Meshuggeneh." He left the room.

"What did he say?"

"It's Yiddish for craziness. He's got it right. We have come to a pass in this country where we will either find a way to settle our differences amicably, or I will need to hire many more deputies, assuming I still have that responsibility in a month. At any rate, to be open and objective, I haven't ruled out random stupidity, mistaken identity, or a psychopath on the loose."

"Take me home," Eden said, "wherever that is today. I need a drink and a think. Oh Lord, what are we going to do, Ike?"

"You'll be fine. It'll be okay." Eden nodded but her eyes remained clouded with doubt. He didn't blame her. He had reasons to doubt as well. He understood more "doctor talk" than she and remembered what Kravitz had left out of his summary just now.

When they reached the parking lot, Ike gave her Ruth's apartment key and directions how to find it. She drove off. Ike called Charlie.

FIVE

CHARLIE PUSHED HIS way into a coffee shop in Fairfax where he'd earlier agreed to meet Ike. He had a manila folder under one arm and his raincoat draped over the other. His expression indicated something had him spooked. Charlie did not spook easily.

"Where've you been? I left you a note to call me when you woke up. Holy cow, Ike, all hell is breaking loose."

"Excuse me? Hell for whom? I'm not aware anyone of my acquaintance, except Ruth, is in any way, shape, or form, close to being in the sort of jeopardy you suggest, and Hell isn't an option for her, thank you."

"Sorry, I didn't mean to…you're right. By hellish, I refer to the preliminary results of your forensics request. I thought you'd want them right away and then you didn't call. Then the Director—"

"Okay, as far as wanting the results? I did. I do. I just didn't imagine you'd have them so soon. Then, I had to meet Ruth's mother at the hospital, get her settled afterward, and talk to the doctor. Then…never mind. So, tell me."

"How is the beautiful Mrs. Eden Saint Clare?"

"As always. With the wind at her back and in the right light, a knockout. The results please, Charlie. To answer the question you are hesitant to put to me no, Mrs. Saint Clare didn't ask about you."

"I wasn't going to ask that. Why would I?"

Ike shrugged.

"Okay, I have the data, but first, I have to tell you about the Director. He heard about Ruth's accident somehow."

"Somehow?"

"Hey, he's a spy, for crying out loud, he heard. Anyway, he cornered me when I arrived at the office and said, and here I quote the Great Man as nearly and as accurately as I can, 'After the business with the terrorists on the Chesapeake Bay last year, we owe him big time, so tell Schwartz we're sorry for his troubles and that the resources of the CIA are at his disposal, night or day.' Impressed?"

"Oh, I am. What does he want?"

"Tut, you have a suspicious mind, Ike, always have. He is only interested in your welfare. And, as I said, he hasn't forgotten the Yom Kippur caper, you could say."

"And, as the Metro cop said last night, 'yeah and I'm...' Who did he say he was?"

"Matthew McConaughey. Who is a movie star or something. Unlike you and your obsession with them, actors and movies aren't my thing."

"I only like the dead ones."

"I don't think I'll dissect that statement just now. So, moving on from the Director's highly appreciated and extremely generous offer, the guys in the lab removed your tracking device and mapped everything that happened to your car in the previous twenty-four hours. They report your car received not one but two major impacts last night. The first, they believe was delivered at the rear end of the car," Charlie glanced at the folder's contents, "passenger side, and the second one, moments later when it broadsided the utility pole. Ruth was rear-ended. That's what caused the smash-up."

"I guessed that. How far back did you say they checked?"

"Just last night, twenty-four hours give or take. I thought that's all you'd want. Oh, wait. You want to confirm that the car wasn't hit before yesterday as well."

"Yes. I'll need more. Nothing about the paint yet?"

"They tried. Remember, we don't do much in the auto accident line over at the Company. If we need a sophisticated analysis, we outsource it. Anyway, they couldn't match the paint to any known vehicle manufacturer. Whoever or whatever hit her must have had a respray at some time. There is a complicated chromatographic analysis of the paint, however. If you can find another program to identify it, you might get lucky and locate the places it might have been done."

"That's the plan. Thank you and thank the techs for the quick turnaround."

"You're welcome. No thanks to the Director?"

"You are joking, right?"

"Yes and no. If he wanted to, he could have put the kibosh on the lab work, you know, but he didn't. Give him a bit of credit, Ike, he may be otherwise motivated, but in his avuncular way he does still care about you."

"Noted."

"It would appear you are looking at a hit and run, Ike. You do realize how difficult they are to track down unless there were witnesses? There are garages and body shops all over this city that will gladly make any damage on a vehicle go away unreported for an appropriate amount of cash."

"I know that, Charlie. I am counting on the fact

that this rear-end was not just an accident caused by a stranger who panicked and ran. I'm betting whoever did this had a plan all along. I just need to connect the dots to unravel it."

"This connect-the-dots puzzle looks more like pointillism than a picture of a bunny and none of the dots are numbered. Where do you start, Ike? Who would do this?"

"Someone trying to send a message to Ruth and/or her committee to back off is my thought."

"Committee? Which?"

"The textbook review committee, the one that will have people riled up all over the country but especially in the extremely red states."

"Oh. You do really think…?"

"There were threats before. It would only take one crazy jingo to carry them out so, yes, I do."

"What's the likelihood, really?"

"I don't know, Charlie, but it's all I have."

"Ike, I know this has hit you hard, but take a minute and think it through. How does a group of people primarily composed of little old ladies with blue hair and old guys wearing Uncle Sam hats and sporting beer bellies over white suede belts translate into an attempted homicide?"

"You are right, it has hit me very hard, but you are wrong in assuming that I am reaching or overreacting. I am not interested in the people the media loves to depict as typical attendees at those States' Rights, we're angry, screw the government rallies. I am concerned with the fringe elements they don't show or even investigate. I'm thinking of the young men and, I suppose, women, who teeter on the brink of sanity and who listen to the hate mongers and radical broadcasters from the far right and left. Add to that the latest incubator of disaster."

"Our what?"

"Look, we have been fighting in Iraq and Afghanistan for how long?"

"Since nine-eleven. Too long."

"Exactly, and in doing so, and certainly without intending to, we have created a whole generation of professional killers. Young men and women who have had to watch as civilians were gunned down for no other reason than they were in the wrong place at the wrong time. They have seen their friends and their buddies blown up by suicide bombers or roadside explosive devices, and other IEDs. They have been asked to kick down doors and lob hand grenades into houses without ever knowing if they were filled with terrorists or innocent women and children."

"I understand the problems created by Post Traumatic Stress Disorder, believe me. The number of suicides, divorces, cases of homelessness associated with it is scary, but what is your point?

"My point? Imagine, then one damaged young man sent home, perhaps both physically concussed, suffering from and mentally. Then PTSD and to this hyperpolarized political system that talking heads have created in the past several decades and what are the chances?"

"Okay, I see."

"Do you really?" Ike's eyes flashed. He banged the chair arm. "One side screams death to the imagined threats to our democracy, the other yaps we should quit, withdraw, and apologize. He comes home into this—"

"Or she."

"Or she, especially she. You're right. We have generations of data on how war affects men, but women in combat is a new phenomenon for us. Are women emotionally different enough that their reaction would also be different, or would they be the same as for men? We don't know that either."

"No telling. I would guess the same and I'm not just being politically correct—certainly similar. Perhaps more… I don't know…domestic."

"I'll leave it at similar. I don't understand domestic. Anyway, he returns and feels used, even betrayed. He meets one of those professional purveyors of truth and freedom, buys into his cant, and believes he can help by taking action, by employing the skills with which his country has gifted him. God help us. What is the future going to look like in another ten years?"

Some adjacent customers seemed alarmed at this last outburst. "Ike, I get it, but surely it's not simply a matter of PTSD sufferers on the loose."

"Of course it isn't. What I'm saying is that there were too many politically ︙ nutcases loose in society already and we are not only ︙ doing enough to reduce their number but, in fact, adding enough to reduce

"You think this scenario is possible. ︙

"Possible? Charlie, I don't have a clue wh︙ through Timothy McVeigh's addled brain when he con︙ cluded blowing the front off the Murrah Federal Building and thereby killing women, children, and low-level bureaucrats constituted an act of patriotism. Or what muddled thinking makes someone shoot a congressperson and a half-dozen bystanders. But compared to that, running a car off the road is pretty small potatoes.

So yes, in the absence of a better explanation, I think it's possible."

Ike slumped back in his chair. "Is all the accident data in this folder?"

"Yes, and here's your tracking gizmo." Charlie dragged the box from his pocket. Someone had thoughtfully put it in a plastic antistatic bag.

"I need a laptop."

"There's a computer café down the street, but can't this wait until you get back to the house?"

Ike thought a second and agreed. He could try to send all this to Frank, but downloading the tracking device's data could be tricky and if he did it incorrectly, he might lose it. And he needed a copier that could send the documents to his PC and then be attached to an e-mail.

"Okay, tonight." He looked at his watch. "It's almost five. How about an early dinner somewhere and then I'll try to get this stuff to Frank Sutherlin?"

"Frank? Your deputy Frank?"

"He used to be with the highway patrol. They do vehicular accidents by the thousands. They can sort through this faster and better than anybody. I will need some help to send the data on the tracking device, I think. You have a copier that loads to your computer, don't you?"

"I do, but have no idea how it works. Don't look at me for any help in that department. I have trouble setting my alarm clock."

"I know that is not true, but if you insist on dissembling about your lack of technological skills in order to be excused from onerous tasks while on the job, it's okay by me. Just know that I know you lie."

"You are a hard man, Ike. Let's blow this place and

find a decent dinner. We could do Italian. I'm up for starch, tomato sauce, and meatballs that aren't Swedish. I know a place."

"You always know a place."

WHEN IKE RETURNED to the hospital, nothing had changed from the previous night. The monitor still beeped, the drip still clacked, and the ventilator continued to gurgle. He took Ruth's hand and began to tell her about his day.

"Everyone is worried about you, but I told them you'd be fine. You just needed to take a time-out. Pretty radical way to go about it, but they know you and weren't surprised that you chose to check into the hospital for the rest cure. As for me, I'm not used to the silence yet, but I admit it is a change. Charlie is in a swivet because the Director of the CIA called him out. He claims the Great Man says he'll do anything for us. I guess that means he has something really bad in mind for me. I have five calls from Abe I have left unreturned. He's worried I will screw up the election and end up unemployed. I can think of a worse state of affairs. You offered me a job on the faculty at a dollar a year last summer, so I figure I have options."

He cleared his throat, afraid to say more; afraid if he did, she'd hear the fear in his voice. Eden glanced up and began to talk to Ruth. Ike only heard a few words, scattered memories of growing up, happier days, a childhood…something about finding her tattered copy of *Uncle Wiggly's Story Book* that Eden had found in the attic before she left to join Ruth in Virginia.

"You remember me reading it? I think it was your grandmother's originally. Funny stories. Do you remember…"

His thoughts drifted to Sunday evening, the setting sun silhouetting Ruth in the window of the condo before he left; before she answered the phone that called her away; before…

Who'd called her, and why?

SIX

CHARLIE GARLAND HAD been Ike's friend for years. First, when Ike was a new recruit at the CIA, and later, after Ike's wife died and he'd left the Company and buried himself in the Shenandoah Valley. *Dying* was an egregious understatement for what happened to Ike's wife, Eloise, which remained a continuing sore point in Langley. Charlie still worked for the Company. He had an ambiguous job description no one dared question. Few people in the organization knew what he did, some suspected, the rest preferred to remain ignorant. By so doing they only had to guard their speech a bit more carefully than elsewhere. In the corridors of the gray building in Langley and in its numerous and anonymous satellites, candor did not always play well.

After visiting hours ended, and Ike had been ushered out of Ruth's room, he returned to Charlie's place and found him sitting in a battered Eames chair, a TV remote in his hand, but with the television screen blank.

"You didn't have to wait up for me," Ike tossed his raincoat on a deacon's bench in the foyer. He sniffed. "Is that coffee?"

"It is, help yourself. It's not that late and do not flatter yourself. As a rule I wait up for no one. But I do have more news."

Ike poured a cup of coffee and collapsed in a chair.

"What kind of news? Good, I hope. I could use some good news about now."

"Pretty good, I think, certainly useful. On their own, or at the direction of the boss, I don't know which, the techs in the communications department accessed the city's tapes from the traffic surveillance cameras for last night. They found a bit of footage of the accident."

"Where? How? Can I see it?"

"Easy. First I have to tell you it is very blurry, night-time, and therefore dark, and remember also that it was raining so there is a lot of glare on the road from the lights—headlights, streetlights. It's not much, but suggestive."

He clicked the TV remote and pulled up My Computer on the menu. He scrolled through a half-dozen entries and clicked on one filed under "Today" and then "RH/Accident." The street that Ike had photographed and paced off the night before appeared on the screen. Charlie was right, it was blurry and the reflected light from the rain-covered paving shimmered so that most of the detail was lost. Ike watched as his car appeared in the distance closely followed by a truck and, at a distance farther back, a few other vehicles. All of their headlights shone and from time to time glared out the camera. Then in the next split second, the truck sped up, pulled behind the Buick, swerved to the right and then to the left. Its front bumper caught the right rear of the car and spun it sideways. The truck bore down on the car's side panel, accelerating it even as the tires on the car locked. Ruth had to be standing on the brakes. Stunned, he watched as the car, shoved by the truck, slued crosswise, jumped the curb, and crashed against the pole. The truck careened on down the street and out of sight. The whole played out soundlessly but Ike could almost hear the squeal of the brakes, the crunch of metal, the shattering of glass. The two men sat in silence for a moment.

"Ike, before you ask, no they could not lift the license plate number from the truck. Question, do you want us to send a copy of this to the Metro Police for review?"

"It can't hurt, I suppose, but what will they do with it?"

"My guess, nothing much. We live in an age of severe budget cuts and short staffing. It has become a time, for example, when burglaries are handled by filling out a form with an inventory sheet of items stolen. You may or may not see your burglars caught and your stuff returned, but only if they happen to fence it to the wrong people. If police departments around the country were spread any thinner, they'd disappear. Will they have the time or personnel to track down the truck? Not likely."

"Send it on, anyway. If the idiot who did that is caught, that is evidence, blurry as it is, and I'm on record as objecting to them having dropped this as a possible hit and run or worse."

"I can do that. They will be annoyed you pushed, not your jurisdiction and all that, they will insist, but you're right. Ruth's accident should be an open case whether they want it to be or not."

"It is clear to me, and should be to you, that it was no accident. That truck deliberately caught the rear of the car and then pushed her into that pole."

"I have to admit it, you're probably right. No accident. But who and why?"

"Run it again and stop when you get the best view

of that truck. We'll save a still of it. Who knows, we might just find it."

Charlie ran the scene again, paused when the truck appeared, slow-clicked the scene until he found the clearest image of the truck, and saved it to a new file.

"What kind of vehicle is that?" he asked.

"It appears to be a standard-looking stake-body utility truck. I can't be sure but my guess is a General Motors product."

Ike opened his laptop and booted it up. He handed Charlie a new flash drive. "Save all that stuff on this and then point me to your scanner/copier."

Charlie did and handed the drive back to Ike. "It's in the corner of the dining area." He pointed to the small room adjacent to the kitchen where what would have been a dinette table was buried in a mountain of paper.

"Next to you, Charlie, I am a neatnick."

He found the device and spent the next half hour scanning the files from the forensics lab into his computer. He then moved them all to the flash drive with the accident video. He erased any trace of the copied files from his laptop and disconnected the thumb drive.

_____ ___ ____ __ __ay Patrol. Maybe they can make
"_o have a _rom it."
tated. You suspected that all along. Again I ask, why?"
"I am a very suspicious person. You, or rather the
people you work for, made me that way. The Company
teaches that things are not to be accepted on the basis
of how they appear on the surface, right?"
"Yes, but we're not doing some field op in Herze-
govina here, Ike."

"No, we're not. We are tucked up safely in the nation's capital where, as everyone knows, there are no intrigues, plots, plans, or malodorous conspiracies flourishing at either national, international, or personal levels. Let's face it, only in this city, as far as I can determine, does the necessity of using a gun to steal characterize lower-class criminals. The upper-class ones don't need them. They use power and influence instead and are probably responsible for more mayhem than the ones with the guns. We call those guys congressmen. Give me a break, Charlie."

"Okay, okay, you win. I just don't want to see you bogged down in some kind of quixotic quest. I know you're angry and…but you do have a life, and Ruth will pull through. Don't you think it would be better to concentrate on that for now and look for the driver of that truck later when you're calmer?"

"You're right, no doubt about it, but I can't be anything more than what I am, Charlie. I have to do something or I will go crazy. I will pursue this until it dead-ends. I need to know if this is just random violence in spite of what we've seen, or a deliberate attempt to hurt Ruth. I need—"

"You need to ie occur
go crazy."

"Something like that, yes."

"You think it was Ruth? What about someone wanting to hurt you? Had you thought of that?"

"Me? You mean like before? No, I hadn't. That opens a whole new can, doesn't it? Either way, I won't know unless and until I find the idiot behind the wheel of that truck."

SEVEN

WHEN IKE WOKE the next morning Charlie had already left for work. He showered and hurriedly dressed. He found a half-filled coffeepot, reheated a cup in the microwave, made some toast, and settled in to eat what would pass for his breakfast while he made some phone calls. He knew he needed to answer his father's dozen or so attempts to reach him and he had to contact Frank with the data on his flash drive. His father, he knew, had become an early riser. "When you achieve your promised three score and ten," he'd said, "much as you might wish it otherwise, the Good Lord don't need you to sleep late no more." Ike had replied that he was in no hurry to test that assumption.

Abe answered on the first ring. Apparently he'd been waiting for the call. "Ike, how're you making out? You need anything? I don't know the crowd up there in Washington like I used to, all them young Turks coming into government nowadays, but I maybe could make a call or two."

"Thanks. I think everything that can be done is being managed here. Now it's a matter of wait and see. So, were you able to handle the Rotary Club okay?"

"Oh yeah. Shoot, those are votes you got in your pocket anyway, but I have to tell you the other fellah is sure making a push out at the university. Faculty types mostly."

"I'm not surprised. I am much too politically incorrect for that crowd and I think they don't like the fact that Ruth and I…" Ike's voice faltered.

"Yeah, well, can't do anything about either of them things. But you need to get back here quick as you can. This election could be close."

"Pop, right now the election is on the bottom of my to-do list. I have good evidence that Ruth's smash-up wasn't an accident. I intend to focus on that for now. The election will have to take care of itself."

"Well, okay. You know I thought you should be looking at something bigger than sheriff but still, I hate losing."

"You're not running, you can't lose."

"I'm managing. I'm working at it and you're my son. If Ike Schwartz loses, Abe Schwartz loses. That's the way it is in politics. You ought to know that."

"You're right, I ought to. I'm sorry but it can't be helped. I have bigger fish to fry right at the moment."

Ike said his goodbyes, adding a "Say hello to Dolly," Abe's recent bride, and booted up his laptop. He inserted the flash drive with the crash scene data and then called Frank Sutherlin.

"Ike. How are you?"

"I'm managing, Frank, thank you. I have some data that I thought you might shoot over to your friends at the Highway Patrol. Shall I attach it as an e-mail or what? I am learning this computer business but it's still a steep learning curve for me. Some of the files are video, some are text."

"How about I put Grace on the phone and she can walk you through it. When you're done, Essie wants to say hi, and I need to talk to you about something."

"Okay. Let me have Grace."

Grace White had joined the Sheriff's Office during the summer. She was a transplant from Maine and the art of manipulating computers and all the bits and pieces involved turned out to be one of her more useful talents. She did not possess anywhere near the skills her predecessor, Samantha Ryder, did, but she was good enough to fill the needs of a country police operation. She walked him through the steps necessary to transfer the data from the flash drive to the Department's mainframe. When she finished she turned the phone over to Essie Sutherlin.

"Ike, holy cow, are you okay? How's Miz Harris? Lord, we've been praying. Well, me and Billy's Ma have been praying. Billy ain't too strong on talking to God, but I'm working on that. We are all so worried. Are you going to be alright?"

"Too many questions in one sentence, Essie, but Ruth's condition remains unchanged, but stable. I'm as fine as can be expected. A word of advice—you and Billy keep each other safe, you hear?"

"You bet. I guess we forget sometimes, don't we?"

"Forget?"

"You don't get no extended warrantee with your birth certificate, do you?"

"No, none, and thanks for asking. What does Frank want to talk about?"

"Oh that. Well, seems like we got ourselves a murder here in town. We can handle it, no problem. You just sit tight up there and take care of your lady."

Frank came back on the line. "Well, you heard it. I thought you'd want to know. We will process this one. No need for you to get involved."

"Who was murdered?"

"Not sure it qualifies as a murder, Ike. Essie notwithstanding, it's a suspicious death as of the moment. One of the maintenance workers up at the college. His co-workers found him in the cab of one of the school's mini-vans. Motor running, garden hose from the exhaust pipe in the window, looks like a suicide."

"But you don't think so?"

"It could be, of course, but there's no suicide note, and he had a nasty contusion on the back of his head. As I said, suspicious."

"Stay on it, Frank. Your instincts are usually pretty good. If it looks suspicious to you, there must be something to it."

"Okay. I'll get on the data you sent off to the Highway Patrol lab today and let you know what they say ASAP. I reckon we should wipe this from the office computer when we're done. You have all of the originals, I assume."

"I do, so do that, yes."

"I know it's too soon to ask, but do you have any idea when you'll be back?"

"I can't say just now. I have to talk to the doctor and then we'll see what happens next."

"Take your time. We have everything under control. Oh, by the way, I almost forgot. Doctor Fiske's secretary called. She said that Fiske was concerned and all that and wanted your cell phone number. I told him we didn't give out personal numbers but if he'd leave his, I'd have you call him."

"That's Fiske as in the Acting President of Callend?"

"That's the one. He wanted to check on Ruth. I guess that's pretty normal."

"I suppose so. Tell him, if he calls again, what I just

told you and that I'll call the university when I have some real news."

Ike hung up and stared at his laptop. He tried and failed to conjure up an accurate face for Scott Fiske. Aside from being tallish, fair-haired, almost an art nouveau throwback look, all he could remember about Fiske was that Ruth had some questions about him. He couldn't remember what they were at the moment. He might later. His absentminded musings were displaced by what transpired on the computer screen. A colleague from another jurisdiction that he'd met at a local police conference the previous year had given him a screen saver. He'd installed it out of curiosity and left it there out of laziness. It depicted a series of chase scenes from actual police footage, including the famous O.J. Simpson in a white Bronco caravanning through Los Angeles. He rarely watched the whole sequence because he either switched to an application or turned the computer off. At the moment he watched fascinated as a police car from somewhere in the Midwest, in pursuit of some baddie or other, pulled to the car's right rear, hooked the bumper, and put it into a spin. Like Ruth's vehicle the night of the accident, it slued sideways. Only this cop did not proceed to ram it as the truck had done to Ruth, and there was no utility pole for it to slam into.

That particular classic maneuver by a police chase car is learned by law enforcement officers on the job. Could an amateur, someone not experienced with it, have done it? Ike guessed not. Whoever smacked Ruth's car that night knew what he was doing. That implied he or she had been, or still served, in a law enforcement capacity somewhere.

What had Charlie said last night?

"How about hurting you? Had you thought of that?"

Could he have misunderstood the message? Who would want him out of the way, and why? It wouldn't be the first time.

EIGHT

KARL HEDRICK AND Sam Ryder would be at work, and what Ike needed to ask of them was best left off a government-monitored phone line. He sipped the lukewarm coffee and made a face. Too late to call them, too early to go to the hospital. He stood and paced. His second ration of toast somehow became stuck in the toaster and began to smoke. He pulled the plug and pried the charred slices of wheat bread from it, tossed the smoking ruins in the disposal, ran water into the sink until the mess disappeared from view, and then dumped the remains of his coffee cup in after it. Breakfast had been a disaster.

Ike was a compartmentalized thinker, or so he claimed. Those who knew him well thought he was anything but. Somehow, they said, he could hold several thoughts, possible outcomes, or probabilities in place at the same time even if one of them conflicted or contradicted another. True or not, he desperately needed to think this through. One thing seemed clear: irrespective of the motivation behind it, someone had deliberately sent Ruth crashing into a pole. That someone needed to be caught and taken care of, and soon. The problem he struggled with at the moment centered on the why of it—the motive. If the act had been aimed at him, a different set of factors and possibilities came into play. If the target was really Ruth, then he'd start somewhere else. But in either case, the task remained the same: find the bastard.

So, do first things first. Who wanted to hurt him but not directly? He'd been through the experience of having a woman he loved shot out from under him, so to speak, and he understood how it might work. His late wife Eloise had been a pawn in such a game. But that happened in a different time and place—a time when he was embroiled in covert work. The instigators of that particular piece of work had wanted him out of the loop but not dead. Killing him would have made what they intended transparent. They wanted him angry and nonfunctional, not dead. The situation differed here. He no longer mucked about in the shadowy backstreets and dim corners of international intelligence. He hadn't for years. He was a country cop. Hurting him indirectly meant nothing. If he stopped being a cop, another would step up and take his place. With the election close, it could happen anyway. He'd not incurred many enemies in his tenure as sheriff, none he could think of who'd vowed some sort of revenge for being incarcerated. Well, there was one, but only one for sure, George Lebrun. But he still sat on death row somewhere and his family, while dysfunctional, was not the sort to take on George's dirty work, and certainly not if it involved the commission of a capital crime.

For the moment then, he ruled himself out as an indirect object of attack. That didn't mean he should forget the cop car maneuver. It added a new and important dimension to the act and said something about the perpetrator. Whoever hit Ruth had most likely been in law enforcement at the street level at one time or another. When he culled through the list of possible suspects he hoped to develop, he would use that as one discriminator.

His stomach began to growl and he felt the need to move, to do something. He decided he would find a restaurant and have breakfast. Some place where they brewed drinkable, hot coffee and didn't burn the toast.

IKE SPENT THE remainder of the day talking to various contacts he had in the several agencies he'd worked with in the past. Ruth's boss at the Department of Education promised to send him copies of any e-mails that were either threatening or suspicious that she might have received in the past two months during her tenure as chair of the textbook committee. He had a long and tearful chat with Agnes Ewalt, Ruth's secretary at Callend. She alternately tried to cheer him up and had to be cheered. She didn't know of any threats, nasty electronic or snail mail, but she would look.

She did tell him that she found Doctor Fiske, her temporary new boss, to be a disagreeable man, and wished she'd accepted Ruth's offer to accompany her to Washington. That brought on another spate of tears, guilt, and hiccups. She said she'd cull through all of the correspondence she had and look for anything suspicious. Ike thanked her and hung up. He made arrangements to have his crumpled car transported to Picketsville. He should have junked it but he felt unless and until the case was resolved one way or another, he should hang on to it.

He spent several hours on the Internet making notes from sites that offered information on automobile impact statistics, safety standards, and survival rates. If these studies were to be believed, Ruth should be dead.

The next car he owned, he decided, would have side window airbags. And maybe a roll-bar installed. Safety standards left something to be desired, surely. He spent the next hour surfing sites that connected directly or indirectly to El-Hi school textbook controversies.

By four o'clock he'd done what he could and drove to the hospital. Eden had beaten him to the bedside and greeted him when he entered the room.

"Look, Honey, here's Ike come to see you. Here let me fix your sheet. Your poor foot must be freezing. She's looking much better, don't you think?"

"Beautiful, except for that overlarge clerical collar. You should see yourself, Kiddo. You look like a nineteenth-century English vicar."

"It's a neck brace, Ike. Don't listen to him. He hasn't had his dinner."

"Have you?"

Eden shook her head but said nothing.

"Speaking of religion, Kiddo, I had a chat with your friend the Reverend Blake Fisher today. He says that at your suggestion, he's taking up Bilphism. Why would you do that to him, I wonder? I thought he had enough problems with his bishop."

"Ike, what are you talking about?"

"Bit of pseudospirituality from one of F. Scott Fitzgerald's novels."

"So you're playing the accordion again?"

"Trying to."

"It hasn't worked yet."

"Not yet, no. But we live in hope."

When visiting hours were over they were all but forcibly removed from the room by a nurse who looked to be about thirteen years old and had a Middle Virginia accent that could have charmed Adolph Hitler. Ike took Eden to dinner. He filled her in on the rough outlines of what he'd been thinking. It was the sort of thing he'd have done with Ruth before—talking a problem through. The difference in this instance was he didn't expect much coming back from Eden whereas he would have from her daughter. Ruth would have found the holes in his narrative. He missed that.

After he dropped Eden off at her car, he sat in the parking lot next to the hospital's emergency room and phoned Karl Hedrick and Samantha Ryder. He used his store-bought throwaway.

"Ike, we only heard today. What happened?" Sam was on the extension. "How is she?"

"In a coma, I'm afraid. She was forced off the road in a rainstorm two nights ago. I need to find out who did it."

"How can we help?"

"You can send me the list of people the FBI has on file, Karl, who are activists in the textbook wars."

"You mean the people, mostly in Texas, who think the history of the United States should be drafted to assure that the Founding Fathers were all Christian, white, and capitalists."

"And not descended from monkeys, among other things, yes."

"Ike, you know I can't do that. The Bureau's files can't be shared that way, especially without a demonstrable national interest or an open criminal case."

"Then I'll ask Sam to hack into your mainframe and get them for me."

"She wouldn't do that."

"Yes I would, Karl. Hey, it's Ike we're talking to here. Give him the lists."

"I'd love to but… Ike, are you on a monitored phone?"

"No."

"Give me your number, I'll call you back. But as of this minute, the answer is no. No for me, and no for Sam." Karl hung up.

Ike understood. He would wait for the call, probably from a throwaway like his or one of the few public payphones still operating in the city. It would take Karl a while either way. He'd wait. He started the engine and drove back to Charlie's.

NINE

IKE'S STORE-BOUGHT phone deedle-deedled at ten o'clock
the next morning. Without waiting for a "hello," Karl
Hedrick said he'd meet Ike for lunch, gave an address,
and rang off. Very good. Any trace on the call might
note his location, but no recipient name, no history,
and, more importantly, no compromising message. He
turned the phone off and would leave it that way and
use his personal phone until he had a chance to talk to
Karl. He looked at his watch and realized he could stop
at the hospital for an hour or so before the meeting.

Doctor Kravitz, as it happened, was on the floor and
had left a message for Ike and Eden to call him. Ike
found him in the Doctor's lounge. He received a few
scowls from the other occupants in the room that he
undoubtedly could have avoided if he had been wearing a white lab coat. Kravitz waved him into a chair.

"Mr. Schwartz, we need to talk. Is your mother-in…
sorry, is Ms. Harris' mother here? No? Okay, you can
tell her what I say. As I mentioned to you that last time
we chatted, your fiancée is stable. There is nothing more
we can do for her at the moment. I also mentioned possible difficulties that could arise. That is a problem for
the hospital."

"What's a problem for the hospital? I'm sorry but
you've lost me."

"Just this, we can do nothing more here that cannot

be done anywhere else by any competent neurologist. Our protocols call for her discharge." Ike started to object but the doctor held up his hand. "This is a tertiary care hospital, Mr. Schwartz, and the per-bed cost is double or triple what it might be in a primary or secondary care unit. My advice to you is to confer with Mrs. Saint Clare and make arrangements to move her to a facility which is set up to care for her special needs."

"You make it sound like you've decided she is not going to pull out of this."

"No, no, not at all. It's just, please listen, this hospital does not provide care past an allotted time for certain conditions. We deal with the trauma, the tricky medical procedures. Care for more than a week, or for what amount to long-term needs, is not something we are set up to do. Other places are. If Ms. Harris' signs were moving toward a recovery in the next day or two, there'd be no problem. Frankly, they're not. That doesn't mean they won't eventually, only that they aren't now, you see?"

"But we're happy with the care she's receiving here, Doc. I can't see how putting more stress on her system by moving her can be a good thing. I'd think you'd keep it to no more than absolutely necessary. I'd as soon she stayed here until you know for certain. Can't you give her a few more days, a week?"

"She is off the ventilator and breathing on her own. That's a good sign. A move should not be too stressful, so I'm sorry, but we are obliged to release her to a long-term care facility. The cost review people, you know, the money crunchers, the suits in the finance office, insist on it. They run health care now, not the doctors. It's all about the money."

"But that doesn't make any sense. If it's about the money, I'd think they'd want her to stay forever. Are you short on beds or something?"

"That's the second part of the decision. At the moment we are not, strictly speaking, short on available beds. Technically the hospital is at capacity, which means we are at somewhere between eighty and ninety percent occupancy. But that is neither here nor there. The policy in the hospital, as a tertiary care facility, is we do not treat chronic conditions. Ms. Harris' initial trauma has been attended to. There is no need for the high dollar medical intervention this place provides. Insurance providers will not pay us, you can't afford it otherwise, so, I guess I'm saying you move her to where you want her, or we discharge her and move her where we want to."

"That's not much of a choice, Doc."

"No, it isn't. I'm sorry. Do you have a place in mind?"

"If she has to be moved, I guess we'll go home. Well, not exactly home, but close. We'll take her to Stonewall Jackson in Lexington. They bill themselves as a critical care hospital but they'll take her. They have a heliport as well. We can fly her down."

"If you can manage all that…"

"I can manage it. You and your bean counters are wrong in thinking I can't pay, but now I don't want them to have my money anyway, so we move. I'll see Ruth's mother this evening and in the meantime, I'll call in some favors and make the arrangements for the chopper and the bed."

IKE SAT IN a booth at the rear of the restaurant Karl had selected. He'd arrived early and had set up a mini-office.

He kept the manager happy by paying for coffee. He called his father who "knew people" on the board of the corporation that ran the Lexington hospital. Abe in turn phoned some people. Ike called in a favor from a med-evac company run by a former spook pilot whose chestnuts he'd once pulled out of a fire in a country that had since changed its name three times. He managed to get Eden on the line and explained what he'd been told and what he'd done since. She didn't know if she was happy or sad. The thought of getting Ruth closer to home, she liked. The idea of a risky flight in a helicopter, she didn't.

Karl Hedrick and Ike had a history dating back to the time Karl spent a season on loan from the FBI to Ike's Sheriff's Department. He'd returned to the bureau and ultimately taken Ike's favorite deputy, Samantha Ryder, with him. For that, Ike assumed, Karl was forever in his debt. Karl did not agree, as he'd nothing to do with Sam's departure and subsequent employment by NSA. But he greatly admired Ike and went along with the illusion.

He sat down opposite Ike and made small talk, ordered lunch, asked about Ruth, and ate. Ike responded appropriately, asked about Sam, and would there be any wedding bells in the future? The crisis in the Middle East came up, as did the weather. Fall was football season and the relative merits of various teams, their coaches, quarterbacks, and chances for a run at the BSC and a championship game were discussed with some enthusiasm. On the whole the half hour passed in a totally uninteresting and one might say boring manner. When Karl finished his lunch he carefully wiped his mouth, stood, shook hands, and left.

Ike apparently mistook Karl's rumpled napkin for his own. He wiped his fingers and then palmed the thumb drive Karl left within its folds. He waited until two men at the counter paid and left before he extricated and pocketed it. He had his lists. Now he could go to work.

TEN

IKE'S FATHER'S CALL and an additional one from Armand Dillon, patron of Callend University and admirer of Ruth, to the corporate office in Roanoke freed up a bed in Lexington that Ike had been told did not exist. Eden had returned to Picketsville the night before and arrived at the hospital early to complete the paperwork for Ruth's admission. Ike saw Ruth onto the helicopter and then followed it by car southwest into the Shenandoah Valley. By the time he pulled up to the hospital's glass-dominated facade, she was safely ensconced in her new room. He couldn't tell whether she was aware of the change or not. As far as ambience went, there seemed little to choose between the one in Washington and this one. A hospital room, like a motel room, doesn't vary much from one place to the next. Ike guessed the helicopter ride would have made an impact, but nothing else.

He spent the remainder of the day alternately speaking to her, sitting silently, and negotiating—with God on the one hand and a hospital administrator wearing an expensive suit on the other. There were times when the tone in the conversation with the latter convinced him they might be one and the same. Ike wasn't raised religious. His father was a nominal Jew, his mother an Episcopalian who decided to be Jewish for his sake, and ended as more Jewish than either Ike or his father.

Today he wished he'd paid more attention. How does one pray to a God that seems so remote?

His father dropped by in the evening with Dolly and insisted he step out for a meal. They dragged Eden along as well.

"You aren't looking well," Dolly said to Ike as they left the building. "You need some food and rest. Are you getting enough exercise?" Dolly was one of those cheerful people who believed that diet and exercise were the panacea for all the ills known to mankind and many yet to be discovered. She believed, as a tenet of her Pollyanna faith, that if a regimen of proper exercise and diet could be achieved, emphasis on proper, all one's problems, physical, emotional, perhaps even financial, would melt away. Indeed, peace would be restored to the Middle East, an end to global warming achieved, and the suffering of countless children in far off and unnamed countries would soon cease.

"I'm fine, Dolly, just under a little pressure is all."

"Of course you are, dear. Now a good meal and eight hours of sleep and you'll be good as new. Mrs. Saint Clare, you look as if you could use a little gasoline in your tank, too."

"Not gasoline in the tank, Dolly. What I need is antifreeze in my radiator. You and Abe need to get me somewhere, pronto, where I can have a stiff drink. Make that two…no, three. Then I will discuss other forms of sustenance with you."

"I got us reservations at Frank's," Abe said. He opened the car door for Dolly and then rushed around to do the same for Eden, but too late. She's already slipped in next to Dolly in the back. Ike took the front passenger seat and they set off.

"Since when does one need reservations for Frank's? I'm amazed he's still in business."

"Now Ike, don't be hard on Frank. He tries hard. I always call for reservations. Makes him feel real good."

"That's very nice of you, Abe," Eden laughed. It was the first time she'd allowed herself to do so in days.

"Besides," Abe went on, ignoring all comments and laughter, "the Lion's Club meets there tonight and I figured after you're done eating or maybe before dessert, you could slip over to the banquet room and have a word with them, Ike."

"Yikes," Eden sat up straight. "Abe Schwartz do you ever think of anything besides politics?"

Abe thought a moment. "Once in a while." He winked at Dolly in the rearview mirror.

AGNES EWALT HAD served as Ruth's secretary for years. Ruth had brought her along when she'd accepted the position of president at Callend. She had witnessed, and not always approved of, the growing relationship between her boss and Ike. In the last year she had become Ike's ally and campus news source, especially if it concerned Ruth in any negative way. The accident had caused her as much mental pain as Ruth must have experienced physically. She would do anything for her boss and regretted her decision to stay in Picketsville and hold down the secretary's position for the acting president.

She sat quietly by Ruth's bed and only nodded a greeting when Ike arrived the next morning.

"She looks so peaceful, doesn't she?"

"What are you doing here, Agnes? The ICU is supposed to be closed to visitors."

"Mrs. Saint Clare told the nurse to let me in."

"Good. Have you spoken to her?"

"Gracious, no. Poor dear can't hear. I just came to be with her."

"You hear that, Ruth? Agnes doesn't think you can hear her. She's looking very spiffy in a flowered gym suit and an antique cloche."

"Sheriff! I do not, I am not. What are you doing? Do you want to upset her?"

"You just told me she can't hear a thing. So, what's the problem?"

"Yes, but…"

"Agnes, you are talking like someone in a funeral parlor. Ruth is very much alive and quite possibly can hear every word you say. If that's the case, she can't respond, which I suspect is driving her crazy. That right, Sweetie?"

"Ike, you can't…you mean…?"

"Exactly. If she's awake in there, I intend to get her so riled up she will come out of that coma if only for a second and long enough to give me hell. Wouldn't you like to see that?"

"Yes, I suppose so, but if she isn't…you said awake in there. What if she isn't?"

"Then no harm, no foul."

"Oh." Agnes let this set of possibilities sink in. "You asked for any suspicious e-mails that might have been sent to her at the college by mistake. I'm sorry, I only found one that qualified as a real threat. The rest were… well, none struck me as really suspicious or threatening. I brought the one and a few of the others anyway, but I really don't know what you're looking for or why, so it hasn't been easy."

"Right. Ruth, you're not going to like this…you either, Agnes, but it is now absolutely certain that you were deliberately forced into that skid and shoved into the pole. I aim to find out why. It would help a great deal if you'd wake up for a few minutes and tell me what you know or remember."

"It wasn't an accident?" Agnes' jaw dropped and her eyes popped a bit more than usual.

"No, sorry to say. I asked for lists, mail, possible enemies, especially those with a problem with her work on the textbook committee, so I can sort through them and begin searching out the SOB that did it. Then—"

"Ike," Agnes interrupted, "I think her eyebrow moved."

"What?"

"Her brow, there on the left side. I think when you said SOB, it moved. She must not like you cursing."

"Good Lord, Agnes, it's hardly a curse and she's heard worse. If it moved it's because of something else I said, or it's a random nervous event. Her good leg jumps every now and again, too. The doctor said that it happens sometimes to people in comas."

The two of them studied Ruth's face for any other signs of cognition but saw none. Still, they preferred to believe that the slight movement was both real and intentional.

And because he wanted it to be so, Ike tried to figure out exactly what he'd said that might have caused an eyebrow to twitch. He couldn't.

ELEVEN

AGNES AND IKE sat quietly with Ruth for another half hour. Occasionally Ike would say something to Ruth. He didn't want to press his "shock therapy," as Ruth's mother had labeled it, too hard. While he believed it couldn't hurt, might help, he did not have the heart to push hard. What he really wanted to do, but couldn't, was to lie next to Ruth and hold her. Eden Saint Clare breezed into the room and declared she'd come to relieve them. Agnes glanced at her watch and rose, flustered.

"Gracious, look at the time. I should be back at the office. Doctor Fiske will wonder what's happened to me."

"How is your temporary boss, Agnes?"

"Oh well, he's fine. He sent me, you know."

"Sent you? You mean Scott Fiske asked you to come to the hospital?"

"Yes. Well, his administrative aide said he wanted me to. I would have anyway, of course, but she said he was anxious to know how Ruth was getting along. He wanted me 'to report back.' That's how she put it, anyway. It seemed a little out of character but I thought it was sweet of him. Don't you?"

Ike had met Scott Fiske once at a reception, didn't like him, and said so. In spite of her own ambivalence about him, Ike had taken some measure of grief from

Ruth because of it at the time. He'd pretty much managed to avoid contact with Fiske since.

"Very. Listen, Agnes. Let me buy you a cup of coffee and you can fill me in on the things you brought me."

"What, now?" Ike nodded and waived her through the door. "Well, I suppose that would be okay. I can't stay long, though, maybe a cup of coffee. Doctor Fiske will be waiting to hear."

"Certainly." Ike found the cafeteria and bought Agnes a coffee and, noticing the attention she paid to a cinnamon bun in the glass case, bought her that as well. "So, tell me about your job with the Acting. I gather from what you said in the room you are not so keen on Scott Fiske."

"I probably shouldn't have said the things I did. He is a very nice man, I'm sure, in his own way, and to some… He's very good-looking, you know."

"Agnes, that is the weakest endorsement of another human being I think I've ever heard. Well, no. My father once described a girlfriend as 'having beautiful eyes.' He was being nice. He is very good-looking, indeed, in a young Richard Chamberlain sort of way if I remember him correctly."

"Sort of a young who?"

"TV and movie actor, very popular in the sixties and seventies."

"You'd know about that. You're the movie buff, I hear. He's sort of willowy, wouldn't you say?"

"How very antique of you, Agnes. Yes, he is. Now tell me. What's the problem?"

"Problem? There's no problem, really, it's just that… well you work for someone like Ruth Harris and anyone else seems pretty small potatoes, I guess."

"Come on, Agnes, we both are fond of Ruth and all that, but she is not perfect and Fiske can't be that bad. Something about him irritates you. What is it?"

"It's nothing. Alright, he just rubs me the wrong way. You know, he came to the school with the merger of Carter-Union College. His administrative assistant came with him. I don't think there's anything going on between those two. Although the way she looks at him— honestly, she's like a kid in a candy store. Well, a little hanky-panky isn't all that unusual in situations where the boss is not married and the secretary isn't either."

"It helps if she's pretty, too."

"Not always, you'd be surprised at some of the… there I go again. Anyway, the story goes that the president of CU was planning to retire about the time the idea of the merger came up. Doctor Fiske assumed he would be elevated to the president's job. Then when the talk of the merger got serious, Doctor Fiske endorsed it. He told everybody that he thought it was a great idea. The Carter-Union people all were for it, I hear. I guess he figured he'd just jump into the head of the newly merged schools. Everyone on that side believed Callend would be absorbed into CU but, of course, the opposite happened. Then their president did retire and Doctor Fiske missed his chance for the top job but stayed a vice president anyway. People said he was lucky to get that, even. I guess he didn't have the supporters he thought he had. Sheila, that's the AA I told you about, implied he was pretty bitter about it. She said if he'd been in charge of the negotiations, Callend would have been the one absorbed, and so on."

"You know that's not likely. Once Armand Dillon was allowed to sit at the table, it could only go the way he said it would. Nothing short of a nuclear explosion would have changed that, and his candidate would be Ruth, so done deal."

"I suppose so. Was Mr. Dillon that involved? I knew he called Ruth and…well, it doesn't matter now, does it?" She blew her nose with a limp tissue and took a breath. "Where was I? Oh yes, before the merger, his AA said Doctor Fiske used to send his curriculum vitae around. He was applying for presidents' jobs all over the place. Then he stopped. After the merger, he started all over again. Sheila, she gets big moony eyes whenever Doctor Fiske's name is mentioned, she said he did it all the time, she said he deserved better."

"Very loyal of her, but is that usual? I'm no academician, but I thought positions at that level were filled by soliciting nominations from outside and then recruiting a candidate, not answering unsolicited queries."

"You're right. I don't know what he had in mind. He even asked Ruth for a recommendation letter."

"Did she give him one? I can't imagine she did."

"No. She explained to him how the process usually worked and said he would need to ask for a different sort of letter, and at the moment, she couldn't see her way clear to putting his name forward."

"How'd he take that?"

"I don't know. Not well, I guess. Shortly after that, Ruth got the call to Washington and the Board appointed him Acting President. He hasn't sent any more résumés since. He's reworked it a few times but not sent any that I know of. Something stopped him, I guess."

"Well, he wouldn't, would he? He's in a position now to function at the level to which he aspires, to build a track record that will attract the notice he needs the correct way. That's assuming he's doing a good job. Is he?"

"Is he doing a good job? Yes, I think so but I'm not the one to judge. I guess you're right about the résumés." Agnes frowned, gathered her purse, wiped the remains of her cinnamon bun away from her chin, and stood to leave. "The e-mails are pretty self-explanatory and none seem all that threatening. Most are old, you know, like, they came in the early part of her chairing that committee. Then I guess they found out her government e-mail address and sent them there after that."

"They'll be useful, Agnes, anyway. I will try to match these early letters to later ones from the same people and see if there is a pattern of increasing anger or threats. Thank you for your trouble."

Agnes left and Ike stayed seated, nursing his coffee and sorting through the documents on the table before him. Agnes had handed him a job-lot of documents crammed into a folder apparently recycled from a wastebasket. The label had once read Dr. F., but that had been crossed out. In addition to the copies of Agnes' take on negative e-mails, she'd included a few sheets that had nothing to do with Ruth. He guessed they had been in the discarded file and Agnes had not noticed them when she collected her papers. He only glanced at them long enough to see that at least one was a marked-up copy of the Acting President's résumé, apparently revised and given to someone for retyping. Ike shoved it and the two or three other papers in the back of the folder, making a mental note to return them to Agnes when he had a chance. Then those papers, along with any thoughts he had about Scott Fiske, slid into that part of his brain where he habitually deposited things to think about later when he had nothing better to do.

A young man in green scrubs sat down at the next table. Ike asked if it would be alright to use his phone in the cafeteria. He'd shut it down on the hospital floor, of course, but wanted to make a call. The young man smiled and said it would be okay as long as he used it only in the cafeteria, the lobby, or outside.

Ike called Charlie. He needed another favor. He had to leave a message. Charlie, it seemed, was out.

TWELVE

BEFORE RETURNING TO his office for the first time in nearly a week, Ike stopped by the mayor's office to fill him in on what he hoped to do over the next few days. The interview did not go well. That may have had something to do with the fact the mayor preferred the candidate running against Ike in the election. He'd decided early in Ike's tenure as sheriff that Ike was too apolitical and therefore not easily controlled. He wouldn't admit it, but his cronies reported the mayor wanted a more tractable top cop.

He denied Ike's request for a leave of absence. He said he expected Ike to be on duty twenty-four seven. Recently, the phrase "twenty-four seven," had crept into and nearly taken over a substantial portion of the mayor's vocabulary. It had replaced "give one hundred and ten percent," which in itself was a small blessing. "Think outside the box" also lingered in the mayor's speeches but, thankfully, seemed to have fallen slightly out of favor.

Ike waved the refusal off and said that since he had leave time accumulated, he would use it. The mayor said he wouldn't approve any leave. Ike said he would take it anyway. The mayor said he'd fire Ike. Ike reminded him he had been elected, not hired, and therefore, couldn't be fired but only recalled. Since there was an election in less than a month, that did not seem to be a worthwhile undertaking. The mayor was not happy. He picked up the phone and, giving Ike a significant look, called the town's attorney. Ike left.

Essie Sutherlin saw Ike first and let out a whoop. Ike smiled an acknowledgement and headed to his office.

"Yo, Essie, how's Junior?"

"Growing like a weeping willow on a river bank. How's Miz H?"

"Holding steady, thank you. Oh, and thanks to everybody for the flowers."

"Ike, the word around here is you don't think Miz Harris' accident was one. Is that true?"

"Yes, I don't consider it an accident. But it's not simply a matter of what I think. There is clear evidence that says her car did not skid because of wet streets. Somebody rammed her and made sure she crashed into that pole."

"Who?"

"No telling. I'm working on it. There's no dearth of suspects."

"No dearth? That means a whole lot, right? I bet I know who did it."

"Really? Who?"

"Jack Burns, that's who, your opponent in the sheriff's race. He has a good reason to, doesn't he?"

"A reason to make Ruth crash? How do you figure that?"

"Not Miz H, Ike, you."

"Me?" Essie, it seemed, shared Charlie's concern that the perpetrator of this mess wanted to get at him through Ruth.

"Well of course. It was your car that got sideswiped, wasn't it?"

"Yes, but I wasn't driving it."

"He wouldn't know that. He knows it's your car and here's a chance to eliminate you from the race. Look, Ike, you got this election all sewed up, everybody knows that, so what else is that carpetbagger going to do."

"First, Essie, he's not a carpetbagger and—"

"He is. He only moved over here from Buena Vista at the invitation of the mayor and just in time to qualify as a resident to get on the ballot. Then he's walking around town talking trash about how big a cop he was over there, and how professional and all, and he ain't."

"Okay, if you insist. But it's a pretty radical idea, you have to admit. What is the likelihood he drove all the way to Washington in a big truck in the hopes of catching me on a wet street in the dark?"

"You don't have to make this complicated, Ike. Maybe it was one of them serendipity things. Say he's up there visiting his old granny or something, and sees your car. 'Ha,' he says, 'I'll notch this dude right here and now.' Then—"

"'Notch this dude?' What does that mean?"

"It's something Billy always says. I think it means to put you down or something. See, he does have motive and opportunity."

"Essie, you've been hanging around cops too long. First, you haven't come close to establishing opportunity. Was Jack Burns in Washington Sunday night? Does he drive a truck or even own one? Did he drive it to DC to visit, as you suggest, his old granny? And why in a big truck?"

"I'll bet he does own one. Everybody in Buena Vista's got them a pickup at least. What kind of truck are we talking about?"

"It's a five-year-old Silverado platform with a modified front bumper, definitely not a pickup truck," Frank Sutherlin said. He'd come in the middle of Essie's Agatha Christie moment.

Ike had not seen him enter and turned. "You have some news for me from the State forensics lab?"

"Preliminary stuff, Ike, but useful for starters. The truck is what I just said. The front bumper had some sort of projections on it and it was not, as far as the techs could tell, either standard or optional manufacturer's equipment."

"A custom bumper then with some sort of hitch, do you suppose? Anything on the paint samples?"

"Not so good there, Ike. Black Rustoleum. Sold in every hardware, paint, and drug store in America. Not even a special order, just your basic black."

"That's not much help."

"Not on the face of it, but then, how many Chevy Silverado platform trucks can there be with modified front bumpers painted with store-bought black spray paint? It won't help us find it, but it could confirm it if and when we do. The next piece of information is better, maybe. The techs were able to enhance the video images you sent. First, the license plate is unreadable because it had some sort of cover, like a rag over it. Second, there were markings on the door panels of the truck but they were covered as well. Duct tape, the techs thought, because of their slight sheen. And finally, they were able to enhance the driver's face."

"We have a picture of the driver?"

"Not really. He had a bandanna over his face like an old-time Western movie bank robber and wore a ball cap low. So, no face, but—"

"But we now know, and without a doubt, that the crash was premeditated. Whoever sat behind that wheel went to a lot of trouble to cover any identifying marks and, it seems, even anticipated the traffic surveillance cameras."

"It would seem so, yes. Whoever did this took the time to think the whole thing through and plan it very carefully."

"Essie, would you bring me a coffee? It smells like somebody made a fresh pot."

"Just this once, Ike, but you know this ain't in my job description."

"Lord, Essie, you're sounding more and more like a federal employee every day."

"Well maybe I do, somebody's got to look out for the rights of working women." Essie put the cup down on Ike's desk. "Frank, you're family. You get your own."

"Thank you, Essie. It appears motherhood has made you feisty. Rights of working women?"

"I'm just looking out for me and mine."

"Indeed. Frank, Ruth received a phone call just after nine. That's why I left DC a little early. I found her phone on the floor of the car. It must have been on the seat when she hit the pole. I assume there is a way to retrieve the numbers of anyone who called her."

"There is. Almost every phone has a call log of some sort built into its memory, but if the guy was careful about covering the markings on his truck, the possibility of surveillance cameras, and so on, what's the likelihood he'd use a traceable phone?"

"Slim to none, but criminals make mistakes. Sometimes that's the only way we catch them. I'll have Grace run the phone log for me."

"I still think it's Jack Burns," Essie said. "Why don't you run him in here and have some face time?"

"Face time? Who are you hanging around with these days? We will not have 'face time' because we have no probable cause, Essie. I'll make you a deal, you find out if Burns has a five-year-old Silverado platform truck with an odd bumper painted in Rustoleum black and no alibi for Sunday night, and then I'll run him in."

"I'll get Billy to do it. He knows all kinds of people up there in Buena Vista. You wait and see, me and him will figure this out."

"Knock yourself out. Frank, is there anything new on your suspicious death?"

"I'm still waiting for an autopsy report. Nothing new."

"Okay. Well, just so you all know, I am in the mayor's dog house—nothing new there—and plan on using up my accumulated leave time. Frank, you are officially in charge."

"What will you be doing, Ike?"

"Trying to sort this out on my own, I guess."

The phone rang. Essie shouted across the room. "Mr. Charlie Garland returning your call."

THIRTEEN

"CHARLIE. WHAT'S UP? Except in the dead of night, in the event of national emergencies, and/or during your rare showers, you always answer your phone, and even then sometimes."

"Ah, you must not take me for granted, Ike. It's unseemly, especially when you call my hygiene into question. I have been busy on your behalf, as it happens."

"Happy to hear it. May I ask in what way you have been busy on my behalf?"

"You may, but I'd rather not discuss it on your very public phone. Meet me for lunch."

"For lunch? Charlie it's one hundred and fifteen miles from Picketsville to DC. If I were to leave this instant, and allowing for the traffic on the 66 and I-95, it would take me well close to three hours to get to there and that's moving some. Lunch will have come and gone before I reach you. You mean an early tea? I never took you for an Anglophile. How about a mid-afternoon snack? I could manage that. Assuming I even wanted to drive to the Monument on the Potomac, which I don't."

"How you go on. No, I mean lunch, or brunch if you prefer. I know a place."

"Yes, I know you know a place. You are one of those people for whom installing a kitchen is both a waste of time and money."

"Perhaps, but one has to have one's oatmeal and coffee somewhere, and what better place than in that room with all the interestingly shaped appliances where I keep my microwave and my Mr. Coffee? Now, are you coming to lunch or not?"

"Whatever."

"Lunch it is, then. There is a woman in this establishment who claims to know you. I imagine it must be so because she described you and your lack of nutritional discipline to a T."

"Does this knowledgeable woman have a name?"

"I'll ask… What's your name, dear?… She says it's Flora Blevins. Does that ring a bell?"

"You're across the street at the Crossroads Diner?"

"Wait, I'll ask… Flora says yes, that is where I am. What a finely honed mind you possess, Ike. No wonder you are such a good detective. You figured that all out in one phone call."

"Shut up, Charlie, I'll be there in five minutes."

Ike shouted to Essie he'd be at the Crossroads and headed to the door. He was met by Amos Wickwire.

"Amos, what brings the number-two man from the accounting office to the Sheriff's Office?"

"Can't say, for sure. What have you been up to?"

"Pardon?"

"The mayor called the town attorney who called my boss and said he—that would be the mayor—needed an audit of this office's use of public property for private use."

"An audit, you say? Anything in particular or is this just our turn for general harassment?"

"Um…cars, photocopiers, computer time, cell phones, things like that. You know."

"Do I? I suppose I do. You are in luck, Amos. Unbeknownst to anyone in this office, and for reasons similar to yours, I recently installed GPS tracking hardware in every car in the fleet. You can install the software you need to read them, have someone from the garage hook them up, and you will have everything you need to know in that department. The computers, however, are password-protected. If you present me with a letter from the mayor requesting access to the hard drives, loggers, or anything electronic, you are more than welcome to pry. As for the copier—good luck with that."

"I don't need a letter."

"Actually, you do if you want a peek at what's in the files. Sorry, but the mayor himself pushed that little statute through back when a Grand Jury requested we look into his correspondence involving the city snow plow contract, if you recall. So, thanks to the mayor's diligence, you will need one here, now. Excuse me, I have a luncheon engagement and must be off."

Amos glanced at his watch. "It's only ten forty-five. It won't be lunch time for another half hour or so."

"Amos, bless your flinty little heart, I am on leave. I eat lunch whenever I damned well please. Have a nice day." Ike stepped through the door and headed to the Crossroads with a grin on his face. The first in days.

Sure enough, Charlie sat in Ike's favorite booth and had Flora Blevins, the age-indeterminate proprietor of the Crossroads, hovering like a vulture waiting for something to die.

"I'm sorry, Ike, I tried to hold off your order but Mrs. Blevins has already decided that you require breakfast, not lunch, and has put the order in. I'm sure she will change it if you ask."

"Charlie, if you intend to spend any amount of time

in this establishment, learn this: Flora does not take advice, cautioning, orders, or requests contrary to what she deems correct and proper."

"Really? She sounds just like my boss. Mrs. Blevins, were you ever employed by the Central Intelligence Agency? Or perhaps you have a relative, a son perhaps, who is employed by that organization in a significant capacity?"

Flora shot Charlie a look and turned to Ike.

"Flora, breakfast will be fine, thank you. Now, Charlie—explain."

"You have friends in high places, it seems."

"What does that mean? How high, and so what?"

"My director is how high. Somewhere along the way you must have impressed him with your charm, though I fail to see it, and he has seconded me to you for the duration."

"That's very nice of him. The duration of what?"

Charlie turned serious. "Ike, we both know you will not rest until you find out who knocked Ruth into that pole. The director, irrespective of what you may think of him, is concerned and he wants to help. He knows we go back. So, voilà, here I am. How are you, by the way?"

"I am managing, thank you. It's easier with Ruth in a hospital close by. Having her mother here helps, too, and I have to tell you I never thought I'd ever say that. But still..."

"Right. How far have you gotten?"

"Not very. The mayor just shut me down as far as accessing national and international databases to find the people I want using the department's equipment. It's the election. He's backing the other fellow. In a perfect world—his perfect world—I'd go away and not force an election. Sheriff's elections, most folks think, should be uncontested. Putting the head local law enforcement on the ballot begs political wheeling and dealing and threatens equal treatment under the law and all that."

"Can't argue with that, though the lawyers have pretty much suborned that portion of the constitution anyway."

"Which portion?"

"Fourteenth Amendment, Section one, equal protection under the law clause. Lately Congress has seen fit to pass laws that apply to the general populace but not to themselves. Lawyers have argued that there are times when congressmen and other subpopulations, in the pursuance of their elected or appointed tasks are not, strictly speaking, equal, and so on."

"Basic tenet in *Animal Farm*, 'All animals are created equal,' to which the pigs added, '"But some are more equal than others."'"

"Exactly. So will you? Resign, I mean?"

"Right now, being sheriff in a town that has an ungrateful mayor at the top and a minority, but still annoying, selection of overeducated idiots on the council no longer holds the appeal to me it once did, but, as it happens, I don't have to. The election could do that for me, I expect, and also, I'd rather not give the mayor the satisfaction."

"No, I don't suppose you would. Never mind the local computer power. We will tap the Company's if we need to. Tell me what you have so far."

Ike filled him in on what he'd managed to get from the FBI through Karl Hedrick, the data from the State's forensic lab, and Agnes.

"Agnes? Indeed. She had useful information for you?"

"Not really. Some e-mails and odds and ends, letters, that sort of thing. Stuff she deemed suspicious. But I will still cross-match them with what the FBI has on their lists. It may be significant or not. Agnes wanted to help."

"Of course she did. We need to set up a clearinghouse somewhere. I would have suggested your office, but as you are persona non grata there, it seems, I suppose we'd better find another place. How about here?"

"You are joking, right?"

"Yes, but you have to admit, it has a certain appeal, ready availability to sustenance and so on."

Flora dropped their plates in front of them with what passed for a flourish in the Crossroads and told them to eat up. She needed the booth for a committee meeting of Red Hat ladies in twenty-five minutes.

"So much for commandeering space here."

"I have an idea. Charlie, we both need a haircut, you more than me. Nothing new there. I think I know a place."

"That's my line."

"Not in this town, it isn't."

FOURTEEN

LEE HENRY HAD been cutting hair for the citizens of Picketsville for years. She cut the hair of most of the town's politicians, businessmen and faculty at the university, at least those who actually had their hair cut. For that reason, she had become one of Ike's more reliable sources of information. Some would call it gossip, but Ike had learned that the "grapevine" that operated in small towns could be considered a primary source and did not mind admitting it. He ushered Charlie into Lee's newly established salon on Main Street.

"Lee used to cut hair in her house on the edge of town," he said by way of introduction, "but success has found her, even in a weak economy, and she now operates this exclusive spa for the town's elite. Lee, this is Charlie Garland, a man of inestimable talents, but not one to attend to his tonsorial needs, as you can see."

"How do, Ike. I didn't understand a single word of what you just said. I reckon you're showing off your college education to this here gentleman who is needing a haircut. If that is what all that lah-de-dah was about, you ain't in any position to comment. You look like you're growing a bird's nest. Sit down and let me tackle that mess. Mr. Garland, you're welcome to wait or you can see Sherleen over there. She's as good as me any day."

"Is Sherleen your partner?" Charlie asked as he eased

into the chair and allowed Sherleen to paper tape his throat and wrap him in a plastic sheet.

"No, she rents the chair. I have me a group of gals that do that. We probably cut ninety-nine percent of the hair in this town between us, don't we, Sherleen?"

"I expect so."

"Ike, I am mighty sorry to hear about Miz Harris. How's she making out?"

"She's…she's hanging on, Lee, you know."

He didn't know what to say, really. How could he tell people he was half scared to death that she might not live, or that she would but as a vegetable, or paralyzed, or all of the above, and whatever the two of them had together might be lost in some sort of post-traumatic disorder even if she did recover? Women, he thought, were so much better at expressing their feelings and fears than men. He envied them that.

"You stay strong, Ike. How about I go up there to the hospital and give her a wash and cut. There's nothing like having someone wash your hair to pep you up when you're lying around in a hospital bed. When I busted my leg that time I'd a given my eye teeth if someone did that for me."

"That's a nice offer, Lee, but she's covered with bandages. She had a nasty scalp wound and cracked her skull. When she comes around, though…" When? If. "…she'll need some pretty fancy styling to cover up the fact that half her head has been shaved."

"It's called a wig, Ike. I got a bunch of them in my back room. I keep them for the ladies on chemo. No sense plunking out them hard-earned dollars on a temporary fix. So, when the time comes, we'll fit her out until she grows out enough to comb."

"Amos Wickwire is still here. He's camped out at the spare desk and wants to know when you're coming back. He needs the password."

"Has he a letter authorizing the search from the ___ ___ two members of the town council?"

___ "

"Sherleen," Charlie said, "how do you spell your name?"

"C-H-A-R-L-E-N-E."

"Thank you. I thought so. Tell me something, Sherleen, I am not a familiar with hair styling and cutting. Why does this salon, and all of the others I've visited—"

"Couldn't have been many of them," Lee cut in.

"Tut. Why do they smell different from barbershops? I would think hair is hair, male, female, or unisex."

"It's probably the stuff we use for giving perms," Sherleen said. "Hold still."

"Speaking of back rooms," Ike said. "Is that one near the alley still mostly empty?"

"You mean the one where I aim to put Margie Tice when she sets up as a massage therapist?"

"That's the one. She hasn't started, has she?"

"Nope. You need it?"

"I do." Ike explained his difficulties with the mayor and the fact he wanted a place to sort through all the data he was in the process of assembling. That Charlie would be helping him and he needed space and privacy.

"You just help yourself, Darling. Margie ain't likely to need it anytime soon. I'll give you a key to the back door and you all can come and go as you please and nobody the wiser."

"Ike," Charlie said, "Aside from these delightful haircuts, am I to understand acquiring the room was the purpose of this visit?"

"More or less. Of course there is the joke of the week. We can't forget that."

"Of course not, but Mrs. Henry does not need to lend us a room. Only a heavy amperage electrical hookup, space on the roof for a satellite dish, and a parking space nearby. I believe there is an alley behind this place and space to locate a van?"

"There is. And you're welcome to that too. I don't know about the electrical stuff but we can get us an electrician in here and fix that up too."

"Thank you. Ike, we will borrow a company surveillance van. They are, or can easily be configured with all the computer stuff we need, including an operator. Now, I need to hear the, you said, joke of the week?"

"He did. Okay, did you hear about the two nuns what were chased?"

"This isn't the one with the Chinese chicken?" Charlie asked.

"Chinese chicken? No, this one is…what? No. See, there's these two nuns, Fiona and Colleen, and—"

"Irish nuns?"

"Is there any other kind? So they're walking home to the convent place where they live at and they hear these footsteps behind them. When they hurry, the steps get to going faster too, so they figure they're being, you know, stalked. 'Sure and begorrah,' Colleen says—"

"Ms. Henry, no self-respecting Irishman says 'sure and begorrah' anymore, and certainly not a pair of respectable nuns."

"Ike, does your friend always interrupt someone who's talking to correct them like that?"

"He does."

"Too bad. Mister Garland, unless you're ready for Sherleen there to give you a high and tight buzz cut, you put a sock in it 'til I'm done telling this story."

"Sorry, continue, you were at 'sure and begorrah.'"

"She says that, and then 'We're being followed?' And

Fiona says, 'Worse. I do believe that man wants to… you know, so—"

"Excuse me again for interrupting, but what do we know? You will need to be specific, I think, Ms. Henry, Ike is not too quick."

"Get out the shears, Sherleen. Th…
ciplining…

een. This man needs dis-
.... Rape, Mister Washington, DC big shot. You happy? So, to continue, them nuns start running, but the man, he runs faster. Now they're sure he's going to catch them so Fiona says, 'We should split up. That way he'll only get to one of us.' So they do. Colleen, she skips off to the right, Fiona, to the left. Pretty soon Colleen is back at the nun house safe and sound. Five minutes later, in comes Fiona. 'What happened?' Colleen says. She's all aflutter. 'Well,' says Fiona, 'he caught up with me out by the riverbank.' 'Oh dear, what did you do?' Like I said, old Colleen is pretty excited, see. 'What could I do? I lifted my skirt.' 'Oh my, what then?' 'Well, naturally he dropped his pants around his ankles.' 'Oh mercy, then what?' 'Not a problem, Colleen. Everybody knows a nun can run faster with her skirt up than a man can with his pants down. So here I am.' It's a dilly, ain't it?"

"A dilly, indeed. You're not really going to use those shears are you, Sherleen? I haven't had a cut like that since my days as a youthful Marine at Quantico."

"Not this time, but you be careful. Interrupting Lee in the middle of a story is considered a capital offense in this town."

Ike's phone rang as Lee finished blow-drying his hair.

"Where you at, Ike?" Essie.

"Down the street. What's up?"

mayor o...

"No."

"Then tell him he doesn't get the password."

Essie passed on the message. "He isn't too happy, Ike. He says he has verbal authority direct from the mayor himself."

"Not good enough. Tell him to go directly to His Honor and ask for it in writing. Tell him I'm thinking of running for mayor myself next election, on a reform ticket. If I win, I'll give him the password."

After a pause, Essie came back on the line. "Wow, I told him what you said and his face got all red and he stormed out. I didn't know old Amos had it in him."

"Life is filled with small surprises."

FIFTEEN

AGNES EWALT PHONED Ike early the next morning. She said she had to rush as her alarm clock had failed to go off, or perhaps she forgot to pull out that little button. She wasn't sure. It had never happened before. She sounded breathless and harried. Ike turned the bacon in the frying pan over with a fork and thanked his parents for not raising him kosher. He shifted the phone to his other ear and shoulder while he loaded bread into his toaster. He heard Charlie in the other room talking on his phone to someone else.

"I understand, Agnes. So, what was it you wanted to tell me?"

"I forgot to mention the other papers in the folder."

"What other papers would that be?" Ike had forgotten the three or four sheets he assumed Agnes had mistakenly placed in with her questionable e-mails.

"I included some things about Doctor Fiske with those e-mails. I shouldn't have. You have enough on your plate and don't need to take on my problem."

"What problem? I'd be happy to help you, Agnes. What is it about Doctor Fiske that concerns you?"

"It's probably nothing but, well I noticed some tiny discrepancies in his résumés and I was worried, that's all. He is the Vice President, I mean Acting President, after all, and I didn't want Doctor Harris… Ruth, to discover too late that he might not be who he says he is and cause a scandal."

"What are you saying, Agnes?" Ike stirred the scrambled eggs in a second pan. He never cooked his eggs in bacon grease, his only nod in the direction of nutritional discipline. He retrieved the toast and signaled Charlie into a chair. He mouthed "Agnes" in response to Charlie's raised eyebrows.

"I think he's padding his résumé, Sheriff. What do they call it? Kiting? He gave me one to retype a while back, and one or two of the revisions he wanted added I thought were pretty big—some publications dating back a ways, actually. I wondered if he really did all those things, and if so, why did he decide to include them on the résumé just now? I talked to Sheila, you know, the one I told you about that came here with him from Carter-Union, and she said he was only updating. She said she thought everyone did. She wears really short skirts and chews gum when she talks. Snaps it like she's punctuating her sentences. Mercy, the way she goes on about him. She is a widow, you know."

"Really?"

"I think he was in Iraq or something, a car accident, and I heard…" Agnes must have sensed Ike's impatience. "I'm sorry, I'm babbling…cafeteria scuttlebutt. Gossip, really. I don't know why I listen to it. Well, so I couldn't very well ask Doctor Fiske myself, could I? I didn't want to start an in-house inquiry in case I was wrong. People would think I was just petty or think Ruth ordered it. I guess you can see my dilemma. I added those papers because I thought you could find out for me what, if anything, on his CV is true."

"CV? Oh, curriculum vitae. I can try, but you understand, I'm kind of tied up with the other investigation. Let me see what I can do. Is there any urgency?"

"No, no, that's why I called. I felt so ashamed of myself for even asking you when you have so much sadness and other things to think about. I called to say you should just forget about it. Just throw those papers away. It's just me thinking the worst about someone I don't particularly like, I suppose."

"I'm sure it's not just you, Agnes. What you suspect is important and does need someone to look into it. And I will, but not right now, okay?"

"I guess so, yes. Thank you. If you go to the hospital, don't mention it to Ruth. We don't want to upset her. Do we?"

"Actually, we do, sort of, but not that way."

Ike hung up and sipped the coffee Charlie had poured for him.

"What was that all about? Or is it personal."

"It's Agnes. You remember I told you she gave me some papers to add to the pile. She included a few copies of the Acting President's CV. She thinks he might be falsifying items on it. She's afraid it could come back to bite Ruth. She understands that is the least of Ruth's worries at the moment, but if the man is a fraud, it could hurt the university, and Ruth by indirection. She wanted me to investigate."

"I heard that part. You have enough on your mind. I have access to the kind of people who do that stuff all the time. Get me this guy's vitals, his Social Security number would do for a start, and we'll outsource that little project."

"It's not that critical, Charlie."

"I know. That's why we will shoot the problem off to Donnie the Snoop."

"Who?"

"A guy I know."

They ate breakfast in relative silence. Charlie said he marveled that Ike could cook. That it was only eggs, bacon, and toast, Ike reminded him, meant his compliment didn't amount to much.

"I've arranged for the van. It will arrive sometime after three. We will need rental cars, and a motel room or two for a while. I figure you can set that bit up, Ike, as you know the area. An electrician and installer will be here around two this afternoon to put in the basic set-up."

"That's fast."

"Time, Ike. The trail gets colder by the minute. We need to start tracking before it is covered with too many footprints."

"Right. Thank you for that, Uncas."

BY THREE THAT afternoon a Comcast Cable van pulled into the alley located behind the strip of storefronts on Main Street and parked by the back door of Lee Henry's hair salon. It would stay there a week. The young man who seemed to be a part of the operation said he would be installing phones and Internet to the salon. The satellite dish on the roof seemed an odd thing for a cable company to install, but technology moved at such a rapid pace these days, so who could say?

On the other hand, what a salon and barbershop needed with that sort of service did raise a few eyebrows. It's not like it's a sports bar, they noted, but then everyone knew Lee Henry was a bit pixilated and you could expect almost anything from her. There was even talk that the banker's wife, Mrs. Tice, would be offering massages there, but nobody believed that yet. Less explicable were the comings and goings by the sheriff and his friend from out of town, in and out of the van, into the salon by the back door, and so on. The town had, however, learned not to question their sheriff's actions. If he needed to check out those Comcast people, it needed to be done. And, as few utilized the alley for anything more than a shortcut to the parking lot in the rear of the sandwich shop next door, it should cause fewer questions than it might have otherwise.

By nightfall, the equipment in the van was up and running, online to the most sophisticated computer programs available anywhere. The screening of Ike's list of potential suspects could begin.

SIXTEEN

ROBERT TWELVETREES, (Colonel, USA Ret.) met Ike outside the Crossroads Diner. Colonel Bob, near to his ninetieth year—people were not sure on which side—found himself relegated to a motorized scooter if he wished to do anything more than be driven to and from places by TJ and his companion, chauffer, likable, but intellectually challenged semi-caregiver. Colonel Bob, who'd served with his hero, General George Patton, during World War II, had required his scooter be painted olive drab, with the insignia of the old Second Cavalry, where he'd first served on horse, decaled on the battery box.

"Colonel Bob, it's good to see you. Are you here for breakfast?"

Ike held the door open for him as Colonel Bob maneuvered his scooter around various objects that normal, ambulatory persons would have hardly noticed, the undertaking made doubly difficult for him due to his advancing macular degeneration.

"Every Wednesday if I can. Flora takes care of me. I keep telling her the EEOC or whatever G-D government agency it is that wants to tell you how to live your life, will be all over her if she doesn't make this place more handicap friendly."

"What did she say about that?"

"She said she still had her old scatter gun and if

some hotshot federal Johnny wanted trouble, well bring it on. I don't know where she gets all that aggression, do you?"

"It's the company she keeps, Colonel Bob. A lot of riffraff hangs out here, present company excepted, of course."

"Of course." Colonel Bob eased his scooter to a table with minimum damage to intervening chairs and stools and yelled for Flora to get his breakfast. Flora Blevins shouted something in return that might, in another age, have been deemed obscene. Colonel Bob smiled and waved in acknowledgment.

"Sorry to hear about your lady, Sheriff. Currently, I am a complete wreck only waiting for the hearse to come and collect me, but if there is anything a half-blind, completely gorked out old Army man can do, you let me know. If I can't get it done, I'll send TJ out to do it for me."

"Many thanks. I will let you know, but right now, I am just trying to figure out where to start. I don't know if the scuttlebutt has reached you yet, but Ruth's wreck was not an accident and I have a lot of questions to put to people. The immediate problem is who to ask."

"Can't help you there. Flora, where's my breakfast? I still have some contacts with the DOD, though most of the people I grew up with in the service are dead. Hell, they're all dead, but still you never can tell."

"Thanks." Ike moved down the length of the diner and found a seat in what he thought of as his booth. Flora plunked down his coffee and stood arms akimbo, waiting. "Just you, this morning. Where's your smart-mouthed friend?"

"If you mean Mr. Garland, he will be joining me

shortly. Also, I think Deputy Sutherlin plans to join us as well."

"Is that the smart Sutherlin or the dopey one that married Essie Falco?"

"The smart one."

"Too bad, I like the dopey one better. He has a sense of proportion."

"He has a what? Billy has a sense of proportion? Billy is moment to moment most days. What do you mean he has a sense of proportion?"

"It means I like him 'cause he don't take life too seriously, unlike some people I know. So how's Miss Ruth doing?"

Ike gritted his teeth. "She's holding on."

What a stupid answer. Ike had become weary of hearing that question. How to answer? Were the folks who asked it really concerned about Ruth, about him, both, or merely being polite? How did he relate to them the turmoil he felt, the emotional swings between guilt, anger, fear, and hope—sometimes alternating, sometimes simultaneous? And did they really want to know? He wondered if people would think him rude or crazy if he printed up little cards that listed possible responses to that question. He could check off one or the other and hand it to the asker.

"Well you let me know if there's anything I can do. They feeding her good up there at that hospital? I could fix up a tray."

"She's fine right now, Flora, thank you. Eating isn't her big problem."

Charlie slouched into the diner, waved a greeting to Flora, which was studiously ignored, and sat across from him.

"What do you recommend for breakfast, Ike, and

why are we here? You made a perfectly adequate meal yesterday. Now, I wake up, you have vanished and left me a note. Not very hospitable, I must say."

"In the first place, I always eat here in the morning if I can. It is one of my listening posts. I'm not officially on duty at the moment, but you never know what I'll pick up. Secondly, Frank is meeting me here because I refuse to go to the office. Oh, and as I indicated to you before, I don't recommend food to Flora's customers. If she likes you, she will select your breakfast for you. If she doesn't, she insists you order it yourself, and then will tell you she's out of whatever you ask for."

"Then the strategy, assuming I am not on her dance card, is to order something I really don't want in order to get what I do."

"You have the proper devious mind to figure that out."

"I've had lots of practice."

Flora brought coffee and glared at Charlie. He ordered a fish sandwich with extra tartar sauce and was told the diner was out of fish. He got scrambled eggs. Frank joined them a few minutes later and sat next to Charlie.

"What's new, Frank?"

"Nothing changes. Amos Wickwire has taken up permanent residency, it seems. The mayor, we assume, is convinced you will return and he will catch you using public, that is to say, police equipment to work your private case."

"Poor Amos. It can't be easy working for the mayor in an election year. Anything else?"

"It appears our suicide, isn't. The ME says he died of asphyxia, all right, but not carbon monoxide intoxication. He surmises that the man was hit on the head and then smothered somehow. Plastic bag, maybe. After that he was dumped in the van. The suicide is a setup."

"The dead man, who is he again?"

"Worker from up at Callend, general duties, janitorial, I think. We're still checking. We're looking into his background now. His name is Marty Duffy. He arrived about the time the school underwent the merger to become a university. He rents in the trailer park, we think. We'll find out more soon enough. Also, I've had a number of calls about the Comcast truck in the alley behind the stores near Lee Henry's back door. Do I need to worry about that?"

"Nope. I hear Lee is installing Internet and TV for her customers. Maybe she'll put in a coffee bar too."

"Great. One last thing, and you are not going to like this. Essie and Billy have been snooping around Jack Burns. I had a call or two from his campaign people wanting to know who authorized the Sheriff's Office to stalk their candidate. They threatened to call the Fair Election Committee and file a formal complaint."

"It's my fault. I told them if they could connect Burns to a truck and so on, I'd consider Essie's idea. Tell those two to cool it. I have enough *tsouris* at the moment and Burns may be a bad candidate for sheriff, but he is not a good one for attempted murder."

"I know, but there is one little problem the two of them turned up. He has no alibi for Sunday night and his cousin owns a platform truck like the one in the video."

"That's not good, but still doesn't move him into the picture. Did Grace turn up anything useful on Ruth's cell phone?"

"The caller used a store-bought throwaway, but she says she's not done with it. Something about backtracking and matching a signal to other calls, locations, triangulation, or something."

SEVENTEEN

FRANK LEFT TO return to the office to work on his suicide/murder, and to ignore Amos Wickwire. He had to tell Essie and his brother to leave Jack Burns alone, at least for now. They were not happy.

Ike and Charlie finished eating and made their way to Lee Henry's Cuttery and Style. They announced their presence, and retreated through the back door to the ersatz Comcast van. A young man Charlie introduced as Travis Blasingame sat staring at the bank of computer screens and attacking a keyboard. Ike could only guess what all that activity meant, but no games appeared on any of the flat panel monitors.

"Travis, are we ready?"

"In a minute, Mr. Garland. I need to sync these two programs so that if one gets a hit, the other won't keep searching for the same person."

"Ike, you have some additional lists and papers. Tell Travis how you wish to proceed."

Ike handed him the flash drive Karl had given him, the folder he'd received from Agnes, and the items forwarded to him from the Secretary of Education's Office.

"There are a lot of names there, Travis. Too many names for us to handle easily, and there are duplicates that may or may not be obvious at first glance or may only seem to be the same person. I want you to merge all of them into one comprehensive list. When you've done that, apply two or three discriminators to reduce the number of people we need to look at closely."

"No problem. Give me an hour to input all this and then I can start culling through the list. What discriminators do you want to use?"

"Okay. First, a prior history of violence, record of arrests, particularly at demonstrations, appearance on a police blotter somewhere, that sort of thing. After that, any time they may have spent in any form of law enforcement." Travis's eyebrows shot up. "I think whoever drove the truck knew something about apprehending a vehicle during a chase. Third, their proximity to Washington, DC. I am assuming for this first cut through the data, that the person driving the truck lived nearby, within a few hundred miles at least. I know some of the more vocal opponents to the committee's work will be found in places like Texas and Idaho, but the guy was driving a truck. That is not an easy vehicle to escape in, nor an easy one to acquire for a one-time use."

"How about we also look for stolen trucks, dark, older Silverados to be precise," Charlie suggested.

"Yes, in the greater DC area. That should include Northern Virginia, Maryland, the south Philadelphia area, and perhaps even as far as the Eastern Shore."

"Can do," Travis said and began typing faster than before. "I'll be awhile. You can wait here as the stuff begins to appear on the screen or go get a coffee somewhere. If you do, bring me one back."

"There's no coffeepot in this luxury home?"

"Could be but with the doors shut, and in spite of the filtered air, the aroma can get pretty overpowering, so no, no coffeepot."

"Lee has got a whole kitchen setup, coffee, pastry,

and so on. You should feel free to step in there if you need to. Oh, and restrooms, too."

"Thanks, that's a relief, or will be."

Charlie said he had some calls to make and would stay in the van. Ike decided to head to the hospital. He stepped out of the van and closed the double doors.

AFTER THE DOORS closed on Ike, Charlie began to work his way through the backlog of calls on his phone. The fact that the director had turned him loose to help Ike did not mean the rest of his projects could be ignored, or that they ceased creating difficulties. Most of them were delicate in the extreme and time-critical, and he couldn't simply drop them. He stayed with it for a half hour and then closed the phone.

"Travis, how about that coffee? If you'd like, I'll check out the kitchen Ike described and fetch you one. Or you could take ten minutes and join me. Either way, I'm headed to the restroom."

"Sure thing. Give me a minute here first, though. There's something I think you need to see."

Charlie rolled his chair down the narrow aisle and sat next to Travis, who touched the screen with the eraser end of a pencil.

"See those names?"

Charlie squinted at the list of four names Travis had isolated from the rest.

"I think they're ours."

"Oh, crap. You're sure?"

"I cross-checked them with our database, Mr. Garland. I'm pretty sure they are. Why are they on these lists?" Charlie tapped his foot and stared at the screen.

"I can think of four possibilities, only one of which

is good. We put them there and the FBI doesn't know, not good. We put them there and they do know, that's the good one. We didn't put them there and the FBI doesn't know, very bad. Or we didn't, and they do, very, very bad."

"What do you want me to do?"

"Hang on, I need to think about it for a second. Damn those FBI guys. Why…?"

"I was wondering the same thing. If they were on the Bureau's list and they know who they are, why didn't they tell us right away?"

"Indeed, why? You are young, Travis. If you stay with us for a while, you will learn that while the several investigative bodies the federal government maintains cooperate, they do not trust each other. The business of keeping the country safe may be the primary task of us all, but behind the smooth façade of interdepartmental good will lurks a nagging sense of distrust born of competition and ego."

"Competition? For what? Don't we all want the same thing?"

"Indeed. That is the one saving constant in the equation. But it is the variables that hurt us, chiefly competition. We compete for the president's ear, we compete for funding. We compete for prestige, for flattering press coverage, all the accoutrements of power and position. There is only so much money to go around and every institution believes it must grow or die. Can you think of a single university that doesn't believe it needs a new student center, gym, research laboratory, and then when it gets it is satisfied?"

"No, sir, I can't. So how does all that relate to this list?"

"It depends on which of the four possibilities I mentioned before are in play. If the FBI knows, it has determined, I guess, that these people pose no threat to the country in spite of their appearance on a roster of some sort. But they also know that we may have some lists as well and assume some of their people may be on them. This list is their equalizer. If we out their guys without letting them in on it, which we might very well do, they will counter with these. It is all very juvenile but what can you expect from institutions built by bureaucrats and funded by politicians?"

"I don't know. So, what do I do with this bunch?"

"Okay, I'm making an executive decision here. I do not believe those birds are in any way a part of what we're looking for. I am hoping for option number two, but I could be wrong. And because they are ours, and because they have access to information and assets which makes wrecking a car in the middle of Washington a very easy undertaking, we will temporarily assume the worst. We will delete them from the main file and enter them in a separate one. You will treat that file identically as the big one, but you will not tell the sheriff what we are up to, unless or until one or the other of them surfaces as a real possibility. And, because they are uniquely positioned, they might have information we can use. I, on the other hand, will notify the director who will, no doubt schedule some serious face time with them. You got it?"

"Got it."

"Good, do that and then we'll go get our coffee."

EIGHTEEN

EDEN SAINT CLARE maintained she married Ruth's father because she caught him on the rebound. In truth he'd run out of patience with a wife who exhibited subclinical paranoia, chronic anger issues, and a tendency to spend beyond their means. Eden, then Paula Cline and an undergraduate student, caught his eye and, as they say, one thing led to another. All of which explained the closeness in the ages of mother and daughter. The first Dr. Harris, Ruth's father, had lately succumbed to Alzheimer's. Once he'd crossed over the line from which no coherent responses could reemerge, he refused to recognize his wife, and when she entered his room, would slip into anxiety attacks or mild violent behavior. On the doctor's advice, Eden stopped visiting.

Since she'd gone from adolescence to motherhood and faculty wife without the usual twenty-something pause at young adulthood, she determined she needed to correct that misstep and had reinvented herself, emerging from spa treatments, surgery, and dubious exotic therapies, as Eden Saint Clare.

Her husband had by then taken up with a fellow Alzheimer's sufferer who bore an uncanny resemblance to his first wife, and he currently resided in a constant care facility in Oak Park, Illinois. Not coincidentally, the facility happened to be close to his spinster sister. As she never cared for her sister-in-law when she was Paula and detested her as Eden, there existed little or no communication between the two—a situation which suited both of them just fine.

Eden finally accepted the sad fact the man she had loved and whose child she'd borne no longer existed. The shell that remained might resemble him in some ways, might have his voice, and bear his name, but it was no longer he. That man had packed his bags and gone to wherever people go when they aren't dead, but aren't alive either. The Catholic Church used to proclaim the existence of Limbo. Too bad they gave that up. It would have provided a comforting destination for so many families dealing with a need for relief from the guilt they dealt with daily because of their inability to care for their loved ones properly, as well as the uncertainty created by a real lack of closure.

Eden had grieved her loss and had moved on, she insisted. Easier said than done. These thoughts and the pain that always accompanied them were on her mind as she sat at Ruth's bedside stroking her hand and murmuring snippets of old memories.

"You remember the time you decided to be a hippie, honey? You had that awful boyfriend who played a guitar and didn't bathe. Your father nearly had a cow."

It had been a huge row at the time, the first time he'd actually yelled at her. He had a position to maintain, he'd said, and as her mother she should bring the girl to her senses, he'd said. Eden smiled at the memory. Could that have been the first sign of the disease that eventually overwhelmed an otherwise extraordinary intellect? Who knew?

Ike slipped into the room.

"Speaking of having a cow, here's Ike, who probably will if he doesn't slow down and relax."

"Nice to see you too, Eden."

"Ike, I have to leave for a few days. I have to fly to Chicago. There's been a problem with Ruth's father."

She lowered her voice so that Ruth could not hear. "His sister, that's Ruth's aunt Joan, is contesting the fact that I receive his university pension and Social Security. She claims that since she is now the primary caregiver, she should at least get the pension. She's hired a sleazebag lawyer and I have to go to Chicago and set them straight. Also," she dropped her voice to a whisper, "the Doc said he does not have much time left, so it's important for the old bag to stick her paws in ASAP. I, on the other hand, need to make the arrangements for the eventual end to this sad story."

"Sorry to hear about all that. Do you have a good attorney? I went to school with a guy who practices out there and—"

"No problem, Ike. When you are married to the Dean of a Law School, you get to know a lot of lawyers. I have whole firms at my disposal."

"Right. Leave me an address where I can reach you if there is a change."

She handed him a three-by-five card. "I'm way ahead of you. I'll be here."

Ike glanced at the card and slipped it in his pocket.

"Have to run, Honey," Eden said, loud enough for Ruth to hear. "See you in a few. Ike will take care of you now."

Did he see her eyelid flicker again? Was anybody in there? He cleared his throat and decided he would read to her from the book she'd started but never finished when the two of them last spent a weekend in the mountains at his A-frame. Something easy and not overly stimulating, but entertaining enough to require the engagement of her faculties, assuming there were some on line—to make her think. He opened the book to the page marked with an envelope which also had a shopping list scrawled on it. They'd made chili that night... that night. He folded it and began to read.

It had started innocently enough. A week after her sixtieth birthday, Darcie saw her cat savaged by her neighbor's pit bull. The image seemed so real that she dashed into the back yard screaming at the dog's owner. He, a glass of lemonade in one hand and a tattered copy of Agatha Christie's A Holiday for Murder *in the other, nearly fell out of his Pawley's Island hammock at Darcie's verbal onslaught. Cleopatra, the cat in question, watched all this with feline disinterest. Her neighbor, momentarily stunned, recovered and had some strong words for Darcie in return. Mixed in among them was the news that Jaws (the name of pit bull in question) had spent the day at the vet's and had not yet returned. At that moment Cleopatra announced her presence by rubbing against Darcie's legs. Abashed and thoroughly confused, she retreated to her kitchen and poured a bowl of milk for the cat.*

Ike flipped the book over to glance at the cover. *Digby,* it read. He did not recognize the author. He checked the inside and saw it was a collection of short stories. He continued to read as Darcie discovered she had been visited or cursed with second sight and in the end had successfully shared some loot with a woman with whom she'd briefly shared a jail cell. The story line seemed a little thin but the O'Henry ending pretty much saved it. He thought that with the right actors and director, a decent little comedy-crime movie might be assembled along the lines of the classic Lavender Hill Mob. The cheerfulness these musings tried to force into his conscience faded, and darkness descended on his psyche again.

He did not see any more movements in her eyes. He hoped she'd enjoyed the story. He'd probably never find out. He wondered if she would ever finish the book. That thought depressed him even more. He left before she sensed his mood, if indeed she could. He didn't know how much she picked up, if anything.

He wanted to hit something.

SCOTT FISKE, PH.D., didn't often feel inadequate. Oh, sometimes one of the younger faculty with a brand new degree and a research grant in his back pocket triggered an old reflex and he got that sinking feeling, but he had conquered most of that and now he was on top. He'd managed to sidestep the difficulties he'd encountered in the past, learned to compensate for the gaps in his background, and as far as anyone knew, he could stand with any of them. Scott might be glib where others were thoughtful, but at his level, glibness had its positives—just check out the majority of the country's elected officials. He talked a good game and thereby gave the illusion of competence. If you didn't look too closely, he was what he pretended to be. And the truth of the matter was, he really did function ably in his current position. The great irony of the academic world is that the qualifications required to rise to the top in administration are not the skills one needs to function in those positions. Scholarly research and a long list of juried publications does not make one a good administrator. Scott lacked many of academe's more conventional trappings, but he did know how to make things happen.

He glanced in the mirror, slicked down his hair and straightened his Italian silk tie. It had cost him seventy-five dollars but Sheila said it gave him a presence, whatever that meant. She was okay, could use some grooming in the right way to have a presence— her word—herself. Content with his appearance he left his office. Sheila sat at her desk as he stepped into the outer office.

"You look nice, Scott, I mean Doctor Fiske."

"Thank you, Mrs. Overton." Had he looked closer, he would have noticed the unabashed look of admiration on her face. Another man would have been genuinely flattered and possibly concerned. As it was, Fiske merely accepted it as his due. He was, after all, the Acting President. He smiled, gave the knot in his tie one last tweak, and moved down the corridor. Sharp.

A wit once described Academe as the last outpost of medieval governance. In it the president assumes the role of the king and deans and chairmen/women, are the barons. The president, like the king, maintains power because he can allocate space and money. In the case of a college or university, that translates to budget approval and the dispersion of the more liquid grant overhead allowances and FTEs. The trick to running a university, a trick Ruth Harris had to learn early, was the judicious allocation of these assets, thus keeping more barons with you than against you. To do so took guile, an iron constitution, and guts.

Scott Fiske, unfortunately, possessed few of the important characteristics. That would not necessarily be fatal. After all, he was the Acting President—allowances would be made. But the fact that he was ignorant of these shortcomings meant that the barons routinely manhandled him like bullies working over a nerdy kid on the playground during recess. When Ruth returned to her office, assuming she would, she would have some serious fence mending to attend to. Very likely, given her private thoughts about her vice president, she had already planned for it.

Fiske proceeded to the administration conference room and joined the department chairpersons for the scheduled weekly policy meeting. Rarely was policy the topic of these meetings, however. Lately they had devolved into verbal pushing and shoving about whatever issue the "barons" seemed to think important. This day the topic would be messy, but Fiske felt he could handle it. How hard would it be to establish norms for Interpersonal Referencing? The term was his. He intended it to replace "political correctness," which he believed no longer passed muster. He'd show them how to run a meeting that produced results.

He just hoped the woman with the degree from West Virginia didn't get smart with his talk about mind control, First Amendment rights, freedom of speech, and coerced censorship. What the hell did that mean? And what was she talking about with Brave New Worlds? Fiske sort of remembered reading that book, and he'd seen the movie *1984* in sociology class twenty years ago, but so what? Everybody agreed some things were not to be said, period. He could live with that and if the hillbilly bitch from the mountains didn't get it, well tough cookies. Time to move on.

NINETEEN

CHARLIE LINGERED OVER his rapidly cooling carryout coffee to chat with Lee Henry. Sherleen/Charlene had the day off and in her place were two other women who, he was told, also rented chairs in Lee's Cuttery and Style. He didn't catch their names, which was unusual for him. He had a prodigious memory for names, places, addresses, and telephone numbers. Ike sometimes referred to him as an idiot savant. Charlie was anything but intellectually challenged and had responded by suggesting that Ike possessed an inordinate quantity of Neanderthal genes in his DNA.

When he returned to the van, Kevin handed him a message. "It's from the director. He wants you to call and he told me to wipe those names we were so concerned about."

"Did you?"

"Not yet, waiting to hear from you."

"Good man." Charlie stepped out of the van and reclosed the doors. He managed to reach the director's unlisted number and an aide on the other end put him through.

"Garland? About those names, am I right in assuming this has something to do with Schwartz's probe into his friend's accident?"

"Yes, sir, it does."

"Okay then. Here's what you need to know about

those four names. They are ours, we put them in there, the Bureau knows they are there and is okay with it."

"Yes, sir. Am I to assume they are plants to monitor possible connections with international organizations?"

"Yes and no. That will do for the moment. I've talked to them all and here's what I want you to do. One of them, Hank Baker, might be able to help you out in this. He has some information that he says could be relevant. I can't see this being the work of someone on the fringes, but I suppose that's all Schwartz has to work with at the moment. Anyway, I don't want Schwartz in this patch of turf at all. I'm just being cautious, mind you, so I want you to interview Baker yourself. Break out of there for a day or two and head to Skokie and hear what he has to say. He may have some other information to pass along to me as well. Two birds, one stone, and all that."

"Skokie? Odd place for us to lurk isn't it?" The director did not answer. "Telephone not good then?"

"For a variety of reasons, that is to say, reasons not related to this business, absolutely no. So, no telephone. Fly out and back and use the information as if you'd gleaned it some other way. Clear?"

"What do I tell Ike?"

"Does he know what you do?"

"He's guessed. Ike is quick. He won't admit it, but yeah, he knows."

"Then he won't have any questions for you if you have to bug out for a couple of days, will he?

"No, sir, I expect he won't."

"Good luck. How's the lady doing, by the way?"

"Holding her own, I think. We remain optimistic."

"But you don't know if she'll make it or not?"

"No."

"Damn."

Charlie spent the next hour on the phone making his travel arrangements, details he could have done in five minutes if he did not have to use the Company's travel booking service.

IKE HAD AGREED to meet Charlie for dinner in Lexington. The restaurant was not far from the hospital and it allowed Ike some extra minutes with Ruth. He arrived at the Palms Restaurant a few minutes before Charlie and had a drink in his hand when the latter arrived.

"Charlie, will wonders never cease? You are on time."

"And you are early. What are the chances of either of those two circumstances repeating singly or coincidently ever again?"

"Not good. So what news do you have for me?"

"Lists are up. Kevin will have the details for you tonight or tomorrow. It appears that as with most groups with an axe to grind with the government, the people you are interested in are primarily headquartered in the DC area. No surprise there. Also, not surprisingly, they have political action committees and money to funnel to congressmen in the form of election campaign contributions and, thereby, the wherewithal to purchase the votes they need to swing the legislation in which they have an interest."

"No surprises there either. As far as I'm concerned, PAC funds are just legal bribes—the oil that lubricates the machinery of government."

"Tsk, you have become a cynic in your old age, Ike."

"Maybe. I'm not feeling terribly bright-eyed these days, that's for sure."

"Justifiably. However, do not lose all hope. As quirky as the system often seems, it is still more open and efficient than most countries I have visited. And if you have a problem that needs solving, you can always start your own PAC and buy a solution."

"Goody."

The server took their orders and refilled Ike's glass.

"I must leave you for a few days, I am afraid. Duty in the dark recesses of the Company requires my presence. But, as the good general once famously said, 'I shall return.'"

"Where are those dark recesses located, or can't you say?"

"No secret, I am off to the Windy City, or near enough. Skokie, I think."

"Interesting. This is real, or some BS you cooked up to make contact with a lady?"

"Ike, is that likely? Why would you think that?"

"Because Eden Saint Clare is also scheduled to travel to Chicago for a few days. It seemed a logical conclusion."

"Very logical and very wrong. Why is the handsome Mrs. Saint Clare traveling to the Midwest?"

"Personal reasons, I think. Her husband is an Alzheimer's sufferer and his sister is after Eden for a piece, at least, of the old man's pension. He is on the last leg of his journey, she says. She goes to Chicago to consult with doctors, lawyers, and Indian chiefs, not to mention morticians."

"Ah, some humor has returned to my dour friend. Shall I call on her?"

"I think keeping an eye on her would be a good idea. She is about to take a dip in a shark tank. Any help you can give to keep her from being devoured by attorneys who, because there is money involved, will be in a feeding frenzy, will be appreciated."

"Give me the address of where I can find her and I will do what I can."

Ike slid Eden's three-by-five card across the table. Charlie studied it for thirty seconds and pushed it back.

"Got it."

IDA TEMPLETON MADE a much needed part-time income by working as a temp at the hospital. She had three kids under five at home and so full-time nursing was out of the question, but like many young couples, she and her husband were upside down in their mortgage and a refi not on the radar. She worked shifts, when she could get them, that were opposite those of her husband's at the county fire department.

Tonight, she'd drawn the ICU. She liked it. Always quiet in the ICU. She looked up from her paperwork and nodded to the doctor as he passed the desk. She thought she recognized him but she couldn't be sure where. She'd only been on this floor once or twice but she was sure it was not in this hospital that she'd seen this doctor. Nice looking, she thought. What other hospital could it have been? Perhaps she'd seen him that week she worked in Roanoke. She shook her head. It would come to her eventually. She gathered her papers together and sat back. An IV alarm sounded. Ms. Harris' room again. She stood and walked down the corridor, the soles of her sneakers squeaking against the

vinyl tile. She rounded the corner and saw the new doc
bent over the apparatus.

"Doctor, I'll do that, thanks."

He stood abruptly and backed away from the machine, dropping the tubing he held in his hand.

"Doctor?"

"Sorry, I never was very good at these things. Carry
on, Nurse."

He turned and slipped through the doorway and disappeared down the hall. She frowned. Doctors seemed
to be younger every year. Or was she getting older?
Nah. She adjusted the IV, replaced the bag. The old
one was nearly empty anyway and she could save a
trip later. Very strange. She would ask who this tall,
slick-looking doc was when the charge nurse came back
from break. She knew most of the nurses in Rockbridge
County by sight, but doctors seemed forgettable. She
wondered if that was a significant psychological insight.
By the time the charge nurse returned, Ida was busy
updating charts and forgot to ask.

TWENTY

IKE MET FRANK SUTHERLIN at the Crossroads for breakfast again. It had become part of his routine. He did not want to go to the office, as much as he missed seeing the staff, because of the presence of the mayor in the person of Amos Wickwire. He also did not want to listen to the phone calls and read his mail, and mostly he did not want to talk about Ruth, to answer the questions, to be reminded. And then there was the election to consider. The job of sheriff seemed distant to him now. He'd stubbornly ignored his father's pleas to campaign. He'd refused to authorize the expenditure of funds for new posters to replace those allegedly defaced by Jack Burns' supporters. His father overruled him and the posters now adorned most of the street lights and intersections in and around Picketsville.

Ike sat in his usual booth, soothed by the familiar aroma of diner food—in the morning, bacon and coffee. Around noon it would shift to hamburgers and grilled onions, and coffee, and by evening, mostly just coffee. Frank sat down across from him and took the cup of tea offered by Flora, who scowled her disapproval at the thought of a policeman drinking tea rather than the high-octane variety of caffeine she regularly brewed, which she believed a necessary part of any man's breakfast generally, and a policeman's, certainly. Frank was, as nearly as Ike could tell, impervious to Flora's disapproval, and might well be the only male in town who was.

"What's new this morning, Frank?"

"Ah, nothing much. A couple in Bolton let an argument about their missing and very expensive pedigreed golden retriever escalate into a smackdown, and somehow the wife ended up sticking a steak knife to her husband's backside. I put Billy on it and told him to stay on it. That way he may stop harassing Jack Burns' people."

"Are they still complaining?"

"Oh yeah, they insist that you have charged your deputies with politicking in your favor, and other things as well. I can't keep an eye on Essie and Billy twenty-four seven so I can't say what they're up to."

"Can't be helped, I suppose. What else?"

"Ike, it's none of my business, I guess, but don't you think you ought to campaign a little? I came over to the sheriff's office from the highway patrol because of what I believed you represented here. I'm not sure I can work for Burns if he's elected. The other guys feel the same way."

"I know, Frank, and I'm sorry. I'll try to make an event or rally here soon. But right at the moment my heart is not in it. Anything else besides the Bolton ruckus?"

"Some developments in our not-so-suicide. It seems one of his neighbors down by the trailer park where he lived mentioned that he was 'on to a big score.' We received a notice from AFIS that his prints matched a person held briefly in Scranton, Pennsylvania, as a possible participant in a drug-related shooting. I called Scranton PD and a very annoyed narc told me that the deceased received immunity for providing information to the cops and that's probably why he ended up, and very dead, in our jurisdiction."

"You believe it?"

"Well, it makes sense. It allows us to shift the investigation back to Pennsylvania and clears one off the books."

"That's true, but that is not what I asked."

"Am I buying it? No, I don't think so. Movies and TV notwithstanding, my experience tells me if he sold out his pals, they would not, more likely could not, have hired a hit man to finish him off while they lolled around in jail. I mean, how'd they pay for it, and wouldn't it be more likely they'd wait until they were sprung and do the job themselves?"

"I think you're right. You probably need to stay on it. See if there is a local connection. 'On to a big score'— that could mean anything, but with his priors all related to drugs, there might be a connection there. I guess the local dopers need to be pulled in and interviewed. As soon as he's finished with the Bolton business, put Billy on that, too. I don't want him to have a life until the election is over."

"Got it. Are you going to eat that donut?"

"No, go for it."

Frank stood, scooped the donut from Ike's plate, and left. Ike sat a few more minutes to finish his coffee and then followed Frank out the door. He needed to talk to Kevin.

CHARLIE PREFERRED ENTERING Chicago by the back door, that is to say through Midway rather than O'Hare airport. Before that mega-airport had been built in Orchard, Midway was *the* entry, but no longer. As he needed as much anonymity as possible in his prowling in "the dark recesses of the Company," a smaller airport suited him to a T. Eden would doubtless land in the larger and better served O'Hare so he did not expect to run into her at all.

He was mistaken. Her flight had originated from Roanoke, wandered across the south, and finally landed a few minutes before his direct flight from Washington. He almost ran her down in his dash to the car rental desks.

"Why Mr. Garland. What a surprise. What are you doing here? Aren't you supposed to be helping Ike?"

"I am, you are correct, but duty called me away for a day or two. You are here on a personal matter, Ike tells me."

"I am. I must tackle a passel of money-grubbing lawyers and their avaricious client, that is to say my sister-in-law, and other things." Her face fell with the mention of the last.

"Yes. Well if I can be of any help, please call me." Charlie made the offer knowing that Eden did not have his phone number or know where he might be reached. He was raised to be polite at least, if not always genuinely accommodating.

"I am fine, I believe, Charlie, but then it is a big town and I have no company this evening. If you are not busy…will you be? If you are not, maybe you will join me for dinner. I am staying at the Drake. You know the Drake?"

"I do. Very nice hotel…lots of history. It's a Hilton property now, I believe. So you're at the Drake?" Charlie, of course, already knew that, but a lifetime of caution willed him to keep it to himself. "I am not sure how engaged I will be, but I think dinner could work. Not at the Drake, however. I am required to be invisible right now. I know a place on the west side where I can be that way. Perhaps you could meet me there, say sevenish?"

"A place? Invisible? Mercy, you sound like a man of mystery. Are you, Charlie?"

"It is all a front, Eden, but for a few days, I need not to be seen. Sorry."

"Really? How exciting. Well, I tell you what, give me the address and I will see you at seven. Oh, wait. What if either of us can't make it. You can call the hotel to tell me, but how will I contact you?"

"You can leave a message at this number." Charlie scrawled the number of an answering service and the address of the restaurant on a piece of paper. "Just ask for Garland. They will find me. Must run, see you at seven."

He left Eden Saint Clare in the wash of travelers flowing to the street and into waiting cabs, cars, and busses. He found his rental and headed north to Skokie and Hank Baker. Why Skokie of all places?

TWENTY-ONE

KEVIN HANDED IKE the completed list of names which met his first criteria for scrutiny. They had to have a history of overt political activism, have a possible arrest on file, and have served in a law enforcement capacity at some time. Ike studied the list of twenty or thirty names, unsure where he should begin.

"I guess Mr. Garland told you about the headquarters of the organizations you wanted to screen being in the DC area. Four of those names are affiliated with one in particular."

"Really? Yes he mentioned the DC connection. Do you have the names and executive officers of the organization in question?"

"Interesting that you'd ask. This guy," Kevin tapped the paper with his index finger, "is the head honcho of Let States Decide. It's the biggest of the groups, and he also used to be a cop in Houston, Texas, fifteen years ago."

"You're kidding—the organization is called Let States Decide? Do you suppose they are aware of the irony in the name?"

"Sir?"

"Let States Decide—LSD? Do you think they are hallucinating up there in Washington?"

"Oh, you mean the drug hippies used in the olden days. No…yes, I don't know."

"Olden days. My God, son, how old are you anyway?"

"Twenty-five. Is there a problem?"

"No, sorry. Growing older can sometime be painful, especially when your doctor looks like she, emphasis on she, is maybe twelve and your adolescence is described as 'the olden days.'"

"Gee, I'm sorry if I—"

"It's not important, Kevin. Okay, so the LSD is head-quartered in Washington, DC."

"Not quite. They are in Arlington. That's across the river from the—"

"I know where Arlington is. You have the address, I suppose. I think I will start with the number-one guy and see where it leads. What's his name?"

"Byron Yeats."

"You're kidding. That's his real name? Someone named Byron Yeats heads up the LSD. That sounds more like a Beatles' song than a suspect."

Kevin nodded. Ike felt certain he'd missed the juxtaposition of two romantic poets in the executive officer's name. Apparently literature no longer received the attention it used to in college. Kevin's face brightened.

"Oh, I get it. His name is from a couple of guys who wrote poems or something and you're thinking he maybe made it up because of the LSD."

"More or less. Give me the address and get on that machine of yours and dig up everything you can on Let States Decide. I want names, the date it incorporated or received its 501.C.3 status, the works."

"I'm on it. Oh, I forgot, someone named Don T. S. sent Mr. Garland a fax but I think it's for you."

"Donte? I don't know of many Dontes and none personally. Let me see it."

Kevin handed Ike a sheaf of papers. The last had "from Don T. S."—Ah, Charlie's contact, Donnie the Snoop. He studied them first in order and then one page a second time. Agnes had been right. Doctor Fiske was an academic fraud. How had he managed it for so long? Ike guessed he knew. People were generally trusting of the claims made by others and academics dangerously so. Ruth would not like this at all. But Ruth wasn't in any position to receive or respond. He would have to talk to someone on the board. While he considered his next step, Marge Tice walked up to the back door of Lee's and smiled a greeting at Ike.

"Are you here to set up your massage therapy room?" he asked.

"Just a preliminary look-see. Lee tells me you have commandeered the space."

"Very temporary, Marge. We can be out of there anytime you want. But now that you're here, I have a problem for you."

"Me? What sort of problem? Do you have a sore back, stiff neck? What?"

"All of the above and others not mentionable in polite company places as well, but that is not the problem I want to hand off to you. Your new avocation hasn't taken you away from the serious life, has it?"

"You mean, am I still married to the town's most important banker?"

"Maybe, but what I need to know at the moment is, are you still on the Board of Directors for Callend?"

"Just for another month. I turned down an offer to serve another term. The school isn't the same since it grew into a university and it needs a more experienced board, I think. So, what's the problem?"

Ike filled her in on what he suspected about Fiske's CV. He left Agnes' name out of the conversation. Right or wrong, whistle-blowers rarely fared well in the aftermath of a scandal, and this one promised to be a doozy. He explained why Charlie Garland—though he did not mention him by name either, but for different reasons—had at Ike's request, commissioned an inquiry into Fiske's credentials, and then handed her the report.

"The guy's a fake?"

"Let's say he's exaggerated his experience more than a little."

"Exaggerated? How?"

"It appears in small, and occasionally, big ways. For example, according to this report several of the publications he lists on his bibliography were authored by a different person with the same initials, S. Fiske, here." Ike pointed to the list, "And there is a Susan Fiske, a woman who dropped out of the academic world years ago. Since her papers are in Fiske's field of study, who'd notice? Then there are fellowships listed that were actually visits. Things like that."

"This is serious." Marge scanned the papers and frowned. "Who is Don T. S.?"

"A friend of a friend. Very reliable, I am told. I did not have the patience to follow up on my own, so we, that is, I, had it done outside the office."

He didn't tell Marge that he couldn't have done it in-house in any event. Not with Amos Wickwire's annoying presence hovering over the department computers making his life more complicated.

"Do you want a copy?"

"No, Marge, I haven't the time or the interest to pursue it. It's in your bailiwick and I have no doubt you will do what needs to be done."

CHARLIE FOUND HANK BAKER sitting alone in the Starbucks at the Old Orchard shopping center. A copy of the *Chicago Sun-Times* completely obscured his face. Charlie recognized the orange-and-black backpack on the floor at his feet. He ordered a tall vanilla latte, which he considered a "chick drink" and so would only sip but not consume. He pulled up a chair at an adjoining table. Baker glanced his way and nodded imperceptibly. After five minutes during which Charlie attempted to read the exposed back page of Baker's paper, he cleared his throat and leaned toward him.

"Excuse me," he said, "but are you finished with your paper?"

"No, not quite. In a minute or two, perhaps. You are welcome to it when I am. Do you work around here?"

"On occasion. I travel. Sales, you know."

"Ah." Baker turned away and continued to gaze at his paper. When he spoke he did so very softly and did not take his eyes off the newsprint. Charlie never looked his way but instead watched three baristas busily scalding milk and making endless cups of strong coffee behind the hissing espresso machinery. He had no idea how that thing worked and did not wish to, but he admired those who did. He fine tuned his ear to Baker's murmuring.

"I have scoured the activities of not only the members of the organization I monitor, but any others I could hack into. I am afraid I don't have much for you. I can tell you that at the lower levels of the organizations, where the zealots and crazies lurk, there is general jubilation at the news the woman was racked up, but no indication that any of them knew beforehand of any attempt being made or who might have made it. Most wish they knew who did it, however. I guess they want to send him a card."

"That's it? No names, no suspicions, nothing? A wild guess would make my trip out here worthwhile."

"Sorry. No, it's not a complete blank. My particular organization, as are others like it, is funded by what we believe is a front for a smaller group of extremist individuals who support other less-than-savory and/or more dangerous undertakings. That is why I am on their membership list."

"I gather the boss believes the agendas of fanatics on the far left and those on the far right sometimes intersect. So who are these baddies that I need to check out?"

Baker stood and put on his coat. He folded his paper, turned to face Charlie, and spoke to him in a normal voice.

"Here you go, friend. I'm done with the paper. Sorry about the crossword puzzle. I'm afraid I started working it but didn't finish it."

"Not a problem." Charlie thanked him and watched him leave. He opened the paper and began reading at the business section. He sipped his coffee and leisurely turned pages, folding the paper and eyeing its contents with studied attention. At the same time he kept tabs on a tall man in a rumpled Burberry hunched over his cup, who had not removed his gloves the whole time he'd been there. It was chilly out, but not inside. Gloves? Charlie eventually turned to the crossword and memorized the information Baker had scribbled in the blanks.

After a minute, he proceeded to fill in the remaining blanks, erase, or overwrite Baker's earlier entries. He stood and left. He dropped the paper in a trash can outside the store, crossed the street, and waited at the corner to see if Burberry would retrieve it. He did. Baker must really be close to something. The director needed to know that. Baker might soon be in need of backup or even be extracted. Before the paper retriever could spot him, Charlie climbed on a bus and let it take him four blocks south on Skokie Boulevard. He would wait another ten minutes and then walk back to his rental in the parking lot. This could get dangerous. Ike needed to know.

TWENTY-TWO

IKE FINALLY YIELDED to his father's pestering and attended a small luncheon of businessmen and potential supporters. He spoke briefly about how he viewed his position and what he hoped to see in the sheriff's office in the future. Picketsville was, he said, a growing community. He wasn't entirely sure he liked that, but it was a fact and the town and its citizens needed to keep that in mind when they discussed budgetary issues. He hoped he sounded thoughtful and sincere. The truth was his mind went wandering halfway through his speech and he had no real idea what he'd said or if it made any sense. The rapt expressions on the faces of his listeners suggested he had.

He then answered questions about why he should be re-elected over his opponent and what he would do differently if he were. The questions were predictable, his responses, perfunctory. He did manage to hang on to his temper when the questions devolved from the obvious to the inane. Traffic patterns on Main Street did not interest him and he was not aware the town experienced a "rush hour," and if so, certainly not one that needed his attention. But he scowled thoughtfully and said he'd look into it.

When asked what other changes he would make, he brightened a bit, thought a moment, and suggested one or two of the town's other municipal offices might be areas needing scrutiny. He'd had some complaints, not substantiated of course, but where there's smoke, and so on. When pressed he shrugged and muttered something about possible instances of undue influence from the administrative branch being brought to bear on the employees of some other departments. He was careful not to use the word "mayor." He imagined the person thus not mentioned would hear about what had been said within five minutes of the meeting's conclusion. His father's expression did not alter during this last musing, but Ike did notice the blood vessel on his temple begin to throb. He received polite, but not enthusiastic applause when he finished. So much for campaigning.

HE SPENT THE next half an hour working his way through the phone system at Let States Decide to make an appointment to meet with Byron Yeats. Then he returned to Charlie's Comcast van to find out what Kevin had gleaned about LSD's Chief Executive Officer. Kevin handed him seven pages, eight-point type, single-spaced. His name really was Byron Yeats, born Byron Shelley Yeats, in fact. His mother once taught English literature and poetry at a community college in western Kansas, which doubtless explained the name. His father was a painter—of houses, not canvases.

Ike retreated to the Crossroads for a BLT, coffee, and a place to read. He had settled into his booth with his sandwich, fresh-brewed coffee, and only a small dose of nagging from Flora Blevins when Agnes called for an update on Acting President Fiske.

"You were right, Agnes. Your temporary boss has padded his résumé over the years, and in more than one area."

"Oh dear, what should I do now?"

"You should do nothing, Agnes. I have turned the documents over to a member of the Board of Trustees and they will deal with it. You do not want an angry Doctor Fiske or any of his friends, if he has any that are involved, after you for blowing the whistle. Take some advice and forget about it."

"Oh, do you really think they would be upset enough to do something vengeful?"

"It's not likely, but you should be cautious anyway. Academe can be a jungle and nobody likes a whistle-blower."

"Well, thank you. If the Board needs to interview me or Sheila, I'm sure it would be appropriate. She's not in today, though. Doctor Fiske asked me where she was, as if I would know. Imagine!"

"Thank you, Agnes, I'll pass that along."

Ike closed his phone and promptly forgot Agnes and her problem. Enough already with the peregrinations of the academic set. He needed to focus. He spread the sheets of paper on the table in a disorderly array. Periodically, he underlined or jotted a note in the margin of a passage he thought might be useful. Byron Yeats had been busy in his fifty-four years.

"I'VE GOT TO run up to DC, Kiddo, so I may not find a way to visit you tonight. Your mom had to go out of town and Charlie is AWOL as well. Sorry about that. I think we are digging up some useful information on who pushed you into the pole but it is still scattered and not too clear just yet."

Ike gazed at an inert Ruth, unsure what if anything

he should tell her. Fiske could wait. That problem was
in Marge Tice's hands. So what to talk about then?

"I wish you could talk to me."

He tried his best to sound cheerful. He doubted he
succeeded. God, she could slide into a vegetative state
and then…not again! Where are you, God?

"You were always able to figure out where I needed
to cast my net. Well, not all the time, but just talking
to you seemed to help. So…" Ike's voice trailed off. It
wasn't the same, somehow, just talking. He needed a
sentient, wise-cracking Ruth to make it work.

IN SPITE OF Ike's warnings and Frank's direct orders,
Essie and Billy left the house, put Junior in the care
of Billy's mother, and set out for Buena Vista. Burns
had to be up to something. A person didn't just walk
away from one police job and shoot for another without
a reason. It seemed obvious to them that Burns must
have been up to something and they aimed to find out
what it was.

Their first stop was at a coffee shop close to where
he lived. The counterman had all kinds of things to
say about Burns and none of them were complimen-
tary, but by the same token, none were suggestive of
criminality either.

"So," Essie said, sipping a very bad cup of coffee,
"what's he really like? I mean, didn't he used to be your
top guy in the police department?"

"You heard that?"

"That's what he says."

"He's county. He was assigned to us, is all. He ain't
no big-deal cop. Only thing I ever found him good for
was to fix a speeding ticket once, and that cost me

twenty-five dollars. Shit, it'd been cheaper to pay the fine."

"Write that down, Billy. We can use that. What's your name, Sir?"

"You writing stuff down? Who are you?"

"Umm, we're newspaper reporters. We're doing a story about corrupt policemen."

"Fixing a traffic ticket ain't my idea of corruption and if'n you want that, go to Detroit or Washington by-damn, DC. That's where you'll get a story. Say, what paper you with?"

"Thanks for your help, I reckon we better go, great coffee. Come on, Billy."

"You didn't get my name. It's Ballard. Edd, that's with two D's, but people call me Tank on account of my size. What's yours?

"Umm, Wickwire, Amos and… Darlene Wickwire. Thanks again."

They tumbled out the door and dashed to the truck.

"Wickwire? Essie, what are you thinking?"

"It was the first thing that popped into my head. You weren't no help."

"You don't look like no Darlene, that's a fact."

"Well thank you for that, anyway. Where do we go now?"

"I saw a bar up the road a piece. Best place to get information is bars and barbershops. We'll do the bar and then I'll get me a haircut."

"Okay, but only one beer, you hear?"

"I know what I'm doing, Essie. Who's the cop here, you or me?"

"One beer, that's final."

TWENTY-THREE

THE NEXT MORNING Ike stopped in the hospital cafeteria for a quick cup of coffee and a moment to jot some notes before taking off for Arlington and tackling Byron Yeats. Frank, Billy, and Essie Sutherlin found him there.

"We need your okay to visit Ruth," Frank said. "Visitors are limited in the ICU. The lady at the desk asked Essie if she was Agnes Ewalt. I guess she has a pass, that right?"

"Ike, I don't look a thing like that dumpy old woman. That nurse had a nerve."

"Indeed you don't, Essie. I think she's a volunteer and wouldn't know either of you, so give her a break. Ruth's mother set up the permission for Agnes, I gather. Do I need to sign something?"

Frank dropped a slip of paper on the table. Ike turned it around and signed. "Not too long and for God's sake, Essie, no talk about Jack Burns and the accident."

"Ike! I wouldn't do that. Shoot we're just going to say 'Hi' and all."

"Billy, Essie, you two go on ahead. I will join you later. I need a minute with Ike."

Frank plunked down opposite Ike. "Couple of things you need to know. I thought you might like an update. We have a connection for the dead guy."

"You pulled in the drug users and dealers?"

"Well, no. We started to and then got a call from the

State Police on the missing-but-not-missing truck. Do you know about the latest theft target? Hay. Honest to God, people are stealing hay out of the fields and people's barns. A farmer up the valley heard about what was going on and went to Radio Shack and bought a surveillance camera with night vision capability. When the thieves hit, he called the cops and they ran the tape."

"People are stealing hay?"

"Hay, yes. With the drought and the increase of small feeder lots and so on, the price of hay and straw has gone up enough to make stealing the stuff worth the risk. It's a big problem in Britain and in Maricopa County, Arizona, too. I saw that on the Internet. Who'd believe it?"

"I guess I heard about it, but it never occurred to me that it would be a problem here. What took the State so long to call us?"

"The farmer's setup wasn't very expensive or very good. The pictures were grainy, if that is what digitalized pictures are—probably not—but anyway, they had to tinker with the picture and then only got a partial on the truck's plate. After that they had to run it through the motor vehicle system computer. They skipped over the college's vehicle because they couldn't imagine it would be a likely candidate. Anyway, after they crossed off every other suspect truck, they called us."

"Did they see who was driving the thing?"

"They didn't say. Some figures in the field but no ID. Like I said the images were kind of raw."

"So this leads us where, exactly? I mean, besides knowing that someone at the college was moonlighting as a hay thief."

"To Bolton and the next item in the story. It's fascinating. You remember me telling you about the couple in the area that had the fight about their dog and the husband took a steak knife in his backside?"

"I do. So, that goes where?"

"To their barn. These part-time residents of Bolton leased it a month ago. The owner called to complain that his tenant hadn't paid the rent, had skipped, and had damaged his tractor to boot."

"But that wasn't what the fight was about that produced the coup de derrière?"

"The what? Oh, no, it was the dog, but it might have been connected. I went out there and took a look. We found the dog dead a few yards from the barn—been shot. I don't know how badly the tractor was damaged or even how the owner knew. He doesn't farm the land but leases it to a factory farmer out of Madisonville. There was evidence that a lot of hay had once been stored there, and a sign had been set up on the road nearby advertising hay for sale. Long story short, he identified a picture of Marty Duffy as the guy who rented the barn. Marty was dealing a different sort of weed, apparently."

"So the big score he bragged about wasn't dope after all. You think it was hay?"

"Don't know, Ike. I'd have to say probably not. I'm thinking it had to do with something else, something bigger. Tell me, what substance which has a high street value and can easily be stored in a hay mow comes to mind?"

"You think?"

"Maybe. A bale of marijuana looks and smells enough like hay to be invisible in a place like that. It's speculation, but think of the possibilities."

"Take the county's drug-sniffing dog out there and see if it confirms the presence of weed. It has a nose that can detect an ounce in a carload."

"Will do." Frank stirred as if to leave. Ike held up his hand.

"Try this while you are poking around looking for trace evidence. Duffy used the truck on the weekends and at night, presumably to haul hay. Leave the dope out of the equation for a minute and consider the possibility that he goes to the university to 'borrow' the truck and while he's at it, he sees or hears someone near it or fooling around. Whatever he or she or they are up to looks like an opportunity for him to blackmail someone and so he approaches him/her/them. But instead of shaking them down, he's snuffed."

"As an alternative, I like it. But until the dog with the magic nose says otherwise, I'm putting my money on the drug deal gone sour. Remember, he plied that trade before he came here. Old habits die hard."

"You're probably right. Did you have something else you wanted to tell me?"

"Oh yeah. Again, you're not going to like this. Essie and Billy were over in Buena Vista snooping around. Apparently they stirred up a ruckus in a bar over there when they started asking questions about Burns."

"Where's the uproar in that?"

"Well, it turns out Billy was over his limit in Rolling Rock and proceeded to get very loud. Then Essie jumped on his case, and the upshot is the county cops were called and escorted them out with a warning."

"Put a leash on those two, Frank. God knows, I appreciate what they are trying to do but tell them it isn't helping."

"I have, and I will again." Frank left to join the others and Ike headed to his car and the trip to Arlington.

Ike closed his eyes and tried to see the humor at the image of midnight hay thieves. It was there but it eluded him. The darkness that followed him through most of his waking hours dropped over his mind like the curtain in a theater. What comes next in this two-penny drama?

"WELL, HEY THERE, Miz Harris. You're looking pretty spiffy today. Billy's here and Frank is coming. He wanted to talk to Ike first 'fore he got away. We can't stay long, just came by to say—"

"Essie, what are you doing? She can't talk. If she can hear you, you're just frustrating the bejeezus out of her."

"What do you know, Billy? I don't recall as how you been to medical school anytime lately."

"It don't take a doc to know that, Sweet Cheeks."

"Well, I still think she ought to know who's here and who's not. If I was laid up like that, you know, and couldn't move or see or nothing, and I knew they was people in the room I surer'n heck would want to know who they was. Scare me half to death if I couldn't yell out for help and all if there was a stranger hanging around."

"Nnngh."

"Did you hear that? She's trying to say something, Billy."

"What?"

"I don't know. Probably agreeing with what I just said…ain't you, Ms. H?"

"Nnngh."

"See, what I tell you. Say, here's Frank come to say

hi, too. Lordy, we hope you pop out of this soon, because Ike, he's a mess."

"Essie!"

"Sorry. You rest easy there. We'll keep Ike straight, don't you worry."

TWENTY-FOUR

IKE RECEIVED CHARLIE'S text message while waiting in Byron Yeats' outer office. At first he couldn't make heads or tails of it. Charlie said he'd gone to Chicago on Company business. Judging from the message, that was not the case. Or perhaps he had gone on one unrelated mission and had stumbled on this information by chance. That did not harmonize with Charlie's normal *modus operandi* and therefore seemed unlikely. Ike scratched his head and reread the text. The oddity was, Charlie never texted. He claimed he didn't know how. Yet here it was, and not a simple line or two with abbreviations that took longer to decipher than it would have required to spell the word out. Here were whole paragraphs with names of individuals and organizations. As he knew less about texting than Charlie, or Charlie claimed to, he assumed he'd figured a way to attach a standard keyboard to his phone or make his laptop function like one. Bluetooth? Who knew? Either way, he was impressed. He would ask Charlie how he did it when he saw him next. He saved the message and rose when Yeats' administrative aide signaled for Ike to go into the main office.

If a call went out for a slightly over-the-hill, middle-aged but fit college professor, probably teaching the Humanities, Byron Yeats could have come from central casting—tweedy, pipe in the breast pocket, horn-rimmed spectacles, and in need of a haircut—perfect. He greeted Ike cordially and asked if he would like something to drink. Ike declined both green tea and coffee. Thankfully, Yeats did not offer the sherry sitting in a decanter on a sideboard. Ike had had his fill of that beverage at the occasional faculty gatherings Ruth dragged him to on Sunday afternoons. Sherry, as far as Ike was concerned, was only good for cooking, and as an adjunct to split pea soup in lieu of vinegar. He'd been told terrapin soup also benefited from it as well. He'd yet to try that. Soup made from a turtle created a gap in his imaginings.

"You are an interesting man," Yeats said as Ike settled into one of a matched pair of leather chairs across from his desk.

"I am? Why is that, Mr. Yeats?"

"It's Doctor Yeats, actually—Sociology, Haverford. You are interesting, at least to me, A, because you are no ordinary sheriff, B, because you are here, I assume, to inquire into the accident involving Doctor Harris, and, C, you are way out of your jurisdiction if you do so. I will refrain from pointing out your past for the moment. It does feature in my estimation, however."

"Since you know all these things, you might not want to set my past aside so quickly. If you looked into it, as I am sure you must have, you will have discovered that jurisdictional issues and the niceties of formal interrogation did not loom large on my horizon in the past. That could be the case again if I am looking for a particular killer or, rather, a potential one."

"Ah, I see. And you believe I may be one, or am I just harboring one?"

"Four."

"Four? And how did you arrive at that number?"

"I have my sources. You do run an organization that has in the past shown very strong contrary opinions to the government in general and certain issues in particular and you have attracted the notice of more than one agency because of it."

"Ah, the FBI?"

"Among others."

"Surely you do not believe opposing the federal government, or any government for that matter, constitutes sedition. We went through all that with the late, unlamented second president of the United States, if I recall my history."

"John Adams, yes and no. I consider it a near sacred duty to oppose authority when there is a clear misuse or abuse of the power entrusted to it."

"Then we agree. So what do you see as objectionable about my organization inasmuch as we are in basic agreement?"

"We are not discussing the fundamental right to disagree. I am drawn here because there is no provision in the Constitution or elsewhere that sanctions violence in the pursuit of that disagreement."

"And you are under the impression that Let States Decide is purveying such action?"

"I am persuaded that possibility exists, though not stated, yes."

"You overestimate me and the group I represent."

"I think not. You have charted a very public course of action encouraging the members of your group to display their anger at the government."

"First Amendment rights, Sheriff. We are guaranteed

the right of assembly and freedom of speech, among other things."

"The operative word in the amendment is 'peaceably.' The right to peaceably assemble. And the First Amendment right to freedom of speech does not, as Justice Holmes said, extend to the right to falsely shout 'fire' in a crowded theater. You are pushing the limits of the Constitution in some of your meetings and assemblies. It has consequences you cannot ignore, much as you might wish to."

"And I would say to you, define 'falsely.' One man's truth is another's prevarication. The difficulties, when they arise, stem from the intimidating presence of police and the FBI mingling among our numbers jotting down names, taking pictures, not to mention a biased media. It is not we who are fomenting trouble."

"I don't know whether to reach across this desk and rearrange your teeth or keep up the pretense that I am a gentleman. You said you investigated my past. Are you sure you want to continue in this way? Yeats, you either suffer from gross self-delusion or have become the worst kind of demagogue. I can't make up my mind which, but in either case I am not interested in debating with you about what I take to be your skewed notions of law and order. I am here because your opposition and reaction to the work of the committee Ruth Harris chaired had near-fatal consequences."

"Consequences? What consequences? We oppose it as we opposed the antecedent legislation that established Federal Curriculum Standards. There is no provision in the Constitution or anywhere else establishing Federal oversight of education in the separate states. The Department of Education needs to be eliminated."

"Except for the composition of the Legislature, the Presidency, and the Judiciary, there is no provision in the Constitution for the establishment of most of the departments of government. But they exist and you and your organization benefit from their existence. If you are so keen on reform and return to fundamentals, consistency would require you also object to the Departments of Health, Transportation, Commerce, Defense, and all of the regulatory agencies that keep snake oil off the market, banks out of your pocket and, more immediately, your current tax-free status. Am I right?"

"You are, like most liberals, blind to the insidious takeover of our rights by a centralized government."

Ike laughed. It hurt to do so. Laughter was no longer part of his program. "I've been labeled many things, but you are the first to pin that tag on me. I am not here to debate this. Nor is it my purpose to play Constitutional chess with you. Too much damage has been done to the fabric of society by people like you already. I am here to request from you the addresses and particulars of the names on this list. They are your members, as you know full well, and they lurk on the fringes of your organization. They are like rogue predators. You have provided them sanctuary and a mission. Any or all of them are capable of forcing Ms. Harris off the road."

"You say it was not an accident?"

"Do not toy with me, Yeats, this is personal and I am not in a mood to play games."

Yeats finally lit the pipe he'd been stroking with his thumb for the previous fifteen minutes, and disappeared behind a cloud of smoke, which had a significant measure of latakia, if Ike guessed correctly.

"I will concede that there are in this organization,

as with every organization, a fringe of, shall we say, zealots—your rogues, if you will. I mean, look at any group and you will find them. Even in police departments. Surely you have among your employees one or two who will step over the line in the pursuance of a suspect or a lead. In point of fact, you are here out of your jurisdiction chasing after what—revenge? Does that not make you a rogue as well?" Yeats read Ike's expression. "Did I hit a nerve? I did. So, how do you expect me to be held accountable for the occasional knuckle dragger who shows up at our rallies?"

"None of my nerves was even in the neighborhood, much less hit. Those fringe elements are responsible for violence that cannot be justified or excused. You know who these people are because, unless you are an idiot, you have them monitored by your own security people. Please don't waste my time. I need their current locations and status."

"Ah, but as we agreed, you are out of your jurisdiction. Forcing that from me would require a warrant of some sort and you can't get one, so sorry, not going to happen."

Yeats leaned back in his chair in smug silence.

"You can wipe that supercilious smile off your face. I have something better than a warrant. I will read you a message I received today and when you've heard enough, you will tell me what I want to know. You must not have been paying attention. I said this is personal."

Ike retrieved Charlie's text and began reading. When he started to read the list of organizations on the Homeland Security's watch list he paused from time to time and looked up.

"Any of these sound familiar? You have a multiplicity of donors, surely one of these… I could ask Homeland Security to check, of course, and then, who knows what might happen? Agents might be here scouring your files, digging into the pasts of your employees and members, perhaps even looking at your books. As I said, who knows where that might lead?"

Yeats held up his hand, pulled a notepad from his desk, and began writing.

Having Yeats offer up the data was a start, but Ike had hoped for something better, something more immediate. The disturbing thought darted through his mind that he might be hunting the wrong animal. He pushed it aside.

TWENTY-FIVE

A FEW MINUTES past seven, Eden's taxicab pulled up at the address Charlie had given her at the airport, a dingy storefront on an equally dingy street. A window to the right boasted a neon sign which flickered, buzzed, and read, "BAR." Another to the left announced that "This Bud's For You." She didn't think so. Two suspiciously green evergreens in plastic tubs, looking a little worse for wear, flanked the door itself. Overhead, the elevated tracks rattled as a train rumbled past carrying the last stragglers from the evening rush hour westward. She hesitated a moment before paying her driver. The door, she noticed, though deep in shadows, was painted a bright red and over it, at right angles but hardly visible from the street, hung a sign saying "The End Run." She stared at the sign for a moment trying to decipher its meaning. She feared Charlie had pulled a very bad practical joke on her. She seriously considered turning back. The cab drove off, leaving her no choice but to push her way in.

The interior of the restaurant surprised her. She relaxed. It seemed he'd invited her to one of those known-only-to-the-neighborhood-and-a-select-few places where the food is always good, never excellent, the service friendly, and the ambience informal. Unless she missed her guess, it would be owned, managed, or dominated by a character.

Charlie waved to her from the bar. He helped her

off with her coat and scarf and took her elbow to lead
her into the restaurant's dim interior. She sniffed at the
mixed aromas of garlic, onions, tomato sauce, and Italian sausage. Things were looking up.

"There's someone I want you to meet," he said, lead-
ing her to a booth away from the front door, the bar,
and any but the most determined scrutiny.

"Well," she said glancing around, "you're right, I
think. You will be invisible here from whoever it is you
wish to be invisible from, if that sentence parses. You
could hide Osama bin Laden in this joint."

"The patrons of this establishment would dice him
and put him in marinara sauce, were that so." Charlie
beckoned for a server. He ordered rye and water. Eden
asked for Prosecco.

"We're celebrating? Good." Charlie canceled his rye
and asked for a magnum of the sparkling Italian wine.
"And bring us flutes, not the white wine glasses."

"Tell me, what's up with this place that I had to take a
cab halfway to Iowa to meet you? Also, I came because
the whole notion of a clandestine meeting intrigued me.
So, why the cloak and dagger?"

"I could say force of habit. Ah, here he is!"

"Who?"

Eden followed his gaze and saw what she guessed
was the character.

"Tony Agnelli, our host."

Agnelli stood six-five. As nearly as she could tell,
he had no neck. His shoulders simply bunched up and
met his ears. He seemed nearly as wide as he was tall
and moved with the assurance of one accustomed to
having others step aside. Judging from his bulk, she
guessed he may have exceeded three hundred pounds.

Harry Potter's Hagrid but without the beard. The closest thing she'd seen that massive and mobile was the USS New Jersey.

"Hey, Chucky," Agnelli rumbled, and shifted course fractionally, enough to miss a table and chair, but not the waitress serving drinks next to it. Eden held her breath, expecting the crash of glassware and crunch of bone and sinew as USS Agnelli ran her down. But she pirouetted away at the last moment. An old hand, it seemed.

"Marie told me you made a reservation. What is this, you gotta make a reservation? This is The End Run. You don't make a reservation." He slowed his pace. Eden could almost hear the orders on the bridge. "All stop. Reverse," and the clanging of the ship's telegraph. He berthed gently at their table and his gaze settled on Eden. "How do you do."

She got her second surprise. However massive and clumsy Agnelli appeared, his eyes were extraordinarily soft, kind, and a startling shade of Nile green.

"Tony, Eden Saint Clare."

"Hi," she extended her hand.

"Tony Agnelli. Nice to meecha. Any friend of Charlie here is a friend of mine."

"Mr. Agnelli and I used to play football together. Tony was somewhat lighter in those days and we were both very much younger. Tony played every down, both ways, while I kept the bench warm for him for the rare moments when he needed a breather."

"We played for the once-mighty Princeton Tigers, a lot of years ago."

"You won a lot of games?"

"We had a few good years and a few not so good."

"In the Dartmouth game, Charlie got mousetrapped and mashed his knee and was out of football forever."

"It was the first and only time I actually got to play a down. I think we were losing forty–zip and the coach decided to rest the first string and most of the second, for that matter, and proceeded to clear the bench. One play and my march to the Heisman ended."

"I haven't the faintest idea what you're talking about, but it sounds awful. What is a mousetrap?"

"You tell her," Charlie said.

"Well, a mousetrap is when somebody on one side is maybe too good and coach wants to make him not so good. So instead of meeting him head-on like you're expected to, you step aside and let him through. He thinks you missed your block. And then two guys who're supposed to be somewhere else come from the right and left and bam, the guy who might be too good goes to the sidelines with his bell rung."

"Or his knee filled with relocated cartilage and ligaments."

"That's awful."

"That's football."

"What happened to you?"

"I ended my collegiate career with a limp as the team's Assistant Manager."

"Charlie was on an academic scholarship and put himself through college. He goes to Desert Storm with the Marines, gets medals, and disappears, only to come out in the spook business. You be nice to this man."

"And what about you, Tony? Did you play any more football?"

"Oh yeah. I had the other kind of scholarship, so I played. The Bears drafted me in the seventh round. I sat on the bench a year and got traded to Miami. I sat on their bench two years and then moved to Buffalo and some other teams. Never made the big time. Quit when the only job I could get was on Al Davis' Raiders and it looked like another year on the bench or maybe the practice squad."

"Tony is being modest. He was a heavy-duty fullback. The game changed around him and running backs got lighter and faster."

"I was a dinosaur."

"So now you work here, Tony?"

"Not work, own. People might have thought I was a big, dumb jock, but while all those high draft choices were out buying pimped-out Caddies, trophy wives, and swimming pools, I bought tax-free munis and blue chips. I built a nest egg big enough so my family can live up north of Winnetka and I can lose money on this restaurant."

"You have a family?"

"Six kids, wife, two dogs, a cat, a rabbit, no mortgage, no car payment, no worries. Football was good to me... Marie!" Tony bellowed so loudly three men at the bar spilled their drinks. "Menus. These people are hungry."

"None for me," Charlie said. "I know what I want already."

"You really don't need a menu, Charlie?"

"No, I always have the house specialty."

"Then make it two," Eden declared.

"Uh, I don't know," Tony said, "it's kind of like, you know, a guy thing."

"A guy thing? You don't mean for men only, do you?"

"Oh no, it's not that. It's just that girls usually don't—"

"Girls? Whoa, this woman can eat anything a man can, ex-football players included."

"Well, sure, but…"

"Eden, you should at least look at the menu."

"Don't need to."

"Sight unseen?"

"Blind." Oh God, she thought, please don't make it mountain oysters.

"Okay, be right out." Tony, engines full ahead, set off toward the kitchen.

Eden studied Charlie.

"Okay. What did I just order?"

"Liver and onions."

She let it sink in a minute. "You did it to me, didn't you?"

"Did what?"

"You guys just mousetrapped me."

Charlie grinned. Eden sat back and twisted her wine glass by its stem. "Can we be serious for a minute?"

"Certainly. What is it?"

"You've known Ike for a long time, right? You're his friend. You'd do anything for him?"

"Probably."

"I worry about him. It's like he's obsessed with this search for the person who hurt Ruth."

"Don't you want to catch the guy, too?"

"Sure, but I want a whole Ruth and a sane Ike more. Look, finding the person isn't going to change anything. And I swear, I sometimes think Ike's head will explode if he doesn't slow down. Tell him to call it off."

"He's a tough guy, Eden, he won't explode."

"Tell me the truth, Charlie. Is all this running around looking for an antigovernment crazy going to work?"

"Probably not—no."

"Then why…?"

"You need to know how personal this is for him."

"You are referring to what happened to his wife in Switzerland, I guess. Ruth told me the story."

"There is that, yes, and other things. Ike is a very righteous man. I mean that in the Old Testament sense. When he sees injustice, he wants to make it right. At the moment, unfortunately, justice is looking like a needle in a haystack. A needle, by the way, that probably isn't really there."

"But why, then, are you all spending so much effort when you don't believe it will work?"

"He will not rest until he's satisfied he's done everything possible. And if you're sincere about wanting him sane, you will understand, it's the way he is. He needs to hunt. After a while, when he steps back from the thing and lets his intuition rather than his emotions run the case, he will focus and finish it. So, that's why I am helping him. He will be okay, trust me."

"I guess I must. Listen, Charlie, I have a big day tomorrow. If you'll call me a cab, I'll take a miss on the house specialty. Tell Tony I said thanks, but no thanks."

"Stay. You have to eat and he won't bring you liver. He will have a small filet and a house salad out here in five. Stay."

TWENTY-SIX

IKE STARED AT his second cup of coffee, oblivious to the sounds and mixed aromas of the Crossroads Diner. On a normal day, if any of a policeman's days can ever be considered normal, those olfactory stimuli would be comforting, a good beginning to the day. But not this morning. Frank Sutherlin eased into the bench opposite and waved at Flora, who rolled her eyes and brought him his cup of tea.

"Any progress on your dead hay thief, Frank?"

"The news is, there is no news, well, nearly none. The drug-sniffing dog did not find a trace of marijuana or anything else. Not even an aspirin. Our guy and his accomplices—we assume there were more involved— were actually stealing hay. Is that weird or what?"

"Maybe guys like Duffy who are attempting to go straight have to do it gradually. Going 'cold turkey' may not be possible, so they move from risky drug felonies with major incarceration consequences to dealing items that can bring punishments approaching misdemeanors, like a smoker and his nicotine patches."

"It's a thought. Not a good one, I think, and it does not explain the 'big score' he bragged about. I guess I should follow your other scenario. He saw something that he believed would net him some money."

"Or, if he's a partner as you surmise, he got cut loose for some reason."

"There is that, too. We, that is the dog, did at least find a wallet buried in the hay. ID and money intact. Probably dropped. Could be the colleague or a customer."

"Whose?"

"A guy named Smith—tricky name—and he lives over in Buena Vista. I'm heading out there today to see if I can determine which of the two he is, thief or customer."

"If he turns out to be one of the hayseed gang and, God forbid, he's an associate of Jack Burns, do not tell Essie or Billy. Please."

"Got it. How's your search going?"

"Badly. There are too many people, too many places to look and, in taking the long view, an unlikely scenario to boot. If I had the FBI's resources on the case, I might be able to wind it up in a month. As it is, if I am going to catch this guy, it will be as much a matter of luck as skill."

"Umm, about that, I… So what's next?"

"I'm thinking a trip to Dallas, but I'm not looking forward to it, I can tell you. Long run for a short slide. What were you about to say just now?"

"Well… There's something else I need to tell you. The mayor has tumbled to the fact that we are talking and he's guessed about that van behind Lee Henry's. He's declared you absent without leave and has declared your office vacant by virtue of desertion. He's aiming to appoint Jack Burns as acting sheriff. If we do anything with you, including having conversations like this one, he says we'll be fired. So, this will probably be the last time we talk—sort of."

"You know, of course, he can't do that. But this close

to an election, and given what I'm dealing with, he
knows I won't take action, so don't risk it, Frank. I will
be available on that cell phone number I gave you earlier if you need anything. Thanks."

Frank left for the office and Ike resumed his concentration on his now-empty coffee cup. The crowd at the
office had not been doing much to help his search anyway, but he did enjoy their moral support. Now that had
been taken away, and Charlie had run off to Chicago as
well. Flora cruised by and refilled his cup.

Ike felt alone. He'd been fighting the feeling for days.
Stiff upper lip and all that but… Ruth was his anchor,
the job was his ship. Now the anchor had slipped and
the ship had started to sink. What next?

He opened his store-bought phone and called Charlie, who once again was not answering. Ike lifted an
eyebrow at that and left a message.

"Charlie, I only hope you are not answering because
you are gainfully employed and are about to strike a
blow for peace and freedom. If not, shame on you. Listen, I have the data for the list of names associated with
LSD. I extorted it from the executive officer of Let
States Decide. I have no doubt that the minute I left his
office he was on the horn to the people he'd just given
up, and warned them away from me. I think it will require someone no one knows is in the hunt to flush them
out. Maybe you could do that or persuade one of your
colleagues looking to get out from behind a desk for a
few hours to do it for you. One of the men Yeats gave
me is near where you are, or where you said you'd be.
With you it's never a certainty. Here's the list and what
you need to know. The last is supposed to hang out on

the South Side near the university. Oh, and where in the hell are you, really?"

Ike read him the information, spelling the names that might pose a problem, and hung up. He left his coffee on the table and headed out the door to the hospital. If he had to fly to Dallas, he was going to get in some serious time with Ruth first. Was any of this making any sense, or was he simply yielding to a combination of anger and the need to do something, anything to stay sane?

IDA TEMPLETON HAD spent the previous week in Roanoke and today marked the first time she'd worked the ICU at Stonewall Jackson since her run-in with Harris' doctor. The head nurse greeted her, and ran through the new admissions and alerts.

"So how is Ms. Harris doing? Did I tell you, I met her doctor? What a good-looking man. He was trying to fix her IV."

"He was? Harris' neurologist is Doctor Neena Patel and she's a woman. I don't know who you saw, but it wasn't her."

"Oh, then he must have been in to visit another patient."

"You're sure it was a doctor?"

"Yeah, pretty sure. I've seen him in a hospital, I know, but I can't remember right now which one. I'm in and out of so many, but yep, he's a doc."

"Good. The trouble with this business is you put somebody in a white lab coat and nobody questions if they belong in the corridors or not. You did see his ID badge?"

"He had one, yes. Anyway he didn't stay long. Maybe he's the new intern I heard was coming."

"Tall lanky guy?"

"Yes."

"That's him. You can't be too careful. Like you said—guy in a lab coat, who's going to question? Okay, Harris had a bad night so keep the visitors to a minimum today, okay?'

"What happened?"

"Oh last night that silly woman Miss Ewalt brought in a bunch of her co-workers, from Harris' office, I think, and it must have gotten loud or something. Her BP and heart rate shot up, the alarm went off. The attending showed up and shooed them all out. Stupid. I don't know what the night shift was thinking about."

"She's okay now?"

"Peaceful. We need to keep her that way. Next week she will be evaluated, and if she has slipped into a vegetative state, Doctor Patel will recommend she be moved to hospice."

"Gee, that'll be rough on the sheriff, won't it?"

"You know what they say, 'Life's a bitch, then you die.' Oops, speak of the devil. Good morning, Sheriff Schwartz."

"Good morning. How is she?"

"About the same. She had a bad night so go easy with her today, okay? No parties, loud singing, or dancing."

"No problem. What caused the bad night?"

"Too many visitors at once, we think. Miss Ewalt brought some university people by to cheer her up and it had the reverse effect it seems."

"Or maybe it was a good sign."

"Mmm-mmm." Ike hated it when nurses and doctors assumed a we-know-it-and-you-don't attitude. "How do you figure that, Sheriff?"

"She is responding to whatever is going on around her—reacting. That's good, right?"

"Well, you have a point but that sort of reaction we would like to have in smaller doses. So be easy with her today."

"Got it."

Go easy? For God's sake doesn't anyone get it? Easy for whom?

TWENTY-SEVEN

RUTH REMAINED STABLE, so that was good and it wasn't. She should have shown some changes by now. Either way, Ike spent a sleepless night. He skipped the Crossroads and made his own breakfast. Charlie still wasn't answering his phone. He couldn't call Frank and he wasn't sure what he should do next. Would Charlie pick up on the names he'd sent? Did flying to Dallas make any sense at all? If he went and if he found the people he was seeking, what then? They obviously wouldn't confess and he had no evidence. He could beat it out of them, but he'd always avoided that approach. It worked for others but he didn't see it working for him. He realized he might have to revisit that notion someday. He hoped not soon.

In the first hours after the wreck, he would have gladly shot anyone he was convinced had something to do with it, and done so without a second thought or remorse. That was then. This was now. He'd cooled down and maybe had a better perspective. Yeats did not have any direct culpability in it, but if you counted his rhetoric into the mix, he had to shoulder some of the blame. His speeches riled the crowds. One of them would only think he was doing the king a favor. Henry II: "Will no one rid me of this turbulent priest?" Oh, he'd have no qualms in tossing the elegant Byron Yeats in the slammer if he could. But he couldn't. And on calmer reflection, wouldn't.

So what now? No Charlie, no Frank, and he'd received a call from Lee Henry that the van had pulled out, so no tech support. No word, no explanation, no warning, nothing. Yeats had said Ike could be considered a rogue. Now, he guessed he really was one. Start over again. Look at the data, the meager evidence, as though he'd never seen it. The problem with sifting through data is that once you've made up your mind how it is to be interpreted, it is difficult to nearly impossible to see it any other way.

Was his notion of a crazed zealot even a remote possibility? In the heat of the moment it seemed self-evident. Even Yeats didn't completely discount it. He stared unseeing at the wall. It didn't really work, did it? He had been clutching at straws. Better start over.

He moved into the dining area and popped open his laptop. He plugged in the flash drive and went through the pictures, the statements, the e-mails, everything. He brewed another pot of coffee and repeated the process twice more.

He stopped at the video of the accident scene. He studied the truck still. The truck. Why did that seem important? Who would drive a truck to pull this off? People drove cars. If they were contemplating a felony or a job like this one, first they stole a car. What sort of person would steal a truck? Not a professional. Probably not one of the possible suspects on his list. So, who? He stared at the screen again trying to make out the masked face behind the wheel. He couldn't see anything except a dab of white, which he took to be the uncovered part

of the face. It seemed to be low behind the wheel. A
short person or one leaning forward?

He sifted through the papers again. One of Scott
Fiske's doctored résumés fell to the floor. He bent and
picked it up. He should toss it and any others like it.
That job was done. His eyes caught one line and his
hand froze in its transit toward the trash can. He read
it more carefully. He found the two other examples and
read them as well. He wished he'd taken Marge Tice
up on her offer to make him a copy of the report from
Donnie the Snoop. He needed to know if this was an
addition cobbled up to pad the résumé or the real thing.
Could Colonel Bob help him? Probably not. He said all
his friends in the DoD were dead. Still, he could ask.
He picked up the phone book and searched for: Twelvetrees, Robt. Col. USA Ret.

FRANK SUTHERLIN FIGURED the only way he could deal
with the mayor's efforts to insert Burns in as acting
sheriff, would be to stay away from the office entirely.
He told Essie he would be in Buena Vista checking out
the owner of the wallet they'd found in the hay barn
and she had better not let him catch her or Billy out
there again.

Frank decided to slide by Jack Burns' old neighborhood on the way. There was a luncheonette nearby and
he'd stop, purchase a cuppa, and ask some questions.
Billy and Essie were way off base thinking Burns could
be involved in Ruth Harris' accident, but there were
things about him, like why quit a job in Buena Vista to
take one like it in Picketsville? That suggested something that needed looking into.

Ballard's Luncheonette was marginally clean and

nearly empty. The counterman, who turned out to be the owner, swatted a fly and wiped the carcass from the counter with a suspiciously gray rag.

"Mornin', Mister. You're a cop, right? You here about them two people raised a fuss up to the bar? Said they was reporters, but I didn't believe them even a little."

"A cop, yes I am, but not interested in phony reporters today. Real ones are bad enough."

"You got that right. So what can I do for you?"

"Thought I'd stop by for a cup of tea and a sinker." Frank hoped he had his lunchroom slang down.

"A what? A sinker? This ain't no bait shop. Don't have no sinkers."

An old geezer in the corner looked up from his day-old paper and said, "He wants a donut, Tank. That's what we used to call 'em back when them USO gals came around. Sinkers, yep. That would be in WWII of course. Did I ever tell you—"

"Yeah you did, Jock. So sinkers is donuts? Shoot, never heard of that." He shoved a cup of hot water and a rumpled tea bag across the counter at Frank and went to a plastic-enclosed case to fetch a donut. "Whatcha want, I got glazed, powdered, honey dip, and one chocolate covered left over from Wednesday."

"Plain will do."

"Did I say plain? Anybody hear me say plain? I said, we got the chocolate covered, the glazed, and the powdered. That's it. Which?"

"Glazed. Do you have cream and sugar?"

The counterman shoved a saucer with the donut on it at him, walked to the other end of the counter, and returned with a handful of creamers and four dingy, paper-wrapped sugar cubes.

"Tea's a buck, donut eighty-five cents." Tank waited while Frank dug two dollars from his wallet and laid them down next to the donut. He stood and left. This had been a mistake.

"Hey, don't you want your eats? What about your change?"

"Keep it." Frank let the door slam. Fifteen cents well spent.

Bob Smith lived three doors down from Jack Burns' previous and as-yet-unsold residence. Frank found him in a toolshed in the backyard inspecting the underside of a lawnmower.

"Bob Smith?"

"That's me."

"You happen to lose a wallet, Mr. Smith?"

Smith turned bleary eyes on Frank, saw the uniform, badge, and gun, and let the mower drop flat on the work bench. Frank wondered if he might make a run for it. He hoped not. Frank never fared well in foot chases.

"I might have. So what?"

"I have it. I came to return it."

"Yeah? Well, thanks. I was wondering what happened to it." Smith's eyes clouded over momentarily. "Where'd you find it?"

"That's why I came by, Bob. I wanted to talk to you about that…where we found it, I mean. Do you by any chance own a gun?"

Smith rubbed the three-day stubble on his face and thought a moment. "I don't see what that has to do with my wallet. Sure, I hunt a little, sometimes. I got me a deer rifle and, well, a deer rifle."

"And a handgun, your record says. I know, it's legal, you have a permit. I was wondering if I could see it."

"Hey, you said you found my wallet and brought it over to return it. So I'll have it and then you can clear off."

"I could take you in and finish this in jail."

"For what? Hell, you ain't even local. You're from Picketsville. You're out of your jurisdiction, Mister, so just hand it over and shove off."

"We found your wallet in a barn over in Picketsville. That barn was at one time filled with hay. And the hay was stolen from some very angry growers in the Valley. That barn puts you in my jurisdiction, Son. You are either—you take your pick—in possession of stolen goods, a participant in a petty theft ring working in the valley over the last several weeks, an accessory to murder, or any and all of the above. Which shall we talk about first?"

TWENTY-EIGHT

IKE HAD FINISHED his call to Colonel Bob and poured his fourth cup when he thought he heard someone outside the door. Who would call on him this early? Most folks had not even finished their breakfast yet. Before he could open the door, he heard a key turn in the lock and the latch snap open. He snatched his service revolver from the lockbox where he normally kept it. Fortunately it wasn't locked. He had the barrel leveled and the hammer back when a disheveled Charlie stepped through the door.

"Jesus, Charlie, I might have killed you."

"Your reflexes are better than that, Ike. You would have shot one of your bad guys, a half dozen or so agents still loose in the world who carry your picture in their wallets, but not a friend, not a child, and not a beautiful woman. I know you. You have rules."

"That is not true. I once shot a very pretty woman."

"Because she had a flamethrower and was about to incinerate a school with you in it, I know. So, there are occasional forgivable lapses in your rule keeping. Besides, she wasn't all that pretty and most assuredly not beautiful."

"Enough. Where have you been, Charlie? I've left you messages and received your text. By the way, how did you do that? You never text and then I get the equivalent of a three-page report from you."

"No magic. Half the teenagers in America can type faster with their thumbs than I can with all my fingers, so no big deal, tech-wise. But you are right, I don't text. I do have access to a very competent, text-enabled aide who tells me her iPad is nothing but an overgrown iPhone. She rigged it to do that and sent the message to you for me. To answer your first question, I visited the greater Chicago metropolitan area, as I told you. I have checked out several of the people on the list and a few not on it."

Charlie told Ike about the CIA names on the list, the director's order to treat them outside the box, and what he'd found in Skokie.

"That contact gave me the stuff you read in the text. So what have you been doing while I have been out in the heartland on your behalf?"

Ike filled him in on his trip to Arlington, the recent antics of the mayor, and the hay caper. "The latter do not feature in this job I don't think, but I never discount anything until it's a certainty."

"Of course. Well, in addition to clearing off names, including, by the way, the man on the South Side—he had an ironclad alibi, he's been serving five to fifteen in Joliet since four months ago. I also did as you requested. I kept an eye out for the lissome Mrs. Saint Clare."

"And?"

"Did you ever meet Tony Agnelli?"

"You took me to his place once. Did the two of you play mousetrap?"

"How do you know about that?"

"I used to be a spy, remember? So you two had dinner. What else?"

"You say that with a smirk and in a lascivious tone

of voice. You should have your imagination washed out with soap. Dinner, period. She is concerned about your health. She asked me to tell you to call it off."

"That is very caring of her. So, are you going to tell me to call it off?"

"No, but not for the reasons you suppose. She seemed a little too eager. You told me to keep her safe from the sharks, as I recall. I checked out the sharks and discovered the reason she went to Chicago."

"I already told you why she went, she needed to fight the sister-in-law about the pension and check out funeral arrangements."

"We shall label that listing as ostensible or in addition to. They were, in fact, two of the things she attended to, but there was a third, and more troubling reason."

Charlie found a chair, sat, and appropriated Ike's coffee cup. He sipped it, made a face, and heaved a sigh.

"Charlie, are you going to tell me what's on your mind or not? What do you think was the third reason?"

"You are not going to like it. I don't like it. We could ignore it, but then it will sit like the proverbial elephant in the living room."

"Charlie, out with it. What did you find?"

"John Harris, Dean emeritus of the New Haven School of Law, father of Ruth, and spouse to Paula Harris, AKA Eden Saint Clare, left a will. A recently written and notarized will, to be exact."

"Is he sufficiently mentally coherent to do that? He's an Alzheimer's patient."

"Indeed, he is. That is the problem for Eden. Can the will pass muster? What will happen at probate? Who knows? But she did not wish to chance it, so she went to Chicago to start procedures for contesting it."

"That makes sense. Why wouldn't she have told me that, I wonder?"

"Indeed. And that leads us to the part you won't like. John Harris wrote her out of his will—totally. She had changed her name, you see, thus denying him his place in posterity or some such nonsense. He doesn't recognize her anymore. He no longer loves her, etcetera. So, he dumped the wife and made Ruth his sole beneficiary. Eden gets nothing when he dies." Charlie paused, lifted and replaced the cup, and exhaled. "But, Eden is Ruth's sole beneficiary. You see where this goes?"

"Charlie, you don't really believe she would… No, that's not possible."

"Motive and opportunity, Ike. I hate to do it to you, but you need to see the possibility."

"This is crazy."

"Murder is crazy. Our problem, my friend, is that you and I have lived within the culture of death so long we find it impossible to rule out anything even when we desperately want to. Did Eden drive a truck into Ruth's car? Nah, can't happen. Or could it? We suffer, Ike, because we were taught by, and ultimately survived the messes the Company put us in, not to trust anyone. It is like a bad tattoo on our souls. Can't erase it, can only ignore it, but it's always there."

Ike collapsed into a chair and reclaimed his coffee cup. He hung his head for a moment. Too much. If he hadn't learned to suppress them as a child, he would have shed tears. Instead he shook his head from side to side and moaned a quiet lament for life in general and for this moment in particular.

"We are very damaged goods, Charlie, you and I. After living in the...what did you call it...the culture of death? We have lived there for so long, the sun can but intermittently shine on us. I will have to order a watch on Ruth now, especially when her mother visits. Jesus, Charlie, I wish you hadn't decided to be my friend, just now."

"You're welcome."

TWENTY-NINE

FRANK'S INTERVIEW WITH Bob Smith did not go well. In the end he had to arrest and cuff him and bring him in.

"You are in big trouble, Cop," Smith snarled. "You don't have a clue what you're getting yourself in."

"How's that work? You have contacts in the Governor's mansion, the White House? What?"

"Jack Burns is gonna be your boss and when that happens you won't have a job. He'll bust you down to Dogcatcher."

"Will he now? How do you figure that? You have a crystal ball or something? Or are you just mouthing off?"

"He's in and you heard it here first. Believe me. It's all fixed up."

"Really? That's very interesting. How is it all fixed up?"

"You'll see." Smith shut up and the remainder of the trip passed in silence.

Things became more exciting when Frank escorted Smith into the sheriff's office. It happened to be the same morning the mayor chose to tour the facility with the very same Jack Burns, his choice to succeed Ike, or so he thought. His efforts to declare Ike absent without leave and his position thereby vacated, had run into a snag with the town council. As with any group of minor elected officials who depended on a day job to subsist, the council first dithered and then sought a second opinion from the town's attorney, who happened to be in Richmond on a private matter. Accordingly, the motion had been tabled and vacancy not declared. Nevertheless the mayor brought Burns to the office to introduce him to his future staff. He received a decidedly frosty welcome from those few who remained in the building. Many had suddenly remembered things that needed their attention elsewhere and left.

All eyes turned and watched Frank drag/shove Smith up to the booking desk.

"Bob," Burns barked, "what the hell?"

"Uncle Jack, this bozo has cuffed me and says I'm under arrest or something."

"What's the meaning of this?" the mayor said. He could not have missed the "Uncle Jack" and even a slow learner, which the mayor most certainly was not, would realize the potential pitfall created by the arrest of a close relative to his candidate.

"This man is here for questioning, Mister Mayor, in connection with a murder, about which we believe he is aware, a larceny charge, possible cruelty to animals—we'll know more about that when we have a warrant and can search his house for a nine millimeter handgun which we believe was used to kill a very expensive dog, and—"

"Whoa up there, Deputy. Where is all this coming from?" Jack Burns appeared about as uncomfortable as a Baptist caught by his pastor in a liquor store.

"—and at the very least, he is in possession of stolen property, specifically, hay removed from several nearby farms and barns."

"I ain't said nothing, Uncle Jack. I ain't talking to

these people. It's their job to prove that one way or other, right? And I figure you probably want to do something about that."

"Mister Mayor, I think we need to talk privately and…"

"Yes, of course. Deputy Sutherlin, I caution you. This had better be a legitimate arrest and not some trick by Ike Schwartz to embarrass his opponent."

"Oh, it's real, sir." Frank turned to his prisoner. "He's your uncle? How very convenient for you. He's a cop and you are a thief. I'm sure you two will have a chat and then you will tell us everything we need to know because, unless I miss my guess, Uncle Jackie will insist on it. He pretty much has to."

Smith muttered something that Frank, had he been paying attention, would have recognized as obscene, blasphemous, or both. He marched him into the back room, booked him, and scheduled an arraignment for that evening. And at that moment, Frank had a brief epiphany. Essie and Billy notwithstanding, Jack Burns needed a closer look. Smith was Burns' nephew. That had to go somewhere. Coincidences might be the stuff of Russian novels, but in his world, they were rare to nonexistent. All Frank needed was a handle. Something didn't smell quite right. Maybe he smelled hay. Smith and hay, Duffy and hay, and then Uncle Jack?

Grace White waved at him from the corridor where she'd been hiding from the mayor. "I have something on that phone call Ike wanted to have traced," she said.

"The call to Ms. Harris the night she hit the pole?"

"Yeah. I don't understand it exactly, but I've traced the origin and identified the phone."

"So WHEN DID you make the decision to remove the van, and why?"

Ike made a fresh pot of coffee and Charlie produced the box of Dunkin' Donuts he'd picked up on his way in.

"The director received a call from your mayor. In fact, he received and ignored several calls from the gentleman. Apparently the mayor then called the governor, who called somebody, who in turn called somebody else, and the upshot was the director received an order from very high up that he should take the call or else. Your mayor wanted to know why the CIA had a van parked in his town and did the director want to answer him or would he rather see this question referred to the *Washington Post*? Since we'd pretty much done what we could with Kevin and his machinery, the decision the director made seemed to be necessary."

"And expedient."

"That too."

"I would like to have known about it, but it's okay. I have had a discouraging morning thus far and you have not added much in the way of cheer, Charlie."

"My bad. What might I have said to change that?"

"Damned if I know. My problem is, I have been pouring over all the information we have. There is precious little here and it occurred to me that if our perp is as I have assumed, he's out there and we will never find him unless we launch a full-scale manhunt. Only the FBI can pull that off, and they can't do that without some reason or authorization. Neither the attorney general nor the director of the FBI is going to expend assets on Ike Schwartz's problem, the DC Metro Police are not going to call them in on a routine auto accident, and if I have correctly figured out the hit, and I am having serious doubts about that now, we would either have our man by now, or we will never get him."

"How do you figure that? You are right about all the rest. The FBI is a no-go and obviously we, that is, my people, cannot operate within the borders, but the rest?"

"Well, you remember my rant about the soldier and the possibilities?"

"Vividly."

"If that were the case—and it need not be a damaged GI. Anyone with a certain twisted mind set could do it. By now he would have told someone, would have made the person he felt had encouraged him know what he'd done. Doubtless the knights who polished off Beckett rushed back to the palace to tell the king and receive their reward. As much as I dislike demagogues, I do not believe they are stupid. If any of them got wind that one of theirs had done something like that, they'd give him up in a heartbeat. Make an anonymous phone call, at least."

"And if, for some reason, our guy didn't run to the king?"

"We're screwed. Unless he talks about it to someone and we pick up on it, we'll never find him."

"So what now?"

"The more I think about it, the more I'm convinced the thing is eccentric."

"Is what?"

"Off-center, it's related to Ruth and what she was doing, certainly, but not as we, or I, first assumed."

"What then?"

"I don't know, but I might be close. One piece and

we will have the puzzle solved. But where do I find that piece?"

The phone rang.

"Perhaps that's the missing piece calling you now."

"I'm not that lucky."

THIRTY

EDEN SAINT CLARE extended her stay an extra day. She wanted to return to Picketsville as soon as possible, but her lawyers were undecided which strategy they should pursue. It appeared that John Harris had executed a series of wills over the last few years. They had to assume that all the will writing and rewriting had been the result of a mind gone gray, but would a court agree? People spoke to him. He understood them or he didn't. One could never be sure that what he heard had anything to do with what was actually said. At the same time, a will, if it made sense, should stand irrespective of his mental state. It wasn't as if he'd left his estate to the home for stray cats.

They were in general agreement, however, that the latest will could be successfully contested, but which of the several previous documents would supplant it? At what point during the process would the will in question stand the test of sound mind? Clearly they needed to inspect them all. To do so, they would need a subpoena to get at them, and might never be sure they had them all. The sister wasn't being entirely forthcoming, they suspected.

"We tried to explain all this to your associate yesterday afternoon, Mrs. Saint Clare, but he seemed only interested in the latest version."

"My associate? Did you say someone spoke to you claiming to be my associate?"

"Why, yes. He showed me some identification and a letter from you identifying himself as your representative. He did say he did not work for you often but, as you were in his neighborhood, he'd offered to help."

"In his neighborhood? You mean he works in Chicago?"

"Yes. He had his business card. He is a partner, it seems, with Gavel and Strock. They are a small legal consulting firm located in Skokie, as it happens."

"What was his name?"

"It was…well here," the young clerk handed Eden a business card. "You can read it for yourself."

She glanced at the card. "May I use your phone?"

"Yes, of course. Is there a problem?"

"You better hope not."

Eden dialed the number and waited for someone to pick up. "Hello, may I speak to Mr. Franklin Barstow, please? What? I am calling about an inquiry he made with this firm, Baker, Baker, and Watts." She waited another minute. "Mr. Barstow, my name is Eden Saint Clare. Have we ever met? No, I am quite serious. I am standing in the conference room at Baker, Baker, and Watts. I have been informed by—" She covered the mouth piece. "Sorry son, what is your name? By a Mr. Andrew Watts, who, I assume, must be a relation to the Watts. He tells me that you were here in this building asking about some matters currently being handled on my behalf by this firm. Since we have never met, I wonder if you could enlighten me on what that was all about. Yes, yesterday. You were. Thank you, sorry to have bothered you."

She hung up the phone. "Junior, describe the man to whom you revealed confidential information. Then fetch your dad, or uncle, or whoever or whatever the senior Watts in this firm is. Mr. Barstow and I have never met, and he was not here yesterday afternoon because he was attending a bar mitzvah in Winnetka. We have a problem."

"Yes, Ma'am. The original founder of the firm, Hiram Watts, is dead. I have the same name but am not related. I'll get Mr. Baker, Senior."

This smelled fishy. Either the devious sister had sent a spy to snoop, or…or what?

"You do that. Then you might want to think about pursuing another profession."

"Ma'am?"

IKE ANSWERED THE call on the second ring after he'd checked the caller ID. Frank on his private cell needed to speak to him.

"Ike, some news. You need to hear what happened today at the office but it takes time. Will you be at the Crossroads anytime today?"

"I could do lunch. You could join me, that is, if you can keep the Pooh-bahs in the mayor's office off your case."

"No problem there. Not anymore. Okay, right now Grace has some news about the phone call Ruth received the night of the wreck. Shall I put her on?"

"Of course." Ike touched the speakerphone button so that Charlie could listen to what Grace White had discovered.

"Boss." Grace came on the line. "I was able to do some fiddling with the cell phone you gave me. I know where the call she got that night came from, its number, and where the phone it was made on was purchased."

"All that? Tell me what you have."

"It's kind of weird." Grace thought most of life in the Shenandoah Valley was weird when compared to her upbringing in Maine. "The call was placed in Washington, DC. You probably already figured that part out. The weird thing is that the person who made it bought the phone in Lexington."

"Our Lexington? Not Kentucky…the one right up the road?"

"Yes. See, once I retrieved the number, I traced it to the manufacturer, well actually the United States rep. The phone came from Asia somewhere originally and—"

"Skip that part, Grace. So they were able to trace the phone consignment that narrowly?"

"I guess so."

"Who bought it?"

"That's the part I don't know. I am calling all the stores in the Lexington area to find out who bought a phone. If I'm lucky, there'll be a time stamp on the sales slip and if I'm luckier still, whoever bought it will have used a charge card. Then we'll have him, or her, but that doesn't seem likely."

"Not a woman? Why?"

"It would take a pretty hefty woman to drive a truck, wouldn't it?"

"You ever drive a truck, Grace?"

"Oh, sure. I sometimes helped my cousin, Rodney, haul logs out of the forest, so sure."

"Big truck?"

"Oh yeah, that sucker ran…oh, I get it. If I can jockey

a tractor and log hauler, someone else could manage a
stake body, I guess. I stand corrected. Sorry."

"Nothing to be sorry for. I don't think you will find
a charge slip on that phone. The attacker built his plan
very carefully. He would have paid cash. But keep looking, you may get lucky. In the meantime, assuming there
is a cash register record of the sale, and assuming you
can locate it, check the time stamp and then see if any
surveillance cameras might have caught the purchase."

"Right. I'm on it."

Ike hung up.

"I guess we put the solitary fruitcake as perpetrator to bed."

"Not quite. I never let something go until I have
something better to take its place. That's not the case
yet, so we'll put it on hold. Lexington could simply be
a coincidence. Anyone coming up the valley on his
way to Washington might very well have pulled off
I-81 and picked up a phone. You'd be pretty stupid to
buy it in your hometown, assuming you knew it might
be traced."

"Point taken. Fruitcakes placed on hold, but not discarded. In the real world, discarding fruitcakes is an act
of mercy. My great aunt Louise exchanged the same
fruitcake with her sister every Christmas for something
like thirty years."

"You exaggerate."

"Only a little."

THIRTY-ONE

As they made their way into the Crossroads to meet Frank, Colonel Bob grabbed Ike's sleeve. He rifled through a rucksack he'd duct-taped to the steering mechanism of his scooter, withdrew a thick envelope, and held it out.

"Here's what I found for you, Sheriff. I called Saint Louis and talked my way into the main records section. Had to pull rank. Damn, but that felt good! It turned out the major in charge of the unit is the grandson or maybe the great grandson, hard to keep 'em straight, of Chesty MacDaniels. You know General Mac?"

"Sorry, no. He a buddy of yours?"

"Chesty and I fought all the way from North Africa, Italy, and Europe together. One time we liberated a whole wine cellar in France and after about three hours of sampling, Chesty decided to steal Patton's six shooters. See, it was…sorry, off the point, never mind. I got through and the major, nice fellah, asked me what I wanted and so on. Well, I didn't really know for sure so I had him fax me a list of everyone who served in that unit you asked about during the years you told me. T.J. printed it out for me. There's a hell of a lot of names, I think. With my eyes on terminal leave, I can't read it, but if your guy was there, he'll be on the list."

"Thanks, Colonel Bob. So, did you actually steal the general's pistols?"

"Nah. By the time we'd generated enough Dutch courage from the wine to do it, we were falling down drunk and our master sergeants had to scrape us up off the floor and cart us back to HQ. I sometimes wonder what would have happened if we had done it, though."

"Thanks for the list." Ike found his usual booth occupied by some travelers on their way to Tennessee and had to settle for a table close by. Charlie, who had remained silent through the colonel's story and the exchange, sat opposite.

"Can you imagine what General Patton would have done to him and the other guy if they'd tried it? What's with the list?"

"Just a hunch. You know, no stone unturned and all that. I saw on Doctor Fiske's highly fictionalized résumé that he claimed to have served in a military police battalion. I wanted to find out if it were true or not."

"Because of the pursuit maneuver, I take it. Did he?"

"Yes. Give me a minute." Ike slit the envelope open with a butter knife and spread the sheets of paper it contained out on the table. "We're in luck, I think. The lists are for each year Fiske claims to have been assigned. They are in alphabetical order by year and by rank, so… checking the F's…nope, nope, nope. He didn't serve as an officer as he claimed, nor did he give himself a promotion on his paper and really serve as an enlisted man either. My guess, he didn't serve in the military anywhere."

Ike read through the list of names again, frowned at one and underlined it, then returned the sheets to the envelope and stuffed it into his jacket pocket. Frank joined them a few minutes later. If a smile can light a room, his would have powered the Las Vegas strip.

"You seem happy, Frank. Do you want to share?"

Frank filled them in on the morning events, the mayor's hasty retreat from the office, and Burns' difficulties stemming from his nephew's arrest.

"So far, Smith isn't talking beyond repeating that he didn't have any part in the death of Marty Duffy, and he wants a lawyer. I think our wannabe sheriff is arranging that for him now."

"Have we got anything on him that we can make stick or will keep him close until we can dig a little deeper into the Duffy killing?"

"I think so, yes. I managed to have the judge hand down a search warrant before I came over. I'll take Billy over to Smith's place and we'll toss it. He has a permit to carry a nine millimeter. Whoever shot the dog used a nine and I'm pretty sure it'll be his. It's not much, but it will do for the time being. We can also put him in the barn. The couple who leased it to Duffy said they can ID his partner, too. So, yes, I think we can keep him for a while."

"That's good work, Frank. And you're telling me that the office is quiet? Amos Wickwire still lurking?"

"He is but he looks a little lost and confused. His line to the mayor seems to be shut down."

"Poor Amos."

"Grace found one of Sam's old programs that she used to track cell phones and calls. She's locked it on the one you're looking for. If it is turned on, she'll know when and where. If a call is made, she thinks she will be able to monitor and maybe even record it."

"Clearly you do not need me or Kevin anymore." Charlie waved to Flora, who made a point of ignoring him. "How does one order lunch here if you are not on Ms. Blevin's A-list?"

"She'll be by in a minute. She is punishing me for allowing you into her bailiwick. But, she makes money selling what passes for food, so she will be along soon enough, never fear."

"What I want to know is, why me? What have I done that she finds so reprehensible that she would black-list me?"

"It's your looks, Charlie. She was once left at the altar by a man who looks remarkably like you."

"No."

"Could be. Entering and then exiting a black hole is easier than delving into Flora's psyche."

"You could come back to the office now, I think, Ike. There is no way the mayor or his mafia will bother you now."

"I appreciate that, Frank. Not today, but maybe later. There are some things I need to do first. Charlie, I never asked. How did you find out about the will?"

"Oh, no big deal. You know I have a habit of picking up business cards when I can. Never know, and all that. When I was in, that is, when I was away this week, I found one in the parking lot near where I was headed at the time. It hadn't been stepped on and seemed in reasonably good shape so I picked it up. Using a found card is always better than one which someone might later remember giving to you."

"So you were who?"

"Franklin Barstow. Isn't that a lovely name? I think it fits me, don't you? Very presidential, very impos-ing. With a name like Franklin Barstow, nobody would dream of asking for anything more."

"What do you do if and when Mrs. Saint Clare tumbles to your snooping?"

"Let's hope she doesn't. Either way…"

"I guess this is a conversation I am not supposed to be following."

"Sorry, Frank. No, it isn't. Maybe later."

"Right. Well I'm off to the office to pick up Billy and head out to Buena Vista again to search Bob Smith's house."

"Good hunting."

"You feeling any better, Ike?"

"Marginally. My chief concern now is protecting Ruth. As long as I thought the idiot who forced her off the road was 'out there,' I didn't worry. Now it occurs to me that he could be closer and maybe will try again."

"Try again? Why?"

"If—this is hypothetical, you understand—if the intent wasn't to intimidate, then it must have been to kill. If we rule out the lone nutcase intent on making a statement for the moment, then we are looking at a new set of parameters. I have been so obsessed with one solution, I have not really considered others, and that has been very careless of me."

"You have an alternative in mind?"

"No."

"I think I know you, Ike. I'm waiting."

"What if…"

THIRTY-TWO

SCOTT FISKE OPENED the top-center desk drawer and slipped out a small mahogany box. He bought cigarettes from an import house in Washington. He'd only recently refilled it with Balkan Sobranie Turkish Ovals. Fiske wasn't a smoker, not in the usual sense. He hoarded the finely rolled Turkish imports and only lit them on special occasions. Sometimes in his office when he'd had a particularly good day or pulled one off when they didn't think he could. Sharp. The trick was to be sharp all the time—stay a step ahead.

If he were honest with himself he'd admit the cigarettes were an affectation he'd acquired after reading a thriller; he couldn't remember by whom or what it was titled, but it featured a protagonist who had been described as sophisticated, worldly, and hugely attractive to women, and who smoked Sobranie Turkish Ovals. Today did not meet his criteria for a victory smoke; it had been anything but a success. Where did these Liberal Arts types get the idea their disciplines were important enough to require more money? Who hired artists anyway? A degree in English literature got you a job as a barista, for crying out loud. He would light one up anyway. An anticipatory puff. Ruth Harris could not last much longer.

He walked to the door to close it. This wing of the building was nominally non-smoking. A pink call slip on Sheila's desk reminded him to check his messages and mail. He walked to the stand with its rows of pigeon holes. His was jammed with notes and papers. He sorted through them, retaining the ones which seemed important, dropping the rest in the trash container placed next to the stand. He turned with a handful of papers in his hand and returned to his office. Sheila probably wouldn't notice the singe mark on her desk top, and if she did…well, a little polish would fix it up.

Back at his desk, he smoked fitfully. Smoking did not come easily to him, as it happened. He pulled the drawer open again and removed the phone. He studied it carefully. It was a flip phone, very compact, very neat, and a convenient aquisition. He liked well-designed things. How many hours, he wondered, remained on the chip or whatever it was inside that kept that record? He hit the red power button and waited while it booted up. The face lit and briefly told him he had fourteen hours left. Not bad. He could always go to the drug store and buy more hours, of course. Should he call someone? He'd call Sheila, find out what she was up to. He punched in her number, waited, nothing. The call went to voice mail. He decided not to leave a message. Where was she anyway?

He did not like it when she took off like that. Sure she was entitled to take off personal days, but what if he needed her to take notes or…something? He worried about that, especially now with his new and probably permanent responsibilities. He'd call her later and ask her to come in early for some dictation. He'd have to think up something to dictate, though.

He used his index finger to twirl the phone on his desk. Its slightly bowed back allowed it to spin like a top. It skittered toward the desk's edge. He managed to snatch it back before it fell to the floor and placed it, no longer spinning, back on the desk. He shut the phone down and put it away with his box of Turkish Ovals. He finished his smoke, snuffed out the butt, and emptied the ashtray into a trash can. Ordinarily, he would have also sprayed the room with an odor disperser, but he let that go.

He would drive to Roanoke, have dinner, chat up some girls at the mall, and call it a night. He paused, reopened the drawer, removed the phone, and dropped it into his jacket pocket. You never knew.

BOB SMITH, with the aid of his uncle and the Picketsville mayor, pled not guilty on three different charges and the hearing magistrate released him on his own recognizance. "Not sufficient evidence," the judge announced, glancing sideways at the mayor for confirmation. Who had the decency to maintain an expression of innocence, that is to say, a blank.

An irate Frank Sutherlin took his frustration out on the box of donuts Essie had brought to the office to celebrate Amos Wickwire's departure.

"At last," Essie had declared from her post at the dispatch desk, "things can get back to normal." She had the phone at her ear, attempting to call Ike and urge him to come in, when she saw Frank scoop up two plain and one with sprinkles.

"Hey, those are for everybody. One at a time."

Frank ignored her, scarfed the sprinkle, and washed it down with the tepid tea remaining in his cup. "You have Ike on the phone?"

"Not yet. What's the big deal, Frank?"

"I need to talk to Ike."

"We all need to talk to Ike. Cripes, Frank, what's your problem?"

"Where's Grace?"

"Her husband had to go to the emergency room or something. Piece of machinery fell on his foot. She'll be out for a while. Billy's taking her shift. He's run over to the lab to get the ballistics on that nine millimeter you all took from Smith's house."

"Too late for that now. They let the horse out of the barn. He'll be long gone before we can do anything with it. Burns undoubtedly told him to get lost, at least until after the election."

"Can't you, like, tail him or something?"

"Forget it, we're temporarily screwed here. You any closer to making that call?"

"Woo, snarky, snarky."

"Just get me Ike."

IKE WATCHED RUTH'S steady breathing, wondering how much longer he could do this. If she didn't come back from wherever she was, the doctors would start talking about sending her to hospice. Doctors, he'd decided, were not known for their patience. Either the person recovered, died, or was shoved out of sight. Too many new and more exciting patients to attend to. But hospice? He could not wrap his mind around it, could not imagine the silence, could not imagine life without her, could not imagine a life alone.

"You need to wake up, Ruth. Come back to me in whatever shape you're in. Even just a small part of you would be better than nothing."

Did he hear a moan? No way to tell. Sometimes her

breathing moved to the back of her throat and caused that little rumble. Like a snore, almost.

"Nnngh."

"Are you trying to say something?"

There was that sound again. Should he call the nurse? What would he say to her? What would she say? Sit tight. If she'd really tried to speak, she would again and again until it was certain. Too soon. He needed to keep his expectations low. Better a surprise than a disappointment.

"You are a heartbreaker, kiddo, did you know that?"

"Nnngh!"

"Would you like to know how the day went? Okay. It was pretty exciting yesterday but all the forward movement seemed to go into reverse today. Did I tell you about the guy we collared for stealing hay? He steals hay, for crying out loud. Turns out he's Jack Burns' nephew. Frank is mad enough to chew nails and spit tacks."

BOB SMITH POSSESSED a low cunning that more or less made up for his limited intellect. He realized that he would not stay free for long. Eventually the Picketsville cops would make their case and he'd be back in the slammer. And when that happened Jack Burns would not be able to save him. In fact, he'd been pretty specific about what he wanted him to do.

"Scram, Bob. Get out of town and stay there until after the election. I can fix us up later, but I can't if they find you first. We'd both go down, so beat it."

Bob had no illusions what the future held if he stuck around. They could just bust him for doing the dog if they wanted to. He had to move on. But that would cost

money and Uncle Jack only had a Benjamin to spare.
A hundred bucks wouldn't get him far or last long. He
needed more cash. He returned to the shed where he'd
been looking at Duffy's book before that cop showed up.
He'd slipped Duffy's notebook under the lawnmower
then. The dopes hadn't thought to check it out when
they searched the place, and hadn't found it. Somewhere in that book, Smith thought, would be his ticket
out of town. Duffy kept records. He recorded all the
hay they moved and who bought it, when they bought
it, and how much they paid. Possession of stolen goods
could be embarrassing. Those jerk-water hobby farm-
ers and horse people might pay for not having their
names mentioned in an anonymous phone call to the
State cops. Duffy had been clear about the names. That
way, he'd said, if anybody messed with them, they had
dates and times when the troublemakers had received
stolen goods, so there wouldn't be any comeback from
them. Just in case, he'd said. Duffy was careful. Well,
maybe not careful enough.

Bob wanted to know if Duffy had written anything
else in his book. He was on to a big score, he'd said.
Maybe he could figure out what it was. Duffy wasn't
going to get that pay-off now, so maybe he could instead. If, one way or the other, he could round up
enough cash, he could head for Nashville and nobody
would ever find him. He rifled through the pages, ignoring the columns and numbers, until he came to the
Sunday Duffy didn't show up with the truck. Then he
stopped and read. He flipped through the remainder.
In the back Duffy had paper clipped some newspaper
articles. Some were old, from before he came to town,
some were later, and one or two were about him. What

the…? But one was more recent. He read it, too. Duffy had scrawled a phone number at the bottom.

It took him another three hours to unravel what Duffy had discovered, but when he did, he smiled. Big score for sure. He'd use Duffy's old phone, make the call, set up a meet, and be in for some money, maybe a lot of money. But he'd need to be more careful than Duffy.

Duffy was dead.

GRACE WHITE WAS not at her desk when the computer program dedicated to tracking the mysterious cell phone beeped. The software logged in as much as it could without her input, then reverted to watch mode. It would go through this series of responses and defaults twice more before Grace could retrieve the information it collected. That would be two days and one additional murder later.

THIRTY-THREE

FRANK AND HIS BROTHER, Billy, drove back to Buena Vista to re-arrest Smith, this time on a cruelty to animals charge. The dog had been shot with Smith's gun and because the ballistic evidence more than supported the warrant, and this was Virginia, after all, still resonating from the Michael Vick business, Frank believed the judge would not be so lenient when they brought him in this time. Smith had to know something about Duffy's death, if not directly then indirectly. Something said or intimated at least. He had hoped to keep Smith close by and lean on him a bit. Putting Jack Burns on the hot seat made the prospect even better.

But, as predicted, Smith had skipped town. Both the man and his old Ford 150 pickup were nowhere to be found. His neighbors had no idea where he might have gone, and of course, Jack Burns had nothing to offer either. Frank called in an APB and resigned himself to waiting until after the election for his man to resurface.

"Billy, I'm telling you this Smith–Burns connection stinks to high heaven."

"You know me and Essie been after him for weeks."

"Oh yeah we all know that. Look, Billy, forget Burns as the guy driving the truck, okay? That dog don't hunt."

"What then?"

"He's got to be connected to Smith, right? I mean, they're related. He works in a small town. People are tight and everybody knows everybody else's business. Smith is stealing hay, he had to know."

"You want us to like, give up our investigation?"

"Not quite. I think you can help out better by not playing rogue cops, okay? The last time you came over here—"

"I know, I know. So what should me and Essie do now?"

"For a start, call around to all his former colleagues on the local force. You know, say something like he's maybe going to be your new boss and—"

"In a pig's eye he is."

"Yeah, yeah. Hey we're pretending here, Billy. And then you ask 'what's he like to work for' and things like that."

"Me and Essie found out he fixes traffic tickets."

"Well, that's a start, but we need some real stuff. I want to nail that guy, Billy."

"We'll get on it."

IKE STILL REFUSED to come into the office even though the mayor and his dogsbody, Amos Wickwire, had removed themselves from the scene. While he seemed less intent on scouring the country for a suspect in the attack on Ruth and, in fact, had serious doubts about pursuing that approach any further, he hadn't completely let it go. He'd left Grace a supplemental list of names to scan into the various police and FBI files. He hoped she could determine where they might have been on that Sunday evening. He really didn't expect much, and since Grace was out with an emergency of some sort, nothing had been done on that project anyway.

The company that distributed the cell phone he as-

sumed to have been used to call Ruth the night of the
crash faxed over information which put the sale in a specific store in the Lexington area. They had managed to
establish the time and date as well. Essie took it upon
herself to call the store and they confirmed they had,
indeed, sold a phone on the date and time the distributor
had specified. She asked Ike what she should do next.

"Ask if there are surveillance cameras in the store
and if there are, ask them if they would provide us with
tapes for the time and day and from any camera with a
view of the cash registers."

They'd replied that they did have tapes. It was good
the office had called when it did because they usually
taped over after two or three weeks. They promised
to make them available. Ike then called Grace, com-
miserated with her about her husband's accident, and
asked her to come in to the office a little early to set up
the TV to run the tapes and, also, to check her phone
monitoring program. She agreed to be in the first thing
in the morning.

EDEN SAINT CLARE went to the hospital immediately
after her return to Picketsville. She had no idea why
someone posing as Franklin Barstow wanted to know
about her husband's will. The young clerk's description could have been for any lanky past-it middle-aged
man—including, she thought, Charlie Garland. But
why would he be nosing around her lawyer's office
and asking questions? He had been in town and had,
as Ike would say, the means and the opportunity. But
what would be his motive? If she saw him again, she
would ask.

She waved to the nurse at the desk as she strode to-

ward Ruth's area. She happened to glance back toward
the central desk just as she reached Ruth's cubicle. The
duty nurse was on the phone; her head lowered, half
turned away from her. She had Eden targeted with the
corner of her eye. What the hell was that all about? A
few minutes later, a young man in a uniform took up a
position outside Ruth's door. She frowned. Something
did not feel right.

"Be back in a minute," she said to Ruth. She marched
back to the desk. The guard avoided her eyes.

"Who's the kid in the cop suit standing outside my
daughter's door?"

"Oh, Mrs. Saint Clare, that's security. It's…umm…
it's, you know, routine."

"How come he wasn't here before? I've been coming
to this hospital every day for what, two weeks? Why
now, all of a sudden, I've got security? You mind telling me what's up?"

"I'm not sure. I think the sheriff asked for it. I understand he's decided that your daughter might have
been a victim of a deliberate attack or something, and
is afraid another try will be made."

"I see. You know…"

"Ma'am?"

"Never mind."

She returned to the bedside and sat quietly with Ruth,
not daring to speak. Ike had known about the crash not
being accidental from the start, so why all of a sudden
the need for a guard at the door? Two possibilities occurred to her. The first was that Ike had more information, or disturbing news about the perp. If that was the
case, she regretted putting Charlie up to asking Ike to
call it off. The second possibility she didn't like at all.

Someone might have told Ike about John's will. In any
paperback novel, that situation would make her a suspect. Did he think she would, or could, do such a thing?
It was a scary thought. Did she qualify? Had she the
means, opportunity, motive? She thought a moment.
Good God, she did. Ike had to call her that night on
her cell phone because she was out. If she tried thinking like him, no mean feat, she realized she could have
been in Washington that night in a borrowed vehicle.
What kind? Did Ike ever tell her? Should she know or
had she said what it was?

"Ruthie, your boyfriend thinks I am a monster. So
does your aunt Joan, for that matter, but not for the
same reason. What do you think? Don't answer that."
She sighed. What a mess.

"Your father, in the depths of his dementia, cut me
out of his will and left me without a sou. He's left his
entire estate, or what will be left of it after two or three
different sets of lawyers finish mining it, to you. My
problem has been whether I should contest it or leave
it stand. Happily, your Aunt Joan has the same problem. She thinks she should be in the will and might
have been in an earlier version. Until I discover what
those other ones specify, I dare not touch this last one.
That fact, however, gives me a motive to bump you off,
Sweetie. Don't worry, there's a guard outside the door,
so you're safe."

Eden started to cry. She had managed to put off tears
since Ike first called her with the news. Either she was
tired, or the possibilities she'd just outlined to Ruth and
to herself, the awfulness of it all, had finally caught up
with her. Probably both. She sat and cried, silently wish-
ing for another life, another day. Anything.

She couldn't really blame Ike. After her chat with Charlie Garland the other night, she realized she didn't know him as well as she thought. But it was enough to know that when it came to Ruth's safety, he would be ruthless, take no chances, and rule out no possible scenarios however unlikely and potentially embarrassing. Not until he'd exhausted them all. She'd heard the stories about him from Ruth. Some she believed, a few she found almost impossible to take in. She conceded that he was the best thing that had ever happened to her daughter, but…

Now that Ike was Ruth-less, he'd be ruthless—nice pun, but no help. Damn it, I'm her mother, Ike! How could you? Then again, maybe he didn't. A guard did make sense. Her instincts told her she might be the problem, her heart wanted to believe otherwise, that Ike had new and disturbing news. She snuffled, and hiccupped, and brought her crying to a halt, took a deep breath, and began to chat with Ruth about her dinner date with Charlie Garland.

The Janus.

THIRTY-FOUR

FRANK AND IKE were seated in Ike's office. He had agreed to come back in, as it offered the only opportunity for him to see and hear the evidence Grace had gathered from her phone surveillance software. Ike surveyed his desktop. Amos Wickwire had obviously been shuffling through his mail and rearranging the carefully constructed mess Ike had made of the papers, reports, folders, and magazines. His trash can, filled with Styrofoam cups and fast-food wrappers, suggested that Amos had appropriated the office as his lunchroom.

"Where do you want me to start?" Grace asked.

"First, the phone calls. Do you have a fix on where they came from?"

"Yes, but 'fix' is not quite an accurate description of what we have. The first one, we know, originated on the Callend University campus. The second—"

"Wait. Did you say on the campus? Where on the campus? Dorm room, faculty housing? Where?"

"Well, see, that's the problem. The best we can do is put it somewhere in or near Old Main."

"I thought the triangulation apparatus could pinpoint the location to a few square feet."

"Sometimes it can. It depends on the location of the relay towers, how many there are and how close. In Iraq, for example, if a terrorist makes a call on a cell phone, the drone pilots can get a reading that close and drop a rocket down the caller's shorts. It's the way the thing was set up. But out here in the sticks, where, let's face it, the terrorist threat is not considered great, we have fewer towers, farther apart, and a lot less accuracy."

"Fewer bars."

"Yes. Now if we were in DC or any city, I could tell you exactly where he was because the buildings and—"

"I get the picture. So, we know the call came from Old Main. You have a time stamp on it, I assume."

"Yes, six-twelve p.m., so it's not likely to be a student. Classes were over and most of that building would be deserted."

"Except for administrative offices, security, and janitorial. Can you at least give us an idea which end of the building it came from?

"South, I think."

"Who'd he call?"

"This number." Grace handed Ike a slip of paper with a number on it. "It's another cell phone. We did a crisscross and came up with a name. Sheila Overton."

"Who is…wait a minute, I'll get it…she's Acting President Fiske's secretary, or whatever. It was her phone?"

"Her cell phone, yes. She didn't answer and the caller didn't leave a message."

"Okay, noted. Next call."

"This is the weird one. It was made from the Valley View Mall near the Roanoke Airport. And there is a conversation but it doesn't make much sense."

"Let's hear it."

Grace punched the play button on her recording device.

Hey, Tina it's me. <Static>

Who?

It's me, Tammy, I had to, like, borrow a phone. My battery is, like, dead or something.

So, who'd you borrow the <static> phone from?

<Voice lowered> It's some old perv, you know? Says his name is Harry. Yeah, like for real?<loud again> So, how come you're not here at the mall like you said?

My mom grounded me.

Why?

Because of Danny and, you know, Saturday night when I said I was with you only me and him were at his aunt's house and—

"I've heard enough, unless 'the Old Perv' is identified. Am I correct in assuming he isn't?"

"He or she. I doubt it's a she, but nowadays, you can never be sure. No, no ID, but we have the receiving party's name and address. So, if you wanted to backtrack to the caller and interview her, you could."

Ike nodded, "I'll send someone from the afternoon shift down. Any more calls made?"

"One more after twelve that night to the same number as the first. No answer, no message."

"From?"

"Oh, right. Same mall."

"So our guy tries to call the Overton woman, fails, goes to a mall in Roanoke, lends his phone to a teen-aged girl, and calls Overton again. What do we learn from that?"

"Whoever used the phone to call Ms. Harris may work at Callend and have access to an office, and knows Sheila Overton."

"Anything else?"

"Anything else would be speculation."

"Right, very good. Let's see the video."

"Okay, before I start, I have to tell you that the time stamp made on the sales receipts and the time stamp on the cameras differ by almost five minutes. They are set by different companies. The cash register time is set via an atomic clock, the cameras aren't. The installer set them. He must have a cheap watch."

"Or an expensive one. So, what you're saying is we have to watch roughly ten minutes of surveillance if we want to be sure."

"Yes, and the worst part is, we have no idea if the person who bought the phone is the same as the person who used it."

"I should think that's a given, Grace. Run the tapes."

The television flickered and then a grainy black and white picture appeared. An elderly woman with a large shopping bag stood at the counter peeling bills from a wad in her change purse.

"I'm willing to concede she's not the 'Old Perv.' Why can't I see the counter and what she's purchasing?"

"The installer must have thought a picture of a face and the folks behind were more important than what was on the counter. He hiked the frame up so you can see if he's holding a gun or not."

They watched for five minutes while the cashier rang up sales, bagged purchases, and took the next customer. Some of the bags might have held a phone, but the buyers did not qualify in anyone's mind as potential killers.

"Whoops, who's that?" A slight figure wearing a hoodie and sunglasses stepped up to the counter, paid her bill and scooted quickly out of view. "Anybody recognize that girl?"

"I'm not even sure it's a girl," Frank said. "I can

make a better case for whoever that is being a boy. Hoodie, shades? How about an underage kid buying cigarettes?"

"Right. Who's next?"

"Little old lady number two followed by…whoa, isn't that Mrs. Saint Clare?"

"It is. And look who she is talking to."

"Doctor Fiske."

"I think we've seen enough, Grace, unless you think we should watch it to the end."

"There's nothing more, really. More kids and more little old ladies—of both sexes."

"Frank, take Billy or somebody and run out to the university and pick up Fiske."

"Ike, I would love to, but on what charge? The call on the phone that night was made in Washington. The attempt on Ruth's life went down there, too. It is not officially a criminal investigation because the Metro Police haven't filed one. I think we need to talk to them first, get one on paper at least. Also, we don't really know it was Fiske who bought the phone. We should get more information, at least enough to drop Fiske on a material witness."

"So we don't have jurisdiction. He won't know. Go lean on him."

"Ike, if we do, and it turns out he's our guy—"

"What do you mean, if?"

"Just that. Ike, I've watched you work, and I trust your instincts, but you are still angry and that could get us into trouble here. We have only the thinnest circumstantial evidence so far that he did anything more than stand in line while someone bought a phone. If we bust him, with no case pending anywhere…well. Even if we manage to turn up something real when we bring him in, and he hires a sharp lawyer, none of what he says or we find can be used in evidence."

Ike stared at Frank for a full minute, then shook his head and relented. Frank was right.

"Alright, here's what you do. First I'll get the DC cops to initiate a criminal inquiry. They have the tape of the so-called accident. Even if it's just a paper chase they'll do it, as a courtesy I think. Then, you go out there and say something like, 'We have a problem, Doctor Fiske, and maybe you can help us.' Tell him we heard of the threats coming to the school and does he know anything about them? Then, when he's relaxed, give him an, 'Oh by the way, where were you last Sunday night?' If he's guilty, he'll show you something and maybe even do something rash. From what I remember of the guy, he's convinced he's too smart to get caught."

THIRTY-FIVE

AFTER AN HOUR of playing phone tag with the DC police, Ike finally located someone who not only would listen to him, but might possibly do something. He explained his situation. He described Ruth's non-accident and his suspicions and the data he'd amassed. The deputy chief, for that was the person he finally wound up speaking with, pulled up Ruth's accident report and read it to Ike to make sure they were talking about the same case.

"There's a note here that says that victim's fiancé, that would be you I guess, acted aggressively and out of control at the station that night."

"Actually it happened the next morning. The desk sergeant was off his feed and I was upset, I guess you could say. I'm sorry about that."

"Understandable, under the circumstances."

"Yes, well, as I said, I'm sorry if I sounded off to the sergeant. Anyway, that's the one. Later that morning I reworked the scene when there was enough light to see," Ike said. He skipped over his opinion of the DC cop's accident investigation. He didn't need to annoy them anymore than necessary. He needed their help. He would cut the precinct cops some slack. "I can send you photos and some other data if you want. You should have a record of the traffic surveillance camera tapes I forwarded as well."

"Okay, I do. Give me a minute to have a look-see."

Ike waited. "Okay, it appears that the truck deliberately hit the car and pushed it off the road into the pole. Is that what you wanted me to see, Sheriff?"

"Exactly. That car belonged to me, Chief, and the driver was my fiancée. I have been busting my butt trying to nail down the why and who of it. I couldn't talk the precinct into a second look that night but I was hoping maybe you could now."

"You want us to instigate an investigation?"

"Yes. I don't think your guys will have the time or patience to do much, but if it's an open case, then I can work it at this end."

"Do you have any idea why someone would do this?"

Ike explained the situation at the Department of Education. The threats and his thoughts on political operators living on the fringes of protest groups. He was pretty sure he no longer believed it, but Washington thrived on the dark side of conspiracies and plots against the government. Anything else would be hard to sell. The Deputy Chief didn't sound convinced, but he bought it.

"Okay, Sheriff. I'll order a case review. That should hold you for now. In the meantime, send us what you have. I can't promise anything, but who knows, somebody has to know something and maybe he'll spill it when he needs a break from the police when he's picked up for something else."

"Thanks, Chief. I'll send you what I have and you can give me a case number."

Ike hung up. Now he'd have to wait and see what Frank found out in his interview with Fiske, and then he would send Elroy to Roanoke to talk to some kid named Tina who would, in turn and with any luck, lead him to Tammy. She could ID the "Old Perv" and that would be that. He cut a picture of Fiske from the Callend directory and clipped it to the slip of paper with the names and an address of the kid for Elroy. He called Charlie and asked if Kevin, relocated back to DC, had anything new for him.

"Nada, so far. Mostly he's eliminated possible candidates. Alibis all."

"How about he adds Scott Fiske to the list. Who knows, maybe he's a sleeper of some sort."

"A thought that is not so far-fetched, considering we do it all the time and so does everybody else. There's no end to spies and spooks lurking in the suburbs, it seems. Old and apparently lost Russian deep plants, Al Qaeda fanatics, and who knows how many North Korean, Chinese, and Venezuelan plants there are."

"Venezuelan?"

"Alas, yes. Not all border crossers are simple folks seeking a better way of life."

"Or drug cartel employees."

"Them too. Then add to the mix your man's predilection to write fiction in his résumé. Donnie the Snoop wasn't tasked to dig into his past, only to check the current listings, but now that you mention it, Fiske could be one of us, so to speak, or maybe once was one of... not us specifically, but us, metaphorically...has a past and...you get the idea."

"I do. I don't think it's probable but, if he was burned or deep undercover for some reason, you could be right. It's much more likely he's hiding from someone or something else. Shady past, perhaps. We, actually that is you—I don't live in that murky world anymore—can appreciate that."

"Never too late to come home."

"It is for me. That life is now just a very bad memory."

"How's Ruth?"

"I don't know. I'm on my way out there now. The last time I visited, I would swear she tried to make noises, but all she could manage was a little gurgling sound."

"Maybe you should ask a simple question and say one gurgle for yes, two for no."

"You should be writing for television, Charlie. The hero asks all the wrong questions, the comatose woman is trying to say, 'Look out behind you!' and he wants to know if she needs her pillow fluffed."

"You saw that program, too?"

"What? No, I…never mind. I'll take a miss on the dramatics, if it's all the same to you. I'd rather not ask any more of Ruth than she already has to deal with. All I know is she is trying to talk. That's a good sign. It means she's gaining. So, I'll wait. Will you see if Kevin can dig out anything more on Scott Fiske? He spells it with a final E but he may have begun life without it. As you say, we have what your pal Donnie says he isn't. I'd like to know who he is, or maybe, who he was."

Ike hung up and headed to the hospital. Maybe Charlie was right. Should he try one if yes, two if no and three for…for what? And what on earth would he ask her? Yes and no doesn't help much if you don't know what you're after.

Jorge Escobar landed the job with the Parks Department three months earlier. He was proud of the fact that in a bad economy, he could find work and support his family. It was part-time and it didn't offer benefits, but the boss told him as soon as things picked up, he'd be first in line to be taken on full time. His duties involved making the rounds to the town's park sites and maintaining them. He drove to the first of the day's jobs, a small park on the west side. He pulled the truck with its trailer full of mowers and tools into the graveled pull-off. Another, older truck sat at the far end of the parking area near an overhanging clump of trees. He scanned toe tables and charcoal pits but didn't see any sign of activity.

He grabbed his tools. He would police the area first. These picnickers, they didn't care how they left things. Bottles, cans, trash everywhere. Cerdos. Then he would mow the grass around the tables, empty the big trash barrels, and check to make sure everything was in good working order. Sometimes the kids from the university had parties here and they would leave things in a mess. Once one of the charcoal grills had been torn off its post and left in the spot-a-pot. He was happy that maintaining that little blue building was somebody else's problemo. This area was small compared to some of the other facilities he had to clean and maintain. It took him a little less than an hour to finish up. He heaved the trash bags into the back of his truck, reloaded the mower onto the trailer, and then went to check out the pickup truck parked at the other end of the lot.

A miscellany of junk and tools filled the truck bed. Jorge decided the owner must be a lazy man to take such bad care of his property. He called out. No answer. No sign of life anywhere nearby. He tried the passenger's side door and to his surprise, it wasn't locked and the window had been rolled down. Not so good an idea to leave a vehicle unattended and unlocked. The mess in the interior of the cab rivaled that in the bed. He poked at the mess with a stick. The carpeting was not wet, so the truck had not been here when it rained. He slammed the door, walked to the rear, and jotted down the license number on the back of a work order. The only explanation he could think of for a truck to be left unlocked and abandoned would be that maybe it had been stolen by some kids and dumped when it ran out of gas. He returned to the cab, rolled up the window, shoved the lock buttons down, and slammed the door again.

He would give the number to his boss and he probably would tell the park police. They would know what to do.

THIRTY-SIX

IKE MET EDEN on her way out as he walked through the hospital's lobby. She started to say something, clamped her mouth shut, and sailed away without speaking. He pivoted and watched her leave. What was that all about? When he arrived at the CCU and saw the guard chatting with the duty nurse, he understood. Eden might sometimes act the part of a twenty-first century version of Auntie Mame, but he knew she was no fool. It must be the will business. She knew that he knew. If she figured out the source of his information, Charlie was in for an earful. And so, probably, was he. Too bad, but no helping it. Until he knew the identity of Ruth's attacker for a certainty, no one got a free pass. He hoped Eden would understand. He doubted she would, but he hoped.

"How's it looking, Nurse?"

"All quiet on the western front, Sheriff. Her mother just left. This is Brian. He's from security."

"I guessed as much. How do you do, Brian?"

"Fine. Um, Sheriff, can I ask you something?"

"Sure. What is it you want to know?"

"Well, there is a rumor. Like, people say you used to be a CIA agent, is that right?"

"I was, a long time ago. Why do you ask?"

"Well, I was thinking I might like to do that, you know. Law enforcement is okay but I'm thinking international stuff would be really cool."

"I see. Brian, let me explain something to you. First, what you are doing barely qualifies as law enforcement. With respect, security officer at a hospital is right up there with mall cop in terms of measurable risk. Second, the CIA is decidedly not cool. Most of it is either sitting at a desk reading other people's mail, listening to their phone calls, or guessing at what someone halfway around the world is thinking."

Brian started to reply, but Ike waved him into silence.

"Or, and this is the part you are fantasizing about, the few field agents we do have, emphasis on few, live in perpetual fear of discovery even when they are home on leave—which, by the way, is rare. James Bond is a figment of one man's imagination, a commercially successful figment, but a figment nonetheless. In the field you have to deal with extremes, between moving about in a normal, however covert, manner or under conditions of extreme hardship. I once spent a week in a ditch filled with ice water, no food, no blankets, and scared out of my wits. It was cold, but definitely not cool. My advice? Stay put where you are safe, warm, and loved."

Ike left the young man with his mouth hanging open, confused and a little distraught. Apparently he had hoped for a more encouraging response.

Ike found Ruth much as he'd left her the day before. Someone had jacked up her bed a little. He sat and, after searching for a topic not likely to upset her, started to ramble on about nothing in particular. When she moaned, he simply said, "I'm with you, Babe, as soon as you can, tell me something, but take your time. In case you're wondering back in that dark world you occupy, I have a guard at the door twenty-four seven now so you are safe."

FRANK SUTHERLIN SPENT an annoying fifteen minutes across the desk from Scott Fiske. First, he had to sit through a rambling lecture by the acting president on the proper way to approach a faculty member if he thought there might be some way he could be of assistance. Frank did not understand a word he said. Then, he had to hear about how busy he was and what a disruption a police inquiry like this created in his schedule. Frank had dealt with stuck-up academics a time or two but they were usually junior faculty still basking in the light of their newly acquired, shiny bright degrees.

"Very fine, okay, sorry to inconvenience you, Doctor, but I still need to ask you a few questions."

"About?"

Frank paused. He intended to paint the misleading picture about the business of the threats and ask if Fiske could help with identifying possible suspects as Ike had suggested, but the combined tensions of the previous week, when added to the anger he'd been suppressing for the previous quarter of an hour, took over. Instead, he leaned forward and fixed Fiske with his "policeman's eye."

"Do you own a cell phone, Doctor?"

"Do I own a cell phone?" Fiske seemed to have been knocked slightly off-center. "Why do you ask? I mean, yes, of course I do. Everyone does. In darkest Africa people have cell phones, though what they do with them is a mystery to me. Certainly I do. So what?"

"May I see it?"

"Why?"

"It may be involved in this case."

Fiske seemed taken aback. "Case? What case?"

"It is certain that your boss, Doctor Harris, was

forced off the road and we are closing in on that some-one, we think. Then there is the underage girl at the mall in Roanoke. Tell me about your phone."

Frank knew he'd stepped over the line and might even have blown the whole investigation. Whatever he learned in this interview, assuming Fiske was their man, might be in jeopardy or inadmissible when it came time to prosecute. But it was too late to Mirandize him now. He would plow ahead and see. Maybe Ike's idea was right after all. He should just slap the cuffs on Fiske and haul his butt in.

Either his tone of voice or his presence seemed to have cowed Fiske. He dipped a hand into his pocket and produced his cell phone. Frank powered it up and read the number on the face as it booted to life. Not the one he wanted to see. He took a chance.

"Where's the other one?"

"What other one? I don't have another one. What makes you think I have another phone?"

Some people can lie, some cannot. A skillful inter-rogator can usually tell if a person is lying, shading the truth, or telling the proverbial whopper. There are those very few who lie with such aplomb that even a trained observer can be taken in. Fiske, however, was not one of those. He all but broke out in a sweat the instant the words were out of his mouth.

"Would you like to reconsider, Doctor Fiske? We have some indications that a person fitting your descrip-tion used a phone recently in Roanoke—"

"This interview is over. I don't know what you are talking about. I wasn't there." Fiske stood up so sud-denly he nearly lost his balance, strode to the door, and left.

"My, my," Frank said. "What was that all about?"

He walked around behind the desk, glanced up and, seeing no one close by, took a peek in the desk's drawers. More inadmissible snooping, perhaps, but worth a peek. If necessary, he could return with a warrant. Fiske had left a notebook on the blotter. He glanced through the door. Agnes was busy at her desk. He risked a quick look at the book's contents. Some dates and phone numbers seemingly attached to them. Local area codes mostly. Some were, unless he missed his guess, from the Roanoke area. Interesting and possibly useful later. He shut the drawer and put the cigarette in his pocket. He left the office. Agnes Ewalt looked up from her work.

"Where's the great man's secretary?"

"She isn't in today. She's taking a personal leave day—again."

"Is that a problem?"

"Maybe not for Doctor Fiske, definitely is for me. I have all of her work plus mine as well."

He waved goodbye to Agnes, and put in a call to Ike.

THIRTY-SEVEN

SCOTT FISKE LEFT the interview with the deputy sheriff determined to find Sheila. She'd been AWOL for two days. What was she up to? Why did the police want to know about the damned phone? He drove to her apartment and rang the bell. No answer. He pounded on the door. Did the curtain flutter? If she was home, why not answer? Really, for an aide she was acting strangely. Why would she do that? He tried to peer through the window but the curtains were too tightly drawn. He tried the bell and knocked again. Still no luck. He fumbled in his pocket looking for his notebook. His heart sank. He must have left it on his desk in his rush to leave. Would that cop stop to look at it? Well, so what if he did? There wasn't anything in there that could hurt him. Just those numbers and…just those numbers.

He found a used envelope in his jacket pocket. He slit its two sealed edges and pressed the inside flat to make a rectangular sheet. He thought a moment and wrote a note detailing his visit with the police, their questions about the phone, and suggested he had some important questions to ask her. He decided to leave that part vague and slightly threatening. That should get a response. Shivering—he'd left his overcoat in the office as well—he tried to slide the note under her door. It crumpled up and would not push through. He guessed the weatherstripping kept it from sliding under. There was a mailbox attached to the wall next to the door lintel. He dropped it in and hoped the box was in fact in use and not merely decorative. So many apartment buildings had installed community mailboxes at various locations in the complex. He guessed the Postal Service must be trying to save money.

"HEY, ESCOBAR, YOU know that truck you reported parked in the pull off?"

"Yeah, so?"

"There was an APB put out on it. The guy who owns it is wanted by the police. There's a warrant out for his arrest, too."

"No kidding. That for real?"

"Yeah. Some cop's here and wants to talk to you about it. Wants you to tell how it was or something."

"Sure, I talk to the guy. Where he at?"

Frank had cooled down a bit after his meeting with Fiske. Ike wasn't answering either of his phones—probably at the hospital. He could have had him paged, but he'd wait. He'd just hung up when he received the call from the State Police who relayed the information about Smith's pickup being found. He figured if he couldn't work Ike's case, he'd work his own.

"Right here. I understand you're the guy who found the pickup we've been looking for."

"Yeah, that would be me, I guess. What'd the guy do? Maybe he kill somebody or what?"

"Shot a dog."

"That's it? He shoot a dog. What kind of crime is that? He kill a dog. Was an expensive dog or something?"

"Somebody else's dog. They were very annoyed.

Animal cruelty is a crime in this state, especially dog cruelty, you know."

"I hear that, yes, but, so, okay he kill the dog. That's all he do?"

"No, there was a little problem of theft and possible accessory to murder. He was a very bad boy. Now, you want to tell me what you found and what you did. I sent a forensics team out there but I want to know everything about how you found the truck. Did you touch anything, for instance? If so, I'll need your fingerprints."

"Why you need my prints? I don't do nothing. I find the truck, I report it to my boss. He calls the policía, yes? That's a good thing, no?"

"Yes it is. But I need your prints on file to eliminate them from any others I might find on the vehicle. So did you touch the truck?"

"Okay, I touch it a little. You don't want my fingerprints please. I only do it a little."

Frank studied the little man. He was more than upset. He looked like he might bolt out the door at any moment.

"Jorge, that's your name, right? Jorge, I'm thinking you might have a problem with ICE, is that right? Whoa, don't run. Immigration's none of my business. That's between them and you. I have a different interest here. Okay, so here's how we can work it. You tell me exactly what you touched. Exactly, you got it? And everything you touched. If you do, I probably can work around without taking yours, okay?"

"Okay. Give me a minute."

Jorge screwed up his face in concentration, clenched his fists, and began muttering in Spanish under his breath. One by one he extended fingers from a closed fist. He stopped at seven, then closed them again.

"Okay. First, I check the door to see if the truck is locked. Is not. Then I walk to the back and look at the bed. No, wait, I have it backwards. First, I look in the bed. I touch the side near the driver side back wheel, you know?" He waved his hands in the air. "So, then I check the door on the same side and look in. So prints on the handle. The window is open and I poke in the mess he make with a stick to see if this truck is there when it rains. Dry floor, so no. Let's see…then I go to the back. Maybe I steady myself on the side again. I write down his number plate. I go back to the cab and open the door again. I reach over and push the lock knobs down on both doors, roll up window, and I slam the door. Palm of the hand for that one for sure."

All seven fingers were once more freed from the palms of his hands.

"That's it? You're sure?"

Jorge nodded, counted out on his fingers once again, and smiled. "Sure."

"Okay. You need to make yourself available in case we need you. No skipping, you hear, or I will make a call to ICE. Got it?"

"Yes. Got it, gracias."

Frank drove to the park and found the pickup. The forensics team had already arrived and had the truck's doors open.

"There's a palm print on this side of that door. Pull it. It's of the guy who reported the thing. You can use it to eliminate any other place he touched. What have you got?"

"Nada, Deputy, just redneck mess in here and back

in the bed. Paper cups, McDonald's wrappers, crushed beer cans, the usual crap."

"What's that on the hood?"

"Oh, yeah. Your guy left a little notebook under the seat. Looks like a record of sales, and the dates they were made. And, there are initials next to each entry. Maybe you can figure out who bought whatever he was selling. There's a few newspaper clippings stuck inside, too."

"Hay. He was stealing hay and reselling it. There's a market in hot hay. You believe that?"

"You're not kidding? He was stealing hay?"

"Yep. Bag the book. When you've finished dusting it for prints, make a copy of everything and then send it over to me."

"You got it."

THIRTY-EIGHT

THE NEXT MORNING, Ike officially returned to his office. The mayor remained in absentia and business returned to near normal. There had been no further calls made on the cell phone they decided belonged to Fiske. Ike sat in his chronically squeaking chair and contemplated the pile of papers on his desk. His father called to remind him he had a rally to attend that afternoon. Essie brought him a cup of coffee and sat down across the desk.

"So, when are we going to bust Jack Burns?"

"We're not, Essie. He had nothing to do with Ruth's crack-up. He isn't our guy."

"I don't mean for what happened to Ms. Harris, I mean for his involvement in the hay thing."

"You think he had something to do with his nephew's midnight business? Why?"

"Ain't it obvious? Look, he's got no job anymore, right? He just moved over here from Buena Vista, but he hasn't sold his house over there, and he's spending money to get elected. So where's the money coming from?"

"I really hadn't thought about that. It's a possibility, very good, Essie. Let me think a minute. On the other hand, if we look into the mayor's campaign kitty, we could possibly find some large withdrawals. You want to do that?"

"Frank has me and Billy calling around. I guess he doesn't want us in the field. I'm sorry about the dust up in the bar over there. Billy gets a little loud sometimes. But if it don't bring down that stuck-up Burns, I guess it ain't worth my time."

"It could. It depends whether he declared the source in his own accounting. If he didn't, or doesn't, he could be cited."

"You think?"

"Maybe, but this is personal isn't it, Essie? You don't just want him because he's running for sheriff or anything recent. What happened between you two?"

"Not to me, to my dad."

"Essie, let it go. It's not worth the effort. Your dad is dead and no one can make that right."

"I got a baby, Ike, and I don't want him to have to listen to all the sh...stuff I had to hear growing up. 'Your daddy's a convict, nyah, nyah a nyah, nyah.' You got no idea how that is."

"No, I don't. But short of a posthumous pardon from the governor, you can't change that either. Not even if we bring Burns down. And, Essie..."

"Yeah?"

"Before you do anything funny, go back and read your dad's case file."

"You've read it?"

"Yes, when I first took the job as sheriff, I checked everybody out. Under the circumstances, I had to, you may recall."

"Yeah, I guess. What did it say?"

"First, as near as I can tell, Burns wasn't the lead in that investigation. Second, your dad was caught pretty much red-handed at the 7-11 with stolen goods and drugs in his possession. The drugs were for your mother, the goods he stole to support her habit. Your mom wasn't much help. I'm sorry, Essie, but it was a clean bust."

Essie sat for a full minute staring at her shoes. "What do I tell Billy junior?"

"He'll benefit more if you tell him the truth, than from lies. Look what your mother's did to you."

Elroy Heath knocked and entered the open office door. Essie rose and left.

"Essie, on your way out, get me Frank on the phone, will you?"

"Yeah, okay."

FRANK HAD STUDIED the little book found in Smith's truck. The entries didn't tell him much but he guessed the newspaper clippings in the back might have something to do with Duffy's murder or maybe his disappearance. Nothing leapt off the pages, however. He drummed his fingers on his desk and, frustrated at what he perceived as a dead end, left to get some air. Maybe drive around.

Whether it was instinct or plain dumb luck, he found himself driving back to the park where the truck had been found. It had been towed away the day before so there was no reason to stop there, but he did. The leaves were in full color, one major benefit granted to people who chose the Shenandoah Valley as their place of residence. Whatever else might be said about the midsection of Virginia, fall was spectacular in the Blue Ridge. He stepped out of his cruiser and circled the area where the truck had been parked. There wasn't much to see. The area had been trampled by the forensic team's footprints. There was no way to tell if the other tire prints were recent or old.

So where was Smith? He walked absentmindedly to the verge and looked at the ground. Something caught his eye and he stepped away from the parking area and into the woods. It looked as if the leaves might have been disturbed. He didn't know why he thought that. The damned things were constantly falling and all over the place, but he could have sworn someone had created a path through them as if they had walked in and out of the woods at this particular point. Leaves that had been scuffed by feet looked different somehow than if they hadn't been disturbed. Had Smith left the truck and walked in here? If so, where did he go?

He followed the path, if you could call it that, deeper into the trees. Here and there the wind had swirled leaves into clumps and piles of various sizes. He kicked at a few of them. The last one did not give to his boot. Perhaps the pile had formed around a stump or a log. He reached down with a gloved hand and scattered the leaves. That's when he saw the boot and the leg attached. He knocked a few leaves to one side and realized why no one had been able to find Smith. He was under the leaves, very dead, and had been for a while.

He called Ike. He got Essie.

"I was just calling you. Ike wants to talk to you, too."

"SHE BEEN CRYING, IKE?" Elroy asked as he watched Essie make her way back to her desk.

"Maybe a little. What have you got for me, Elroy?"

"Well, it took some doing. I had to borrow a cop from the Roanoke force to get to it, but I finally dug out a description of the man who leant the phone to her." He inspected his notebook and read the name. "Miss Tammy Bonwell. I had to find her friend, Tina, first. Tina didn't want to talk to me. Her parents raised a fuss about me being from out of town and such. That's when I had to call in the Roanoke officer. Then she dummied up. Finally, I had to tell her it was an investigation into an attempted murder and withholding information could be considered obstruction of justice. That's when her old man got all nervous and said she'd tell what she knew or she'd be grounded for life."

Ike gestured for Elroy to take Essie's seat.

"It turns out that these girls, maybe five or six of them, meet at the mall and they tease older men, I guess you'd say. They flirt with them, get them to treat them to pizza and so on and then duck into the restrooms and ditch the guys. It's a little like playing chicken, I guess. They think it's funny. I mentioned the few cases we have had involving teenaged rape and disappearances to her, but I don't think she heard. The Roanoke cop was taking notes, anyway."

"Okay, so what did you learn, besides something about the abnormal psychology of hormone-driven teenagers?"

"She finally gave up her friend, Tammy, who is very much into this stuff. I found her at the mall chatting up a banker from Toledo who blew into town for a meeting. He beat a quick retreat when I flashed the badge. Tammy, after a little persuasion, gave me a description of the so-called 'Old Perv.' She claimed she didn't know his name. I got the impression she didn't dump him right away like the others and that maybe she had a sideline going. I am not real sure about that but, well, I told the Roanoke guy what I suspected and he said they'll keep an eye on her. The description she gave me matches your man. I showed her the picture. I'm sure she recognized it, but she played dumb."

"Not dumb, Elroy. Stupid."

THIRTY-NINE

IKE STOOD AND gathered his duty belt and jacket. "I think we need to find Scott Fiske and haul him in, don't you, Elroy?"

"Sounds like a plan."

"Have you reached Frank, Essie?"

"He just this minute called in, Ike. He says he needs you out at the park where they found that truck." Essie held the phone in her hand.

"Can't it wait?"

"He says it's real urgent. He found Bob Smith, he says."

"Okay. Tell him I'm on my way and to stay put. Elroy, see if you can locate our acting president. If you do find him, sit on him until I can join you."

Ike drove to the park. The forensics van pulled in ahead of him. Frank had called them back to the scene again. He parked and followed the path Frank had marked with yellow crime scene tape back into the woods.

"You found Smith, Essie says."

"I did. I think he's been dead a while. Question is who did him in?"

"Indeed. What got him?"

"Looks like a single shot to the back of the head, well not quite the back—more like on top. It's a funny angle, like he was bending over to pick up something and never made it back up. The ME can tell us more, I reckon. But it's pretty clear he had no idea it was coming. Whoever did this must have covered him up with leaves afterward. Lord knows we might never have found him 'til spring if I hadn't been curious about what I took to be a path back to here."

Ike bent over the body which, fortunately, the cool October air and blanket of leaves had kept partially refrigerated. "Anything interesting in his pockets?"

"All turned out. Whoever killed him was thorough. There's not even any pocket lint. We do have his notebook, though, from under the seat of his pickup. I am still working out what significance it could have, but since I think he hid it there, it must have some."

"We'll look at it when the evidence techs are done here. A single shot, you say?"

"As far as I can see, yeah."

"In all this," Ike indicated the leaves covering the forest floor. "I don't suppose you found a shell casing?"

"Sorry, no. It would be near impossible to do it, for sure."

"We'll have the ET team rake the leaves back. Maybe they'll be lucky. If they miss the shell they might at least find something else. A footprint would be nice. I had it in mind to drop in on Scott Fiske when you called. The kid in the mall ID'd him. At least her description is a match. The picture Elroy had with him didn't click, but she had some reasons to be cute. I'm guessing Scott Fiske may well be hearing from her soon, if he hasn't already. Kids! They watch too much television and take too many risks. The way she's headed, that child won't live to see twenty."

"Not following you, Ike."

"Sorry. Elroy got the impression the kid was playing at being a tramp for pizza and presents. Not sure how far she went, but the fact she's being coy about the picture suggests she might be thinking about upping her game."

ELROY TRIED FISKE'S office and then his house on the Faculty Row. The last time he'd visited this end of the Callend campus things had been considerably more hectic, he remembered. Cops, Feds, bad guys, strobe lights, bull horns, and confusion. Working with Ike was a lot of things, but boring wasn't one of them.

Fiske had a place near the end of the street. He knocked but no one answered. He walked around to the rear and peeked in the kitchen window. There didn't seem to be any sign of life. No car in the driveway, either. He circled the house but found nothing of interest. He called Ike with the news.

"IF WE CAN'T find Fiske, how about we look for the secretary, what's her name?" Frank said.

"Sheila somebody—Overton."

"Agnes Ewalt said she hasn't been to work for a couple of days."

Ike held the phone to his ear again. "Elroy, run out to Overton's place and see if you can pry her loose. Call Essie for the address. Tell her it's in the University Directory." Ike hung up.

"In the meantime, Frank, how about you and I see a judge about some warrants and then we'll have a look at Fiske's office and house. Oh, and I had an idea for you. Actually, it was Essie's."

"Essie's? Now what?"

"Tell you on the way to town."

They drove out of the park and headed back east.

"Right. Now here's something else I want you to think about. Burns is financing his campaign somehow. He doesn't have an income. His house is still on the market and he's separated from his meal ticket, that is to say his wife who is a manager at the supermarket. Does any of this give you ideas?"

"If he wasn't being financed by some outside source, he had to have an income from somewhere. Who or from whom do you think? Where in the system is that notebook?"

They drove back to Picketsville. The county judge was just leaving his office. Somewhat grumpily, he returned to his office, heard them out, and reluctantly signed off on the two search warrants.

"Ike, why weren't you at the meeting this afternoon? Your father had to fill in for you. He didn't look too happy, if you don't mind my saying so."

Ike stopped in his tracks and slapped his forehead. "I completely forgot, Your Honor. He'll be fit to be tied. Well, can't be helped."

They left the courthouse.

"I wish you'd take this election more seriously, Ike. You know the mayor will keep a lid on the connection between his boy, Burns, and the dead hay thief, I mean thieves, and that means you could still be in trouble."

"Frank, the only way I know how to show people why they should re-elect me is to do the job they elected me to do in the first place. We have murders piling up. One killing is bad enough but now we have a second one and nobody but a fool thinks they're not related."

"And you have Fiske to collar. Not a murder, but…"

"Close enough. Personally, I can't distinguish between an attempted homicide and a successful one. For me it's a distinction without a difference. In each case the intent is identical, as are the measures taken. The fact the perpetrator failed should be unimportant. The punishment should be contingent on the killer's intent, not his success. We don't reward failure in business, school, or life in general. There ought not to be a reward for incompetence in criminal behavior either."

"Now that is a bit of philosophy I would dearly love to see debated on Sunday morning television."

"Don't hold your breath."

Ike's phone buzzed. Elroy again.

"Ike, the lady is missing too."

"I think we need to execute our search ASAP, Frank."

FORTY

AGNES EWALT LOOKED UP, startled when Ike and Frank strode into Old Main's administration wing.

"Sheriff Schwartz, how nice to see you. How is Doctor Harris?" Even though everyone in town and on the Callend campus knew that Ike and Ruth were engaged, in her public moments, Agnes maintained the fiction that the relationship did not exist. Ike didn't know why, but that was Agnes and there'd be no changing her anytime soon.

"Ruth is coming along nicely, Agnes, thank you. We're very encouraged."

We were? He fought the stab of fear that hit him in his solar plexus every time the thought of Ruth lying unconscious in the hospital forced its way to the surface.

"Frank and I are here to speak to Doctor Fiske. Is he in?" Ike felt sure he wasn't but he had to ask.

"No, he rushed out of here after Deputy Sutherlin spoke with him a while back and I haven't seen or heard from him since. Sheila either, for what it's worth. I already told that to one of your men."

"Yes, thank you. We'll just have a look around his office then."

"Oh, I'm not sure that is…would be appropriate. He likes to keep it locked and after you all left, I pulled the door to. And then, well, there's a matter of—"

"Not to worry, Agnes, we have a search warrant, and we won't take much time. You say the door is locked?"

"I believe so. That is what I meant to do." She went to the door and tried the knob. "Sorry, yes it's locked."

"Is there a spare key? Surely he left one here for emergencies."

"Maybe in Sheila's desk." Agnes sat down at a large desk to the right of Fiske's door and tried the drawers. "This is locked, too."

"Let me try," said Frank. He produced a large pocket-knife, freed the main blade, and slipped it into the space between the drawer's top edge and the desk. He gently wiggled the blade while lifting on the desk's edge just above the drawer's lock. There was a soft click and the drawer slid open. "If this desk is anything like mine down at the office, the rest of the drawers lock when this one does. They should all be free now." They were. They found the spare key, conveniently tagged, in the left-hand top drawer.

Fiske's office had the sterile look of a place used only as a base to do business, nothing more. There were no personal touches anywhere. He had no family which explained the absence of framed pictures on the desk, but there were no mementos, no souvenir paperweight, no magazines, or any indication that Scott Fiske had ever inhabited this space. It could have been a demo unit in a furniture store.

"Look in the desk," Frank suggested. "That's where he keeps his personal stuff."

"You've already looked?"

"A little, yeah. He smokes fancy cigarettes and has one or two girly magazines tucked under that address book."

Ike put on latex gloves, removed the articles from each drawer, and placed them in order on the desktop and the matching credenza behind him. There wasn't much to see. Besides the wooden box containing the Turkish cigarettes and the magazines, his desk was as antiseptic as the rest of the room.

"Do you suppose he cleaned this place out?"

"No idea. Possibly. I don't see anything here that would tell us where he went. His address book is filled with names of people with out of town addresses. Then there's his little notebook with initials and phone numbers only. That could be interesting."

"Put it in an evidence bag and record it. Maybe one of those numbers will turn up something. We'll run a criss-cross on them and see." He turned to the door where Agnes had been watching the search. "I guess we're done here, Agnes. If Fiske returns, tell him we were here, that he should come into the police station at once, and then you call me, and tell me he's here anyway."

"Should we post someone to wait for him?"

Ike thought a minute. "We could, but there are too many ways in and out of this building. A watch would have to sit outside the door to be sure. If he's on the run, and does come here for some reason, he'll see our guy before he's seen and he'll be off. Still, we probably should. As soon as Elroy's done talking to the neighbors over at Overton's tell him to come here and stake out this office."

"Right. Now we go to his house?"

"We do."

Frank drove the car and told Ike about what he'd come to believe happened to Smith. His best guess, he said, was that Smith and Duffy had a disagreement over profits. The notebook he'd found seemed to be a record of sales and so on, and they must have argued.

"So you're not buying the notion Duffy overheard something or saw something and perhaps got in over his head and Smith found out. Or, instead, he was a witness to the Duffy hit?"

"I can't rule it out, Ike, but I like simple answers. In my experience, people like those two bozos tend to be greedy, and stupid, and often sell each other out."

"Then, who killed Smith?"

"Maybe a friend of Duffy who we haven't turned up yet, or Jesus, how about Burns?"

"Wouldn't go there, Frank. In a world where anything is possible, we still deal with probabilities. Burns is an improbable killer—at the moment, he has no compelling motive."

"But if he was mixed up in the robberies and—"

"That's a big if. Without the connection—not compelling."

"Smith took the trouble to hide that book, there had to be a third party involved somehow. Hell, it could have been his uncle trying to get him out of the way and that went south."

"Could have been works, but without a connection there's nothing there. You're sounding like Essie. As I said, won't work, not yet. Frank, he's a loser as a cop. He's the mayor's 'flunky of the week.' And he is shady, but he knows what happens to them when cops go to prison. No, I don't see him as a killer."

"So who, then?"

"I don't know. To be honest, I haven't really given your two murders much thought, sorry. I hear what you're saying about seeking simplicity, but my instincts tell me it's a lot more complicated. As far as we know, Smith didn't have a problem until after you busted him.

Maybe he remembered something or heard something during the course of his stay with us. If it weren't for his uncle Jack, he'd still be in jail and alive."

"There you go, Burns."

"It's at best only a distant maybe. Look, Smith goes home, digs out the book, and within twenty-four hours he's dead. I think you need to look at that book. But that will have to wait until we're done with Fiske. As soon as we take him down, we'll go after your guy."

Elroy Heath's call interrupted Ike.

"What do you have, Elroy?"

"Well, before I left to sit on the office, an old lady in the neighborhood stopped me and wanted to know if I was the one asking questions about that Overton woman. That's how she put it, 'that Overton woman.' I said, 'Yes I am,' and she said, 'Well you should know that that woman had a paramour.' That's what she said. Turns out she meant boyfriend. Anyway, she has a daughter works up at the school and that's what she said, she said…you know what I mean. She also said he was there earlier and seemed upset when he left. Paramour, for God's sake. I had to ask her to spell it out. I thought she was telling me the woman owned a lawnmower. Okay, I'm almost to the school."

"Thanks, Elroy. I don't know what it means but we'll keep it in mind. Lawnmower?"

"Yeah, sure sounded like it."

"Right, thanks, Elroy." Ike closed his phone and scratched his head. "Paramour? Oh… I must have lost a step. Frank, turn here."

"I know. What about a lawnmower?"

"Tell you later."

FORTY-ONE

FRANK PULLED INTO the driveway and settled the police car with its front bumper touching the rear bumper of what he assumed must be Fiske's car. If Fiske had returned, as it appeared he had, and if he tried to make a run for it, the only way he could use his car would be to drive it across his backyard and through a chain-link fence. The fence had a gate and it was open but too small to allow an automobile to pass through.

"You take the back, Frank. Most of these houses have an exterior cellar stairway so stand a little toward one side or the other so you can watch the back door and the stairwell at the same time. I'll go in through the front. I'll call you when I have him, or am sure he isn't in the basement. Keep your radio on."

"Roger that."

Ike waited until he was certain Frank had positioned himself, and then climbed the three steps to the porch. He crossed to the door, rang the bell, waited, and then pounded on it.

"Fiske, open up. It's Sheriff Schwartz. I have a warrant to search this house and for your arrest."

The second part wasn't true, but he hoped Fiske might be more amenable to giving up if he thought the game was over for him. There was no answer. Ike shouted and banged on the door twice more. He stepped back, took aim, and kicked the door open. His entry was quick but cautious. The front room was clear. There was no other sound in the house besides the pounding of his heart. He asked Frank if anything stirred out back.

"Nothing much. The grass hasn't been mowed for a while and you can make out where somebody walked from the back gate to the house recently. Nothing else."

"Hasn't used his paramour lately, I guess."

"What? That's what you all meant. Paramour!"

Ike moved to the adjoining room. He found Fiske slumped over the dining room table as if asleep. One arm dangled from the side of the table and a Colt .45 lay on the floor beneath it. Ike shook Fiske's shoulder and then stepped back as he collapsed in a disorderly heap next to the gun. Scott Fiske had taken at least five bullets, four to his core, and one, complete with powder burns, to his head. Ike marveled how that could have happened and not have made him fall out of his chair.

"We're clear in here, Frank. You can come in. And then call in for the evidence technicians and anyone from the day shift that's not busy. We have another homicide on our hands."

Frank entered while calling in the shooting. "Essie, dispatch the ETs, and send over as many guys as are available to Faculty Row—Fiske's house." He stopped short of the dining room table and stared at the corpse. "Well, it looks like Fiske wasn't your guy after all."

"You think? What the hell did we miss?"

THE HOUSE HAD been sealed off and yellow crime scene tape festooned the porch and yard. Evidence technicians filled the house. Cameras flashed, men dusted for prints, and Ike retreated to the porch. Billy Sutherlin, who had been on patrol when the call came in, kept the crowd of gawkers behind the crime scene tape. Ike watched as a man approached him. Billy listened and then waved him through to talk to Ike.

"Sheriff? I live next door. I told your deputy that I heard shots earlier and I thought I ought to say something."

"Shots? When did you hear them?"

He looked at his watch, thought a second as if the math might be difficult, "Two and a half hours ago. Two hours and thirty-seven minutes to be exact. I heard, blam, blam, blam, blam, a pause and then, blam—five."

Ike exhaled. "We've been here an hour. You heard the shots an hour and thirty-plus minutes before that. Why didn't you call 9-1-1 right away?"

"Well, I couldn't be sure, you know. I mean it could have been—"

"Stop. Please don't say 'a car backfiring.' Cars rarely backfire these days. And even years ago when they did, five times in a row would never happen."

"Well, look, I'm just trying to cooperate here."

"Appreciate that. You are?"

"Harvey Applegate. I am in the Physics Department."

"I see. Well, Doctor Applegate—"

"It's Mister. I'm an A.B.D., not Ph.D."

"Sorry, good luck with that, Mr. Applegate. Just give your name to the deputy and make yourself available in case we need to take a formal statement from you. And thank you."

He walked Applegate back to the tape and noticed a woman standing on the porch of the other adjoining house. He slipped under the tape and strolled over to her.

"Your neighbor on the other side said he heard the

shots that killed Doctor Fiske. Were you home two and a half hours ago, and if you were, did you happen to hear the shots, too?"

"Not really. I heard something that in retrospect I assume must have been shots, but that is not what I thought of at the time."

"You thought they were what?"

"Someone hammering. Look, I have my studio on the opposite side of the house and on the second floor. It's as close as I can get to a north light. The walls are draped and stacked with canvases. So any sound that I hear is usually muffled. I like it quiet when I work."

"I see. Is there anything you can tell us that might help?"

"Maybe. I don't know if it's relevant or not, but he has a cleaning service that comes in once a week. Today was their day to clean so…"

"Any prints we find, at least on the more obvious surfaces, would be new today."

"That was my thought."

"Did you recognize any other person—man, woman—with him?"

"Sorry, no. I was turning to go back into the house."

"Thanks. Someone will be by to take a statement from you later."

Ike walked back to the crime scene and entered the house. The ME looked up from examining Fiske.

"What have you got for me?"

"Very interesting, Ike. The first four shots were fired directly at the victim. The shooter was sitting at the opposite end of the table like they were having a meeting or something. He must have had the gun in his lap—"

"You're assuming the killer was a man?"

"No, just trying to save time by not having to say 'he or she' all the time, but you just ruined that. Anyway he or she must have had the gun in his…crap…in his lap. He gets to the point in the conversation when shooting becomes the preferred option. Raises it to tabletop height and shoots. Look on this end of the table. There are powder burns in the finish. Okay, he squeezes four straight in. The guy is heavy and so is the chair. By the looks of the entry wounds, I'm guessing the slugs are small caliber, .32, or maybe .25—a lady's gun."

"Or a professional."

"A pro might choose a small-caliber gun, but he wouldn't need five shots to get the job done. I wouldn't put any money on that horse. My money says, not a pro. And since there isn't a lot of punch in a weapon like that, he wasn't knocked backwards out of the chair. The shooter pumps four in and your victim is sitting there trying to figure what hit him and sinking fast, if I judge the wounds right, and the perp gets up, calm as you please, walks around the table, puts the gun to this guy's head, and delivers the coup de grâce. Deep powder burns on the forehead and upper face."

"Saw those. A very cool and deliberate character, whoever he was."

"Looks like."

"So the .45 on the floor definitely wasn't the gun used to shoot him?"

"No way, but I can tell you something about it. It has been recently fired and that's not all."

"What else?"

"The fingerprints on this piece are not right. If I didn't know better, I'd swear the gun has been wiped and then one set of prints applied to it. If I had to guess, the gun was pressed into his hand after he was shot."

"But you don't know that."

"As I said, of course not, but what sort of a person wipes his own gun down after firing it, but doesn't clean it at the same time?"

"All kinds. Maybe he just started to clean it and… I don't know. You said it had been fired recently. That's interesting. Send the report over as soon as you can. Oh, and the ballistics from the stiff in the woods, too. Anything else I should know right now?"

"He had two cell phones. Is that important?"

"I think so, yes, it depends on their numbers." Ike returned to the porch.

A car pulled up and a woman got out. She stared open-mouthed at the police cars and crime tape, then started for the house. Billy held up his hand to stop her.

"What's happened?" Her voice carried to the porch. "I have to see him. He's in danger."

Ike took the porch steps in a single jump and walked over to the woman.

"And you are…?"

"I'm his A.A."

"Why is he in danger?"

"He said he'd received threats. He said someone was trying to blackmail him."

"Who?"

"I don't know, but he said he wasn't going to pay, and that he had a gun, and if anyone tried anything, he'd handle it."

"But you don't know who that somebody might have been?"

"No, he wouldn't tell me, but he did say they were 'pretty high up,' whatever that means."

"I'm afraid your boss wasn't successful in handling it after all."

"What?"

"He's been murdered."

Sheila Overton's eyes rolled up out of sight and she folded gracefully to the ground.

FORTY-TWO

FRANK LEFT IKE at Fiske's house speaking to the paramedics, and returned to the office. There wasn't anything more he could contribute to that scene and his two murders, as Ike had called them, were on his mind. He picked up the notebook found in Smith's truck and carried it to his desk. Something had been nagging at him for hours. Had Ike said something about the notebook? Burns figured in the two deaths he's been investigating somehow, he was sure of it. He carried the book to his desk as if he'd been entrusted with the Rosetta Stone and it would soon reveal its secrets to him.

"What you got there, Frank?" Essie might show respect for Ike—sometimes—but Frank was family, Billy's older brother and, in her often-expressed opinion, a pretty dull guy.

"Something I hope will make you and Billy happy."

"What's that supposed to mean?"

"Patience, mother of my nephew. I have work to do. I am hot on the trail of your candidate for bad man of the year, Jack Burns. You want to help?"

"I thought we already were. We've been looking into the mayor's campaign funds like you said."

"Any luck?"

"Do you have any idea how hard it is to get that kind of information from politicians? It's like they're holding on to the formula for classic Coca-Cola or something."

"It will probably take an application of the Freedom of Information Act to get it and then you can't be sure which set of books you'll be looking at. More importantly, what have you found out with your calls to Burns' former associates?"

"You mean the cops he worked with over the years? Not much we didn't know already. He's a little dirty but not enough to make a big difference. Most of them weren't too happy about talking to us—Band of Brothers kind of thing. Probably in it with him."

"Ike said you had this idea about his financing. That's why I asked. You are not going to find much in the mayor's books, either the real or the cooked versions. The answer is in here." Frank held up the book. "Where's he getting the money to run a campaign, Essie?"

"Not the mayor?"

"Don't think so. Not enough to pay for his campaign or get the mayor in trouble. Our fearless leader acts like an idiot some days, but he's smart enough to stay clean. So where is the money coming from?"

"He fixes tickets and takes money for that."

"Essie, dentists get rich doing root canals, plastic surgeons get rich from performing boob jobs, bankers get really rich by bundling bad paper with good. Fixing tickets gets you beer money, not rich."

"Then what?"

"I'm thinking hay."

"You got to be kidding."

"Watch and learn."

It took over an hour for Frank to sort out the entries in the book. The columns of figures didn't always total in the places he assumed they would or should. Duffy or Smith, he had his doubts whether the latter kept the books, had developed a unique method of bookkeeping. After he'd established a pattern, he began writing. He leaned back in his chair and looked at what he had.

"Essie, you're good with figures. What does this look like?"

Essie flipped the pages Frank had assembled and scowled. "Which? These scratchings you wrote or this old book?"

"The ones I wrote."

"Looks like my Ma's egg records. That would be before she gave up on chickens. You got the source, which chicken, and next to it the number of eggs it laid each day. Only this is different and we ain't talking about chicken or eggs, are we?"

"No. But you are right. This is a record of the hay stealing, bales swiped, bales sold and—this is the good part, on this last sheet, the split."

"So you know how much Smith and how much Duffy took home. Is there a bribe in there for you know who?"

"Close enough, but no bribe. A three-way split, Smith, Duffy and…?"

"There's another partner? Not…?"

"It sure looks that way. Get me the State Police and ask for the guy who was investigating those robberies."

It took three transfers and one rude operator, but Essie finally got through to the corporal who'd been saddled with the task of sorting out the robberies. He sounded less than pleased to hear from the Picketsville sheriff's office as they had pretty much co-opted his investigation.

"So, what do you need now? We gave you what we had and next thing I hear is two guys are dead. That's rough justice, Deputy."

"Never our intention to have it end this way. It appears they got tangled up in something bigger than lifting bales of hay from local farms. What I need to know is, were there people in the video the farmer shot, the one with the truck?"

"Yeah, but we couldn't make anything out. It was night and the equipment pretty primitive."

"Can I have the video on loan?"

"Sure. You want me to upload it to your computer?"

"That would be great. Listen, we think there may have been others involved. If we catch them, you get the nod, okay?"

"Thanks. Pictures on the way."

While Frank waited for the transfer, he dug his calculator out from his desk drawer and began adding and dividing. He made three columns and totaled them separately. His next stop was Grace's office. She was on her way out the door but he asked her to stay.

"There's a video coming in. See if you can enhance the people in it, will you? See if there is anything on the edges of the surveillance tapes that might not have showed up in the first transmission. If you have trouble, call the Highway Patrol. They have really good video equipment."

"Sam Ryder left some stuff on this rig," she said, sweeping her arm across the array of electronic equipment. "I haven't had an excuse to use it until now. I'll give it a go."

"Good, then I want you to check this guy's bank records."

"I'm not sure that's legal, Frank."

"Trust me, it will be. You may have to run it again, officially, but right now, it's part of an investigation. Tell the bank he's a person of interest in a murder and we can have a warrant to him in the morning if we have to, but he can save us a lot of time if he'd give us a peek."

"Burns is a person of interest in a murder?"

"I'm hoping."

"Okay, if you say so. Does Ike know you're doing this?"

"Sort of. Doesn't matter. We have too many murders on our books to start getting picky just now. Just run it and set it up to repeat—" he checked his pocket calendar "—let's say tomorrow."

"How about I just see if I can't get into their records on my own first. Then, if we need to, we can make a formal request."

"Works for me."

"IKE, YOU ARE going to love this."

"Love what?"

"Well, running unopposed, for one. And then closing the hay business for another."

"All on the same day? That's nice. May I ask how or who? What?"

"As you suggested. No, I mean as Essie intuited. I about took this book apart yesterday and you'll never guess who was on the payroll besides Smith and Duffy."

"You're kidding."

"I had Grace run Burns' bank records. He has periodic deposits into his account—in cash—on a variety of dates, none of which match his normal payday, for which, by the way, he has direct deposit. This book shows, among other things, how the proceeds for the sale of hay were distributed. Here's the good part, it was a three-way split. The third split matches the cash deposits in Burns' bank deposit."

"Good, but still iffy, Frank. Can you put him in the truck or…a payoff for what? For not arresting the other two?"

"Better. I had the State Police send over the video that caught the truck that night. Grace enhanced it. There are two people in it. Duffy is easy to recognize. Smith is still blurry, but that doesn't matter. When the picture was stretched you could see a car parked in the shadow of the barn. It is very dark and you can't tell if anyone is in it, but—"

"A car? What sort of car? You can read the license number?"

"Better. You can read a number painted on the trunk lid right under the words, get this—POLICE."

"It's a police cruiser? Nobody is that stupid."

"I guess there is a first time for everything. It was signed out to Burns that night. I know that doesn't put him in it, nor does it guarantee that he was even there, but it'll for sure be a tough thing for him to explain away. He will attempt to weasel out in a dozen different ways, but at the very least, it's enough to get us an indictment. And you will be, for all practical purposes, unopposed. Billy and I are out the door to arrest him now."

"Make sure the mayor is around when you bring him in."

"Already on it. Um… Ike?"

"Yeah?"

"You have any objection if I take Essie on the bust? She earned it, I think."

"Get someone in to cover the desk and take her

along. But, tell her no yelling and yahooing. We want a dignified arrest suitable for the seriousness of the occasion, right? Oh, and you might want to consider it your civic duty to call the local paper."

"No yahooing at all? I can try, but—"

"You'll do your best, I'm sure."

Frank left the office and apparently talked to Essie. "Yahoo!"

FORTY-THREE

IKE SHUFFLED THROUGH a fistful of reports from the ETs and two more from the Medical Examiner. He desperately wanted to find a pattern, something, anything to move him off the dime. His case had come completely unraveled. Make that, cases. Charlie Garland knocked, waved a greeting, and set a cup of coffee on the desk.

"Good morning, Charlie, I thought you'd left this sinking ship for safer passage in DC."

"Now why would I do that?"

"Well, for one thing, to hide from the probable impending wrath of Eden Saint Clare."

"Ah, that. I did, indeed, withdraw, but not to abandon the field and certainly not to escape a wrathful Eden Saint Clare. I left, but briefly, to do your business. You may recall you had a few loose ends from your search among the radical right or radical left or whichever they are. I can never keep them straight."

"Depends on whose ox is getting gored, I guess."

"Precisely. At any rate, with the connivance of the director, and a blind eye cast by our friends in the FBI, we cleared your list of potential bad people as far as we could."

"Why, Charlie?"

"Why what? Why did we do it?"

"Yes. Why does the director care, why did the FBI accede to all this?"

"Ah, two reasons. First, as much as you would wish it were not so, everybody sees through you, Ike. They know that in spite of your dismissal of the company in the past and your public disdain for it currently, you would, if called on, do the same for us. You have in the past and doubtless will again in the future. You are a Boy Scout, Ike. You do your duty to God and your country. Second, you are one of the good guys. Everyone wants you to stay that way, the thought of you going rogue is not a happy one for any of us. Now, as I was saying, we can't pin this thing on them. That doesn't mean one of them didn't do it, of course, but the trail in the surreal world of radical politics has gone cold. But then, you'd already assumed that."

"I had, but thank you and the director for all the trouble. It must have been a great deal of work. And I am not a Boy Scout."

"It was. You're welcome, and yes you are, but I won't belabor the point. I am not finished here. You asked Kevin to add your man Fiske to the list. That did turn up something."

"Not in time. Fiske found himself in the path of five small-caliber bullets and didn't duck in time."

"He's dead? How very convenient for him."

"How do you figure that?"

"He is a person of interest in one or two minor fracases some years ago, when he called himself Frank Scott."

"Anything I should know about?"

"Not anymore. As nearly as we could reconstruct the man's past, he had a rocky childhood, scrapes with the law, and disappeared at about age sixteen. He turned over a new leaf, it seems, reformed, changed his name, and completed his education. Not at the places or to levels he listed on his CV, but he did. Oxford, Mississippi, is not Oxford, Great Britain, but the process is approximately the same—he graduated. So, fill me in. Is his death related to Ruth's wreck and if so, how?"

"I thought he was the guy behind the wheel of that truck. In fact, I thought I had him dead to rights, as they used to say. Frank and I went to his house to arrest him. Instead, we found him sitting at his dining room table with four neat holes in his chest and one really nasty one in his forehead. I had it wrong, it appears. Now I am back to square one, and you tell me there is no use going back and picking up the other line either. Just as well."

"That's it?"

"Well, no. Frank has some evidence that the man who would be sheriff was also involved in the business of swiping hay with his nephew and, as we speak, is attempting to raise bail. Strangely, the mayor seems to have forgotten Burns' name and has been acting nice to me. He said he would like to endorse my candidacy."

"Lovely for you. You are the man of the hour. And he will do that because…?"

"Frank let drop the possibility he is considering contacting the county attorney to investigate local campaign finances in light of the arrest."

"Is he?"

"Probably not, but he could. That's the point."

Ike's intercom buzzed. "Ike, Ms. Overton is here like you asked."

"Thank you, Essie. Put her in the interview room. I'll join her in a minute."

"Who is Ms. Overton?" Charlie asked.

"Scott Fiske's lawnmower. Charlie, you have a good

feel for these things. Sit in on this interview and tell me what I'm missing."

"Lawnmower? She cuts his grass?"

"Metaphorically speaking, perhaps. I don't know for sure and at this remove, I do not care. Come on."

Sheila Overton perched on the edge of the oak chair. She wore a simple light gray suit, cream-colored blouse with a dainty, paisley foulard tie at her throat. She apparently had neglected to apply her makeup. Dark circles under her eyes gave her a gaunt and sorrowful look. The white knuckles on the hand that clutched what appeared to be a scuffed Brighton purse were the only indication that she might be nervous. Ike sat across the table from her and Charlie took a seat in the corner, where he could observe her face and body language.

"Thank you for coming in, Ms. Overton. I know this can't be easy for you. How well did you know Doctor Fiske?"

"How well? We were pretty close, you know. Like, I'm his A.A. and so I had to know lots of stuff…things."

Ike riffled some papers in front of him and then fixed her with an icy stare. "That's it?"

"Okay, so yeah, we were very close."

"You were lovers."

"No, no we weren't. Not because I wouldn't have… you know, but it wasn't like that. He wanted to wait."

"He wanted to…wait?"

"It's hard to explain. We were more, you know, like, engaged, but he didn't want to move on that right away. Not until he managed to land a big job."

"How does that work? I thought he had a big job."

"Scotty was ambitious and he worried that if he was hooked up with somebody like a secretary, you know, someone with no college education, it would hurt him during interviews. You can't imagine how snobby those academic types are."

"Oh, I can. I'm curious. Why did you show up at his house yesterday when you did? Did someone tell you about the shooting? What caused you to come by just then?"

"I just had this bad feeling, you know? He'd come by my apartment earlier. He was, like, all shook up or something. I said to him, 'Doctor Fiske—'"

"You called him Doctor? No first-name basis? I would think, off-duty and away from the office, after the years you spent working together, a Scott would be acceptable."

"Well, okay, yeah I said, 'Scott, what's the matter?' He said something about how the police came to see him. That would be one of your guys, I guess. So I asked what about, and he says he's done something and there's this phone and—"

"He said phone? Do you know what he meant by that?"

"No, I'm not real sure. I think he must have bought one of those throwaway things and was using it from time to time. He didn't tell me why. It was maybe about that, but I can't be sure. He could be a little crazy, you know? He liked having secrets. I guess the phone was one of them. I didn't think much about it after that except you guys wanted to know about it. Why did you, by the way?"

"We had reason to believe it was involved in a child harassment case."

"A child what?"

"Another time. What else did he tell you?"

"No, tell me. Child harassment. He was…?"

"Chatting up teenagers at the mall, we think. It's only an accusation as of now. You didn't know?"

Something in the woman's expression shifted—just for a split second, the tick of tick-tock, a bird flying past the sun—a brief moment of shadow, then—nothing.

"No. He did that? Well, who would have thought? So, okay, then we talked about his CV, you know, his curriculum vitae, and I said to him that I thought he was in big trouble. See, there was this woman from the Board that came asking about it and I happen to know some of the things he wrote on it he made up."

"Anything else?"

"No, only he really looked worried. I said, 'Scott, what'd you do?' because I didn't think your people would be talking to him just about a private phone. Am I right? I didn't know about any child harassment stuff then, see? That's for real? You said child harassment?"

"It's peripheral."

"Peripheral? Um, like I said, I asked him what he done…he did. And he says 'nothing.' Then he tells me he'll call me later and he left. I got to thinking about it and I started to worry. That's when I drove over to see if he was all right."

"Did he mention anybody who might be after him? You did say he was being blackmailed, I believe."

"Yeah, I did. The only thing I can think of is whoever he did something to, whatever that someone was, maybe he came after him for it."

"But you don't know who or what he did. Any guesses?"

Another flicker behind her eyes. "No."

"Can you tell me where you were Sunday night two weeks ago?"

"Me? Funny you should ask about that. I was in my apartment waiting for him, but he never showed. Like, it was a sort of anniversary thing and I had this dinner and a bottle of wine open, not cheap stuff either, and he's a no-show."

"Did he say why he missed your dinner?"

"He said something came up that he needed to do. He was sorry."

"This was the next day?"

"Yeah. Monday morning."

"How did he seem to you then?"

"He was really tired, you know, like he hadn't slept much, but at the same time he was really excited about something, too."

"But he never said what he had to do or where he went?"

"No. I didn't push it. I figured he'd tell me when he got around to it. But I did ask him if he needed his CV updated. He'd said something to me about doing that the Friday before, so I asked him again, and he said, 'That won't be necessary anymore.' I didn't know what he meant. Then when we heard about Doctor Harris' accident and, well, I wondered, you know?"

"You wondered what, Ms. Overton?"

"I don't know. Like, um…like maybe he thought his acting president job would last longer or something like that."

"He said that before you heard about the accident?"

"Did he? I don't know. Yeah, I think so. He must have heard before, right? I don't know, he didn't seem shocked at the news, so maybe he did."

"I see. Is there anything else you can tell us?"

"Not really. Am I in trouble?"

"Trouble? No, I don't think so. Thank you for coming. Mrs. Sutherlin will show you where you can write out your statement."

Sheila left and Ike watched as Essie placed her at the spare desk and set her to work.

"What do you think, Charlie?"

"Splendid performance. The naked truth mixed in with a few teeny and maybe important lies. Very adroit, is your Ms. Overton. She was genuinely shocked to hear about Fiske's trips to the mall to talk to teenaged girls. I find that curious, don't you? And, the smudges under her eyes may be the product of well applied makeup, but without an opportunity for a closer look, I can't be sure. Also, for the record, she knows very well what Fiske did, but she won't say. Now why is that, do you suppose?"

"Question for another day. Misplaced loyalty, perhaps. She all but indicted Fiske for Ruth's accident. So she and the sheriff's department seem to be in agreement on that. Which then raises the question once again, if he's the culprit, who would want him out of the way now, and why?"

"Who? Oh come on, Ike, think a minute. Who has been after the person who forced Ruth into that pole like an avenging angel for the last few weeks? You know who. You would. You are the prime suspect in the poor man's demise."

"Me?" Ike thought a moment. "I guess you're right. Lucky for me, I have an alibi for the time of the shooting or I'd be on top of my list of suspects. So, if it wasn't me, it had to be someone else, and the question remains, who killed Fiske and why?"

Charlie frowned, started to say something, then shook his head and shrugged.

FORTY-FOUR

IKE AND CHARLIE returned to Ike's fishbowl office. He cleared more space on his desk and piled all the folders and files he'd assembled over the previous three weeks in front of him. After pausing a moment, he discarded the files relating to the various political groups and the suspect names. He arranged the remaining by case and then by date. The answer, he thought, had to be hiding somewhere in that mess. Frank pulled a chair in from the outer office and sat next to Charlie. He held the notebook the ETs found in Smith's truck in his hand.

"I'm done with this, Ike. Burns is in the slammer and lawyering up. He had to use a public defender, by the way. You still want to see this?"

"I don't know—maybe later. Where's our mayor?"

"Last I heard, planning a family vacation to Florida."

"He should fit right in with the gang at Disney World."

"Anyway, you did say you wanted to look at Smith's book after we closed the Fiske case. I guess that's not necessary now."

"I guess not. And we haven't closed it yet, Frank, that's the problem. He's dead. Someone shot him. If he was the masked man we saw behind the wheel in that enhanced video, why would someone shoot him now?" Frank opened his mouth to respond. Charlie raised his hand to silence him and shook his head. "Either someone, like me, who was angry at what he did to Ruth, and took it out on him, or—"

"Or you had it backwards from the start and have to start over," Charlie finished for him.

"Exactly, but, I don't think we should go all the way back to where we started. If that line didn't work then, it won't work now."

"So where do we start, then?" Frank looked puzzled.

"With the obvious: we have not one, but three murders in Picketsville. Three murders, I should say, and an attempted murder. That makes four acts of violence in a little less than three weeks. And, unlike the killings we have had in the past in which, by and large, the victims were from out of town, these are all local. What are the odds of that happening in the first place, and then as three separate and distinct crimes?"

"Don't forget the dog," Charlie said.

"Actually, I hadn't. But I am pretty sure he doesn't figure into this scenario. The odds, as I was saying, are huge. Picketsville is not Juarez or Detroit. It is a sleepy little town in the heart of Virginia. It's not Grover's Corners either, but it's not close to being a high-crime venue. So, we take a different tack. Up to this point we have pursued the killing of Duffy and Smith separately from the attempt on Ruth, and assumed Fiske was connected to her. What if we have that backwards?"

"How's that?"

"We have several choices. First, they are not connected. Duffy died for one reason at the hands of one killer, Smith at the hands of another, neither is connected to each other or to Fiske and/or Ruth. Possible? Yes. Probable? No. What have we then?"

"I have no idea." Frank's forehead began to take on the appearance of an old-fashioned washboard.

"Second, they are connected someway and the connection is in that book of yours, Frank. Much more likely Duffy and Smith are connected. Third, all three murders, Duffy, Smith, and Fiske, and, therefore, the attempt on Ruth, are all connected. Again, possible? Yes. Probable? Well, I admit it's a stretch."

"Ignoring Fiske for the moment, how do you connect the murders of two local yokels engaged in petty larceny to an attempted murder in Washington, DC?"

"I don't know. I'm just saying. Maybe I should have a look at the book."

"You left out a fourth scenario," Charlie said.

"What's that?"

"There is the will business which we can probably discount, but one person has the same cause to be angry, maybe even murderously so, and wish to bump off Fiske, as you do. She also has motive, means, and opportunity, and she listens."

"Who? You don't mean…"

"Eden Saint Clare."

"No, I'm not going to go there again, Charlie. I concede that on paper it's a remote possibility, an extremely remote possibility, but I'm not willing to even consider it now, thank you. So where are we? We need something to link murder number one to number two, one and two to Washington, and so on. Frank, take us from the beginning. Start on Sunday."

"Sunday? Well, the attempt was made on Ruth that night and—"

"No, wait. Go back. Monday morning, or was it afternoon? It doesn't matter. When I called you, you said two things happened Sunday night or thereabouts. A ruckus at the Roadhouse and a truck was reported missing and then not missing. Have I got that right?"

"Yeah, but I don't see what—"

"I don't either but we need to put down everything. So Roadhouse—not likely, and a truck reported out of place. Jesus, the truck. Frank, tell me about the truck."

"What's to tell? In addition to being used to steal hay, which probably explains why it ended up in the wrong place that morning, we know it belongs to Callend. They use it for general hauling, trash, leaves, deliveries, and so on. In the winter they attach a...oh my God."

"They attach a snowplow. The bumper of that truck has been modified to accept the low-blade snowplow the school occasionally needs to clear its parking lots and driveway. How much do you want to bet they also painted that bumper with black Rustoleum after they made the modifications?"

"It was black all right, and scratched up a bit. So you think Fiske took the truck to DC and waited for Ruth? But how would he know when and where to find her?"

"Ruth received a call that evening. She didn't tell me who called or why. It was not like her, but she didn't. I assumed it had something to do with me and she preferred not to say anything just then. We know from the ME's report," Ike shuffled through the stack of papers on the desk and pulled up a sheet, "that Fiske owned the phone or at least had it on him when he died. If the surveillance tapes from the drugstore are to be believed, Fiske bought the phone and had it in his possession that Sunday night. He calls, tells Ruth something she can't repeat to me, and arranges to meet her at a specific place and time."

"He waits, sees the car and his opportunity, whacks the car, and hightails it back to Picketsville. In his excitement, he parks it in the wrong place. But why a truck?"

"He needed something that had three things going for it. It was big and heavy. It was available, and it would be the last thing a suspicious mind would think was following him, or in this case, her."

"So you are back to Fiske. Fine, and that connects to your other two murders, how?" Charlie said.

"I don't know, do you, Ike?"

Essie stepped into the office and dropped the ME's reports on Ike's desk. He glanced at them, started to put them aside, and then looked more closely.

"Well, this is interesting. Ballistics shows that the automatic found at Fiske's house is the gun used to shoot Smith."

"We're getting somewhere—Fiske killed Smith."

"Not yet. All it says is the gun was the one used. You are assuming Fiske fired it. But, it's been wiped and then one set of very iffy prints were found on it." He read further. "Fiske's. No other prints."

"So, it could have been a dead hand and drop."

"Could have. Or not. Let's see how it fits first. Try this: our hay heisters have been using the truck for a month or so. Duffy goes to collect it that Sunday night and it's gone. 'What's this?' he says, and calls Smith to see if, by any chance, he's beat him to it. He hasn't. Duffy is interested in who else is moonlighting with the school's equipment and periodically checks to see when and by whom it is returned. He sees our guy. He thinks that's interesting. He wonders if he can stiff the guy for a few bucks by threatening to report him for unauthorized use of school property. He doesn't know that the stakes are considerably higher and he discovers that fact only after he's conked on the head and killed."

"Very neat," Charlie cut in. "But you still have to weave in Smith, and even when you do that, you still have a very dead Fiske to explain away."

"I know, I know. You don't have to remind me. If Smith went with Duffy, they'd both be killed at the same time. If he didn't, what put him in harm's way?"

"Do we start over?" Frank looked weary. He placed the notebook on the desk. "I need a break. Anyone?" Ike waved him off. Charlie shook his head. Frank left and rummaged through the drawer of the credenza holding the coffee urn. "Essie, what happened to all the tea bags?"

Essie looked up from her crossword puzzle. "Amos Wickwire used them all up. I told him we would bill his department, but he only gave me a dirty look. Drink coffee."

"I hate coffee."

Ike picked up the reports again.

"They found a .45 shell casing in the woods near Smith's body with a thumbprint on it."

"Fiske's?"

"No, not his. That doesn't any make sense. Maybe it's from another time and…no, what are the chances? I mean, how many .45's are discharged in the woods right where we find a body? Something is screwy here. Someone else had the gun first."

Charlie scratched his chin. "Which begs the question, does it not? Was the gun found in the house the one that shot Smith? Yes it was. So then, did the gun actually belong to Fiske? Maybe not. We have doubts, yes? And finally, maybe it was his, but someone else loaded it. That opens another door. Do you want to go through it?"

"Later if I have to. There are antecedent things to be considered. Too damn many things to be exact. Let me see that notebook."

Ike retrieved the book and slowly leafed through it. He paused once and then began again at the first page. "I didn't make Smith out as much of an organized man, and I don't think he would keep records like these. This must have been Duffy's book."

"That was my thought, too." Frank had perked up.

"If so, when Duffy didn't score his big hit, but ended up suffocated in a school vehicle instead, Smith must have wondered. He found the book and, as unlikely as it seems, he figured it out as well. Then he went for the score himself and ended up the same as Duffy, only shot, not asphyxiated. The gun suggests it was Fiske whom he met."

Charlie tilted back in his chair and closed his eyes. "Smith and Duffy notwithstanding, the real question is, as I have said repeatedly, who killed Fiske? If you don't unravel that one, you have nothing."

Ike nodded and sifted through the contents of the notebook. He removed the newspaper clippings and arranged them on the desk. "What are all these about?"

FORTY-FIVE

FRANK LEANED OVER Ike's shoulder. He sorted the clippings by date and then pointed at each in return.

"The older ones are articles about Smith or Duffy, mostly Duffy, their arrests, a softball game in which one or the other played, and so on. And there's this old coupon for a discount on an oil change."

"An oil change coupon? Why would he keep that? It's lapsed."

"Probably forgot about it. My mother has a drawer in the kitchen overflowing with lapsed coupons. Ask any coupon clipper and they will tell you the great drawback with coupons is they lapse at different times, and unless you are super organized and cross-reference them by type and date, you will, on any given day, have many more useless coupons than good ones."

"Am I hearing the voice of experience?" Ike picked it up and frowned. He tossed it back on the desk and it fluttered and turned over, revealing its reverse side. "Wait. It's not the coupon. This is an article about Ruth and what they were calling her accident. That's odd. Why would Duffy have saved that?"

"You're sure it's not the coupon? It makes more sense, given Duffy is doing the clipping."

"No. I'm not sure. But, let me think a minute." Ike picked up the clipping again and read it. It wasn't easy, but he did. At the bottom, he saw an awkwardly written series of numbers. "What's this?"

"Numbers. A date?"

"No, can't be. Too many digits. There are ten in a row. Dates have a minimum of four and a maximum of eight. What has ten?"

"A phone number?"

"Exactly. So, whose phone number did he write on the clipping and why?"

"You could call it and see who answers."

"Wouldn't do that," said Charlie. He lowered the front legs of his chair to the floor with a crash. "Look it up. If it's connected to the rest of this, and you call from here, it could spook the party at the other end."

"Essie," Ike yelled through the door, "look up this number." He read off the digits.

"Don't have to," she yelled back. "I already know whose it is."

"Who?"

"It's the Overton woman's direct line at the university. I just called her back. She left her raincoat. Why do you want to know?"

"Overton? What the hell?"

IKE INSTRUCTED ESSIE to have Sheila Overton wait in the interview room while he shuffled through the papers on his desk once again. He read, paused, and closed his eyes. His fingers drummed rhythmically. He repeated the process. Papers moved from left to right and back again. His face brightened. He walked to Grace White's bailiwick and handed her the file with the findings about the shell casing from the woods. While she manipulated her computer to log onto AFIS, he reviewed the surveillance tapes from the drugstore. Grace typed in a query to the DoD and Ike made a call to the president's house at Callend. All this took twenty minutes.

Finally, Grace handed him a sheaf of print-outs, her eyebrows forming a ragged question mark. Ike smiled his thanks and then, face set, he entered the interview room.

Sheila Overton sat exactly as she had earlier, her raincoat in her lap, and a worried look on her face. Ike laid a stack of papers on the table between them.

"I'm sorry to have to inconvenience you again, Ms. Overton, but since you were here earlier, some new information has come to light and I need to ask you a few more questions."

"Sure, what do you want to know?"

"How do you know Martin Duffy?"

"Who?"

"Duffy, Marty Duffy. He worked in the maintenance department at Callend. You must have seen him around campus."

"Gosh, I guess I might have, but I don't know. Maybe."

"I ask because your direct-line phone number appears on a slip of paper we believe he carried before he was murdered."

"He was murdered. I thought it was a suicide."

"You know about his suicide? You said you didn't know him."

"I just remembered. I mean, I work...worked for the acting president. We knew, of course."

"Of course you would. So you did know him."

"Like I said, I worked in the... He had my phone number? I don't see how. I mean, no, I didn't know him like that."

"I see. Tell me something else, then. You mentioned in your earlier statement to us that you were aware that Doctor Fiske padded his CV. Is that correct?"

"Yes."

"You also mentioned that you thought he was being blackmailed. Is that also correct?" Sheila nodded. "Is it possible that the person blackmailing Doctor Fiske was Duffy?"

"I don't know. Why would he—"

"Or Bob Smith. Might he have been the person blackmailing Doctor Fiske?"

"Who is Bob...who did you say?"

"Smith, Bob Smith."

"I have no idea. You think these men were blackmailing him over the CV business?"

"Not quite. You mentioned that Fiske said he'd done something. When I asked you what is was, you said you didn't know. But you do know, don't you?"

"No, I don't know what you mean."

"Come, come, Ms. Overton. What is it you believe Fiske did?" Sheila's lower lip began to quiver. "It's no good, we know you know. You all but told us and then you pulled back."

"I didn't want to say. He was my partner, I loved him, you know, and since he was dead I didn't think it mattered anymore."

"What did he do?"

"He said he tried to kill Ms. Harris. The reason he missed our evening together was because he was in Washington trying to make her car crash."

"We thought so, too. We were at his house to arrest him for it, did you know that?"

"Arrest him? No, how could I?"

Ike shuffled through the various reports on the table again. "He had a second cell phone. It was that phone we queried him about, and he panicked after that and came to you, is that right?"

"Yeah, I guess so. I should have told you what I knew

but I thought, well, like I said, we were more than close. We were supposed to get married, but I guess he wanted to wait until he got a president's job."

"He said that?"

"Not in so many words but, anyway, it wasn't working. God knows he tried, but no matter what we did, he never connected. I don't know why, but it never happened."

"It never happened, Ms. Overton, because he was a phony. Academics tend to be fuzzy about most things in the real world, but they know their turf. Your boy tried but never quite got it, and eventually they would have suspected something was not right. So, he was never given a shot. Probably never would be. Doctor Harris all but told him so."

"That snotty bi…. Yeah? Well, he said he was tired of all that and he decided if he knocked off President Harris, he would naturally fall into her place—worst case he'd have a couple of years as Acting to make a record and land what he wanted. I don't know, but I didn't approve, of course, naturally, but it made some sense, you know?"

"Your boyfriend had reached his position in accord with the Peter Principle—he'd attained the highest level of incompetence. It's unlikely he would ever advance from there. And it was only a matter of time before he was exposed. Indeed that process was already under way, as you know. If you hadn't been besotted, you'd have seen it. But that's neither here nor there. Someone shot him and my job is to find out who pulled the trigger."

"Who did it?"

"Indeed—who?"

FORTY-SIX

IKE SHUFFLED HIS reports again and kept Sheila Overton in the corner of his eye. Her nervousness seemed to escalate with every page he turned. She crossed and uncrossed her legs almost synchronously as each piece of paper moved from left to right. She searched her purse and then popped a stick of chewing gum in her mouth.

"You know, I am easily distracted sometimes, Ms. Overton. For reasons about which I am not proud, I generally think of a man when I'm looking for a person who has committed a crime of violence. Doctor Harris is always taking me to task about that. She says I am a male chauvinist. She's probably right about that, actually. Anyway, it makes it difficult for me in those few instances when the criminal is female, you see?"

"See what? Who do you think killed Scott?"

"In a minute, in a minute. You used the words, 'someone higher up.' What did you mean by that?"

"Umm…"

"Did you think someone like me might have killed Doctor Fiske? Perhaps you thought I found out about the phone call and put the picture together and killed him, right?"

"Well… I mean…"

"In some police departments, the chief, or in my case, the sheriff, sits in an office and directs traffic, so to speak. He could slip out, knock off someone like your friend, return, and who would suspect him, right?"

"I'm sorry, I didn't mean anything, but I guessed you'd be pretty angry and all, and it seemed like it could have been you or one of her friends."

"No, no, Sheila, this won't do. You've drifted away from your story. You told us that he intimated there were 'higher ups,' not you."

"I...did I? I meant the other."

"Did you? I have problems with how this plays out. Maybe you can help me. You've had some experience in these matters, correct?"

"Me? Experience? I don't know what that would be."

"No? You said you helped Fiske rework his CV. At some point he decided he needed a mention of military service. But he had none, and I'm guessing he didn't even know where to begin, so you supplied it for him, right?"

"Well, I might have said something."

Ike slid some sheets of paper from the stack in front of him. "I have here a list of all the people in the Military Police battalion your ex-boss claimed to have served in and guess what? His name is not here, not as Scott Fiske, not as Frank Scott, the name he was born with, but I did find a Sheila Phillips. That would be you, wouldn't it? Or it was before you were married to Staff Sergeant Nelson Overton."

"Yeah, okay, yeah, that's me. My husband died, you know. So, okay, I was just trying to help him out."

"You were stationed briefly in Iraq, I gather, both you and your husband."

"How'd you know about that?"

"Come on, Sheila, I'm a cop. We're both cops, or you were. It's what we do, right?"

"Yeah, I guess. I don't see where this is going, though."

"Going? Maybe nowhere. You worked a desk back then, or did you do duty outside?"

"Both. I drove patrol when my name came up."

"Car?"

"You kidding? It's Iraq. Hummers and trucks. IEDs were bad enough in something big. Drive around Baghdad in a car? It'd be suicide. Still, one got my husband anyway."

"I'm sorry."

"Yeah, yeah, everybody's sorry. We go over there to clean up somebody else's mess, get blown to pieces, and back here, you're sorry. Thanks for nothing."

Ike stared at Sheila for nearly a full minute. He started to say something but Sheila cut him short.

"Do you have any idea what that was like, Sheriff? To see your friends blown up, body parts all over the road. Kids—kids shot by some rag-head fanatic. My platoon leader? He went frickin' nuts right in the mess hall. Started crying and calling for his mommy. He was sent home with a Section Eight. We thought he was the lucky one."

Ike sat back and listened. He remembered the rant he'd made to Charlie. When? Three weeks ago, about battle-traumatized veterans. Was this woman one of the war damaged? He shook his head and turned over more pages in the reports in front of him. When Sheila seemed to have calmed down he turned to her.

"I must inform you that we have a warrant to search your house. What are the chances we will find an automatic there? The ME says it should be a .25 caliber. Is that about right? Nasty little thing, wouldn't you agree? Every cop knows that small-caliber bullets have no stopping power whatsoever, but if you use something like a .22 or .25, and your aim is good, or you can shoot at close range, the bullet, because of its lack of velocity, will penetrate but not exit. Instead it will tumble and ricochet around and do all sorts of damage. Especially in a head shot, right?"

"I don't know. If you say so. Wait, you're not thinking what I think you're thinking, are you? So what if I have a gun? Lots of people have guns. There's no law that says I can't own a gun. That doesn't mean I used it."

"No there isn't, and no it doesn't. But you did, I think, and recently. Is your little gun registered, Sheila?"

"Look, I don't know what you're getting at, Sheriff, but you got no right to search through my stuff and I resent even the implication that I done… I did anything. Jesus, I lose everything, I mean everything, in Iraq, and this is what I get back?"

"Everyone suffers losses, Sheila. I have, you have. Life's tough but we learn to take it as it comes. So, our problem is maybe gun registration, a lack of an alibi, some fingerprints on shell casings, and on and on. Ballistics will determine if your little .25 is important, unless you dumped it. We did find the shell ejected from the .45 in the leaves out in the park, by the way. Too bad about that. Who'd a thought? It all just piles up and finally spills over, you know?"

"Spills over? What spills? I don't know what you are talking about, Sheriff, and I don't like where I think you're going with this. I shouldn't talk to you anymore."

"No, of course not. You wouldn't like the direction

this is taking, so let me explain. As I was saying earlier, have you ever noticed that when you fixate on an idea, it is nearly impossible to stop thinking about it? It's the same with murder investigations. How many bad guys have gotten away because a cop, for instance a cop like me, couldn't see the evidence right under his nose? I made that mistake and it cost me valuable time, and maybe resulted in an unnecessary murder or two. I'm sorry about that part. You were a cop once. You would know all about that, of course."

"I got nothing to say to you anymore. This is ridiculous."

"Really? What I'd love to know is how you managed to get the phone into Fiske's hands."

"What phone?"

"The one I told you about. The one used to make the call to Doctor Harris the night she was forced off the road. That phone."

"I don't know anything about a phone."

Ike sighed and held up the stack of reports. "Sheila, how many more of these reports do I have to read from before you tell me why you did it?"

Sheila's lips appeared as if drawn by a very sharp red pencil. Ike heaved a sigh.

"Sheila Overton, I am arresting you for the murders of Robert Smith, Martin Duffy, Scott Fiske, and the attempted murder of Ruth Harris in Washington, DC. You have the right to remain silent. Anything you say can and will be used against you in a court of law. You have the right to speak to an attorney. If you cannot afford an attorney, one will be appointed to you. Do you understand these rights as they have been read to you?"

"I didn't do it, he did."

"No, Sheila, it won't wash. Now tell me why."

Sheila stared unfocused at the wall for a minute. After her outburst earlier, Ike figured she would either break, or slip into catatonia.

"It was the phone that screwed up the deal, wasn't it? You thought it was his. That's why you went to arrest him." She plucked absently at the buttons on her blouse. "I tossed it, you know. How'd I know he was a dumpster diver? If anything, I thought one of the maintenance guys would find it." She straightened up and some life came back into her eyes. "He wrote me a note when I refused to open the door for him. I don't know why I did that, you know. I should have let him in. Maybe I could have explained and he would understand it was for him. In the note he said you'd connected him to the phone. I didn't even know he had it, for God's sake. He wasn't stupid. I guessed it would only be a matter of time before he figured out the rest and then he'd drop me like a hot potato."

"Maybe. That would depend on his part in this."

"He didn't know anything. He talked all the time about getting ahead, about how he came from a bad background, and that's why him and his kind never got the breaks. I could, like, you know, identify with that. We are the people who're asked to do the scummy jobs, to put our lives on the line, while the stay-at-home Ivy League hotshots get all the goodies. That afternoon when he came over after you guys hit him up about the phone, I wanted to tell him I loved him. I would do anything for him, even if the Board found out about his CV. You do know what I mean about doing anything? We were in it together—us against them others. We were the little guys, the ones who get shoved around, and sent to fight wars for fat cats and Halliburton, and have their loved ones splattered all over some god-awful road in some desert a zillion miles away."

Ike tensed in his chair, watching her eyes and trying to guess which way she would jump. She sat with the palms of her hands flat on the table, leaning toward him, her eyes flashing in anger. Real anger, Ike realized. After a moment, she slumped back in her chair, defeated.

"You know what he said to me later when I went to his house and told him how I felt and what I was willing to do?" Sheila's eyes began to tear up. "Honest to God, Sheriff, he said 'That's nice.' Do you believe that? That's nice? I kill for him to make his damn dreams come true, and it's nice? So, it turns out he was just like all the rest. All show and no go. He didn't care."

She sobbed, blew her nose, collected herself, and straightened up, suddenly calm. "So, I say to myself, 'Okay, Mr. That's Nice, you take me or you take nobody.' I mean, after all that, what else was I supposed to do?"

FORTY-SEVEN

CHARLIE WATCHED AS Frank booked Sheila and escorted her to a holding cell.

"Your case is pretty circumstantial don't you think, Ike? Are you going to be able to convince the county attorney to prosecute?"

"It's tight even if she hadn't semi-confessed, Charlie."

"Semi-confessed, what's that mean?"

"She admitted to it, that's what I mean. I don't have her statement in writing and she's lawyered up now, so now I won't get it. That's why its semi."

"Then how do you put it together? Pretend I'm her lawyer. Irrespective of what she said to you, you can't use it in court if she denies ever saying it. She was upset, didn't understand, under emotional stress, lost her friend in a brutal murder, blah, blah, blah. You only suppose, Sheriff, that she set the thing up, and you assume she pulled the trigger. On what grounds? She knew about the killing and didn't say anything? So what? Obstruction of justice, maybe, but... A good lawyer will have a field day. The fact she did a stint as an MP won't buy you much, either. On the contrary, if she saw combat, he'll use it against you, probably."

"Okay. You know what your problem is, Charlie? You are in the spy game. You look at things differently than I do. If I hadn't let my concern for Ruth and my initial anger at what I thought caused her crash get to me early on, I'd have had this thing nailed down tight weeks ago."

"But you didn't."

"No I didn't and that turned out to be a tragic error—at least for Fiske. When I finally stepped back, things began to fall into place. As for the circumstantial bit, I had Grace run the surveillance tapes from the drugstore again. Overton is clearly visible on a different camera as she enters the store with Fiske. I called Eden and she confirmed it and also, that she was wearing a hoodie and sunglasses. Eden thought it odd at the time because it was a cloudy day. Overton became separated from Fiske because Eden, as is her wont, locked in on, as Agnes aptly described him, the willowy Doctor Fiske. Overton bought the phone and Overton made the call to Ruth."

"You're sure?"

"Yep. I will check, but yeah, she made the call. Overton made one serious mistake and a couple of little ones. The problem with automatics, if you are in the business of murdering people, is they eject shells all over the place. You have to pick them up and get rid of them and that takes time, assuming you can find them, and also, that you have the time to do it. But it's something you must do because, unless you have been careful when you loaded the clip, your fingerprints will be on the casings and, furthermore, ballistics experts can sometimes match casings to firing pins. The normal drill is to shove each bullet into the clip with your thumb. If you are not sure you will have time to police your brass after you've shot someone, you will need to use an autoloader or you must wear gloves. Also, people forget that when they clean a weapon, they have to disassemble it, and that means the parts inside the gun proper can also be a repository of fingerprints."

"So you found her prints in the forty-five?"

"Not yet, but now that we know it was originally hers, we know what to look for. She, being ex-MP, would know all about that, so she may have wiped the inside and the remaining shells in the clip."

"So what was the big mistake?"

"In a minute, indulge me. Her next mistake was having Fiske find the phone. Actually that was more in the line of bad luck. If she had dumped it right away, in DC, we might never have picked up on him. Very foolish of her. She tried to be too tricky and it came back to bite her. The wrong guy, Fiske, found the thing."

"And you're sure she didn't want him to?"

"Not consciously, perhaps subconsciously, who knows? Give that question to a shrink. The big mistake was leaving the .45 behind. She did it to implicate Fiske in the killing of Smith, but it was over the top and badly executed. She didn't need to do that."

"Anything else?"

"Yes. When she shot Smith in the woods, the shell ejected from the .45 into the leaves. She couldn't find it and short of setting the woods on fire, never would. She hoped no one else would either. Also, at the time, she didn't realize she'd be giving up the gun later to implicate Fiske. I asked the ETs to rake the leaves. Actually they used a leaf blower and they found the shell, a little wet but not wiped."

"The report said it had a thumbprint."

"It did, and Grace went into the DoD's fingerprint

file and found a match for Sheila Phillips, her name before she married when she was in the MPs."

"Why, Ike? Why did that mousey little woman do it?"

"Who knows? Poor woman, I think she really believed he would be pleased that she set him up to succeed Ruth. You remember my barking at you about the concussed and damaged men and women returning from the deserts and mountains?"

"The ones with PTSD? Vividly. She was one of them?"

"I think so, maybe. Her husband was blown up in Iraq. She returns, drops out of the service, and ends up with Fiske. God only knows how. She fixates on him and wants to please him the way my imagined vet did with a political cause. Hers was not political but clearly as deeply seated. When she realized he did not see her as a lover, wife, partner, or anything significant beyond a compliant and willing secretary, her world came crashing down around her ears. She realized if he discovered what she'd done, he would undoubtedly throw her under the bus. My God, but that had to hurt. So, a woman scorned, and all that—although I'm thinking he had no idea he'd done it. The guy was too self-absorbed.

"She followed him home, came in the back way, which probably symbolized their relationship better than anything. She slips in, wants to have it out at the dining room table. They talk, she doesn't hear what she needs to hear, snaps, and pops him with a different gun. Billy is searching for it even as we speak."

"Premeditated then?"

"Yes and no. I don't think she was thinking rationally. She just went into combat armed."

"I guess that's a wrap, then, and you were right about the PTSD."

"Not quite. Right church, wrong pew."

Charlie stood and walked to the door. "I must remember to be nicer to my secretary in the future. Time for an early dinner?"

"But not too much nicer, Charlie. You turn that society charm on her and she might kill for you."

"You think?"

"Actually, no, and dinner will have to wait. Right now I need to go to the hospital and play one grunt for yes, two for no with Ruth to confirm that Overton made the call that night. Then it'll be a wrap."

FORTY-EIGHT

As USUAL, Ike hesitated outside the entrance to Ruth's cubicle. He needed a moment to get his emotions under control and slow his heart rate. He never knew if Ruth would be better, worse, or remain the same. Only the first option gave him any hope or peace of mind. If he were a praying man, he'd have been at it daily. As it was, he'd had a few conversations with the God he remembered having been introduced to by his mother as a child. The outcome of those chats had so far seemed inconclusive, but he kept the door open, just in case. He took a deep breath, cleared his throat, and entered.

"I must say, you are looking pretty perky this evening, Ruth. The nurses are all smiles. In fact, they look like teenagers at a slumber party telling secrets, like they know something I should know. Do they? Yes? No? Look, I have to ask you some questions. I think you can make a sound, so if you can, give me one for yes and two for no, okay?"

"Nnngh."

"Good. You can. I thought so, but dared not try before. Okay, the call you received that night was to meet Scott Fiske at a time and place specified, right?"

"Nnngh."

"It wasn't Fiske who called, was it?"

"Nnngh, nnngh."

"The caller was Sheila Overton?"

"Nnngh."

"Great. That locks it up. You may have to testify. I don't know if grunts will be acceptable as evidence, but the DA will find a way to get them in front of a jury somehow. But surely you'll be up and around by then. Turns out Overton was the one who stole the truck and smacked you. She also bumped off two other guys. One must have seen her return the truck, then read about what happened to you, added it up, and tried to blackmail her. The second guy must have tried it, too. You alert enough to follow this?"

"Nnngh."

"Great. It came as a terrible shock to her when she realized that handsome, shallow Scott Fiske was not interested in her, was not going to marry her, did not even appreciate all the things she'd done. Imagine sacrificing everything for someone on whom you doted and have it amount to zilch? Anyway, when it appeared her notions of their relationship went away like snow in Phoenix, and he would inevitably dump her, she flipped. She had a busy couple of weeks. The upshot is, you are out an acting president. Sorry about that, but we're finally finished."

The voice was weak and raspy, and sounded more like someone gargling than speaking, and just barely recognizable.

"So, wha took you s'long to ask me queshions, Sher...lock?"

"You can talk? You're awake?"

"Course can. Look, no tubes in, and, yay, no tubes out! Also no beeping, burbling, or drip...ping. Doc Pa... tel sez th'ortho...peed doc give me a walk'n cass next week."

"That's great."

"Yes, v'been ly'ng here try to com...comu...talk you

for long… Time not same in your head as out. N'all you do is read me dumb story about a dopey woman and cat."

"How long have you…? Wait a minute, what's up with all the grunting just now?"

"Gedding bak a you for playing accordion, Bus…ter."

"I could kiss you."

"Brush my teef firs'. Morning mouf for three weegs s'murder."

"Can you hear yourself?"

"Wha?"

"You are in no position to leave, Sweetie."

"M' too…n' gonna. Ged dressed." Ruth held out her hand. "Hand up."

Ike took it and eased her to a sitting position. She gasped.

"You just turned whiter than the linens on the bed. Take it easy there, Wonder Woman. You've been sliced and diced and non compos mentis for a long time."

"Woof. Guess need rest minute." She lay back again.

"More than a minute, I think. You don't wake up from a three-week nap and major surgery and bounce out of bed like a gymnast."

"I'm plenty compos menes…not bounzing…try get up 'gain."

"You can, and then what? Ride your Harley to work tomorrow?"

"I don't have a Harvey. You c'n buy me one for birth…day?"

"You're lucky you're alive to have one—a birthday, I mean. And no, I will not buy you a motorcycle. How about something nice from the Scooter Store instead?"

"No. Check outta here now, Ike. Go the A-frame and you be… Nurse Jane Fuzzy Wuz 'n bring apple dum…lings."

"Not going to happen, Ruth. Tell you what. I have an election in a week. Not the big deal it almost was since Jack Burns is now in the pokey and hopefully will stay there for something like five to fifteen years. So, it appears I'm running unopposed. Abe is happy as a clam. The mayor is reconsidering his position on campaign financing while taking in the sun and fun in Orlando with his kids, and I have got a lock on reelection. So, you behave, play nice with the folks from physical therapy, and when that's done, and if Patel says so, we'll go to the A-frame for a week or two. R and R for you, and post-election decompression for me, okay?"

"Don' nee it."

"You do. You're going to need it because, after that, when you get back on the job, you will have an administration in chaos, the university's reputation in the toilet, a new vice president to hire, not to mention the grief you will be taking from both your faculty and Board of Directors. Fiske getting himself shot was just the beginning of your problems, Kiddo, not an end."

"Goin' home."

"Soon, babe. Not today."

"M' fine."

"Really? Repeat after me. She sells sea shells by the seashore."

"See zells she gels byda zee shhh…or."

"My point, exactly."

"Not important. Doctor gave me painkillers, s'all. Makes me wobbly."

"Among other things, and that tells you what, exactly?"

"I'm fine. Need to go home."

"You need time to recover, Ruth. You need to build your strength up. You need to be on the top of your game when you hit the streets again. You'll be sprung from this joint just as soon as Doctor Patel says it's okay. Maybe next week, two at the most."

"But… Look, the doc gave me crutches." She waved in the general direction of the door.

Ike eyeballed a pair of crutches leaning against the wall in the corner. "Good. Tomorrow some bright-eyed twenty-something will drop by and make you walk with them. You will end your day hating that person's guts. Trust me, been there, done that. P.T.s show no mercy."

"Not going home?"

"Not right away, Sweetie. Soon."

Ruth closed her eyes. For a moment, Ike thought she had gone back to sleep. Then the corners of her mouth turned up.

"Love you, Ike."

"Love you, too."

"You're my hero."

Ike smiled and patted her hand. "Thank you for that, but you aren't going to sweet talk me into taking you home today."

"Bastard."

"There you go. See, you're beginning to sound like your old self already."

* * * * *

For those who might like to read the story Ike read to Ruth about the "woman and her cat" in its entirety, I have added it here. Enjoy.

FINDING GOD IN DIGBY

IT HAD STARTED innocently enough. A week after her six-tieth birthday, Darcie Starling saw her cat, savaged by her neighbor's pit bull. The image seemed so real, she dashed into the back yard screaming at the dog's owner. He, a glass of lemonade in one hand and a tattered copy of Agatha Christie's *A Holiday for Murder* in the other, nearly fell out of his Pawley's Island hammock at her ver-bal onslaught. Cleopatra, the cat in question, watched all this with feline disinterest. Her neighbor, momentarily stunned, recovered and had some strong words for Darcie in return. Mixed in among them was the news that Jaws (the name of the pit bull in question) had spent the day at the vet's and had not yet returned. At that moment Cleopa-tra announced her presence by rubbing against Darcie's legs. Abashed and thoroughly confused, she retreated to her kitchen and poured a bowl of milk for the cat.

The following day, Cleopatra was, in fact, crushed in the jaws of Jaws, so to speak. In a déjà vu moment, the scene from the previous afternoon was played out once again. This time the neighbor, frantic at the prospect of losing his dog, apologized profusely and begged her not to call the authorities. He would make it up to her, he promised. Darcie called the police anyway. They, in turn, took a snarling, unrepentant Jaws away. Her neighbor muttered something about getting even and she guessed that was why she now sat handcuffed in the backseat of a police cruiser. But this would come much later—after the holdup and shooting at the Digby Savings and Loan.

Indeed, two and a half years would pass between those two pivotal events, years during which Darcie saw many more things about to happen. They came to pass on the day following the vision. Like the mythic Cassandra, she felt overwhelmed by omens and portents. Impending disasters robbed her of her sleep. Since she assumed this pernicious gift had been His, she prayed to her God to take it away. She'd been raised a low church Episcopalian and the God that made his home there did not, as a rule, respond to petitions. He, Darcie had been taught at an early age, remained an aloof but distant Presence. And as for his son…well, he was rarely, if ever, mentioned except when featured in the Sunday readings. For the most part, the Almighty was simply referred to as "the Lord." Darcie always imagined the name set in bold face, capital letters—THE LORD— and given the respect the title carried. No other demands were made on Him…or his. In this, she discovered, churches on her side of town were in general agreement.

Darcie's butcher's daughter, on the other hand, attended the First Assembly of God Church out on the highway. She declared that God answered prayers all the time and recounted in great detail instances when divine intervention had, in fact, saved one or more of her friends. Given the vagueness of theological thought that permeated the churches near her, and the insistence by most of her caste that religion was to be a private, that is to say, an unspoken matter, she was led to wonder if her God would mind very much if she were to drop in on the one at the Assembly of God Church and do her praying over there. She really did not want this awful gift and would try anything, even a visit to the Holy Rollers, which is how she thought of the butcher's daughter's place of worship. She finally decided against it.

She had strayed from the correct, that is to say Episcopalian God, once before with disastrous results. When she was sixteen she desperately wanted to be asked to the junior prom by Erik Fosom. Her friend, Bridget O'Reilly, persuaded Darcie to accompany her one evening to the Irish Catholic Church, Our Lady of Perpetual...something. There, immersed in the mixed scents of incense and hot candle wax, they prayed to God's Mother to intervene on Darcie's behalf. The next afternoon Erik slipped from a wagon filled with freshly cut alfalfa and caught his leg in a silage chopper. Naturally, the invitation to the prom never arrived. Bridget insisted it had something to do with the fact that Erik was a Lutheran and you know how God's Mother felt about them. Darcie thought, but never said, that going around God's back and praying to his Mother had probably provoked him into reverting to his Old Testament self. Either way she could never look Erik Fosom in the eye after that. She felt certain her indiscretion with the Irish deity had cost him his leg.

So, in the present instance, even though Christmas did involve God's Mother somewhat more than usual, she decided the risk was too great and resigned herself to five minutes daily on her knees discussing her problem with the God of her upbringing who, she sensed, had no more interest in it than Cleopatra who had, by that time, succumbed to her terrible fate, but who would readily have made some sort of feline petition had she been able.

IT WAS A SHOCK, certainly, that the police would call in such a manner. The front door slammed against the wall, bounced, shuddered, and slapped shut again. Darcie, mouth agape, stood as her father's picture wobbled on its hook in the foyer, seemed to hesitate, unsure if it should, and then plummeted to the floor with a crash, scattering glass shards across the floor. Seconds later, the Digby police, search warrant in hand, pushed their way in, this time more gently, and proceeded to search her house. Ransack would be a more accurate description of what they were about. Clumsy and heavy footed, they tipped over her Christmas tree, the almost new artificial one which she'd bought at the Goodwill Store. Drawers, cabinets and her purse were unceremoniously dumped.

Her beautiful faux alligator luggage, a high school graduation present, lay on the floor; lids flopped back like filleted fish. She'd only used the set once forty-five years before when she went east to college. The huge state university campus and its masses of students so intimidated her that, except for trips to the bathroom and to purchase peanut butter crackers and soda pop from machines, she refused to leave her room. She never registered, never unpacked. Several visits from the Dean of Students and a Health Service nurse could not move her. Mercifully, at the end of the fifth day of her holdout, her father called her home to care for her critically ill mother. And when that good woman died, Darcie stayed on as her father's housekeeper and hostess, not that the Regional Superintendent of Schools required much in the way of the latter.

For over an hour the police traipsed though her house like a herd of errant hippopotami, crushing fallen

Christmas decorations under foot, knocking over lamps, and displacing furniture. They ground the delicate ornaments into the carpet and left footprints of brightly colored crushed glass in the foyer. They dumped her dresser drawers. Her face turned bright crimson when a grinning, gap-toothed cop pawed through her underwear. And as if that weren't enough, protests ignored, she was arrested, handcuffed, and stuffed into the backseat of a police car.

The ride downtown through the slush and gaudy Christmas lights seemed interminable. Cheery versions of Rudolph the Red-Nosed Reindeer racketed along the route as the cruiser splashed to the police station. Her mood did not match their happy cadence. Handcuffs pinioned her hands behind her back. Their sharp steel edges cut into her flesh. No one spoke to her, no one answered her questions, and the heater didn't work. Finally overwhelmed by frustration and discomfort, she began to cry. Not sobs. She had been schooled as a small child to never lower herself to expressing base emotions. But in the rear seat of that icy Crown Victoria, tears streamed down her cheeks as she choked back the howl that sat poised somewhere just behind those two lumpy things in the back of her throat.

When the cop in the front seat Mirandized her and she heard the word lawyer, she settled down. She didn't know any lawyers. The church seemed full of them but she made a point of ignoring them, politely of course, as a matter of principle. Her late father had a low opinion of any profession that would knowingly protect a guilty man. However, she did know Judge Horace Graybill. She remembered that prisoners were allowed to make one phone call. She knew the judge's phone number and she knew he could straighten out this mess in a heartbeat.

She started to feel better.

JUDGE HORACE GRAYBILL had the voice of an Old Testament prophet. When he spoke, people, even those merely within earshot, fell silent and listened. His critics, primarily those in the legal profession and who had to try cases before him, said that voice notwithstanding, most of what proceeded from his mouth made little or no sense. The County Bar Association routinely reported to the Governor the all too frequent instances when the judge's rulings were reversed on appeal. Nevertheless, he had a constituency which regularly reelected him, and the judge remained sublimely indifferent to his record. In his view, one he expressed often to his cronies at the Digby Country Club, the Court of Appeals had been stacked with liberals by President Carter and what else could you expect. The fact that Jimmy Carter had been out of office for decades and the court in question had one or two sitting judges on it who were not even born when he left office did not dissuade him from that view.

"So what's all this fuss and feathers about, Dorothy?" He insisted on using her real name. Darcie was a corruption of Dorothy and a name she'd bestowed on herself at age two when she had attempted to pronounce Dorothy. Almost nobody called her anything but Darcie. But the judge, being of a formal disposition and accustomed to having correct nomenclature used in his court, insisted on Dorothy.

Once, she had changed her name. About the time she had her fixation on the not as yet one-legged Eric

Fosom, she started signing her name D'Arcy. She thought it had a romantic French look to it. She reverted to Darcie after the incident with the silage chopper and never used that spelling again.

"I have no idea, Judge," she said. "These people seem to think I had something to do with a shooting this morning and they arrested me."

"Nonsense. Pure hoo-haw if you ask me. Wait here."

Since she'd been put in a jail cell, they'd called it, she was not going anywhere. Had it been a weekend, she might have had to share the space with any number of felons and miscreants but luckily, it was late Monday morning and, except for her, the cell was empty. She slumped back on the narrow cot and tried to think. Her attempts at cognition were disrupted by the extreme lumpiness of the mattress and the stench it emitted. She stood and moved forward and tried to see into the corridor. Nothing. She heard singing off to her right, mournful, Negro singing. African-American had not made it into her lexicon and as far as she was concerned, it never would. All nonsense, stirring people up against one another. Amy, her black nanny, had looked after her as a child and into puberty. There was never any problem with saying Negro to her. Not the other "N" word, of course. The Starlings were not bigots, everybody knew that. And Amy said so, too. Darcie could not remember Amy's last name. She wondered if she ever knew it—not that it made any difference. Amy was like one of the family and that was all there was to that, thank you very much.

She paced the cell, measuring its length and width, and tried to ignore its pervading aroma of urine and Lysol. Horace Graybill reappeared.

"All hoo-haw, Dorothy," he repeated, "but I can't get any help here. They say they have a witness who's on his way down here to ID you. And because I've known your family since forever, they recused me. What's all this about a witness?"

"My neighbor. He has it in for me. I had his dog arrested for murder and he never forgave me."

"Well, I'll find you an attorney. In the meantime you just sit tight. You have money for a lawyer, Dorothy?"

"Umm… I can probably find some."

In truth, Darcie was as poor as a church mouse. When her father died, he left sums for her support. He had no concept of inflation and believed that with a Republican administration firmly in charge of the nation's economy, he'd set enough aside to last her lifetime. The bulk of his estate went to his son, who played the guitar and lived somewhere in Mendocino, California. No matter how she scrimped, the money dwindled away. The house, the only other thing she'd inherited, was mortgaged to the hilt. Darcie had no marketable skills. How she would pay a lawyer would have to come from some other quarter. She dropped to her knees and concentrated on the Holy Roller God. She would pray to him here in the holding tank and Eric Fosom, or whoever else might be at risk, would just have to take his chances.

The cell door screeched open and a large black woman staggered into the cell.

"In you go, Dolores," a guard said, and slammed the door closed. The woman collapsed on the cot.

"Whoo-ee," she said. "This is not been a good day. What you doing on your knees, Lady?"

"Praying, or I was about to when you came in."

"Well, don't let me stop you. Lord always have time to listen to a sinner."

"It wasn't like that—I mean about the sinning. I wanted him to take something back."

"Take somethin' back. Somthin' that he give you and you don't want no more? Maybe he give it to me instead. Can't have too many blessings, no sir."

"You wouldn't want it."

"Depends on what it is. How about you let me decide?"

"No, you don't understand. I don't think it's transferable. It's the gift of Second Sight."

"Second Sight? You mean like you can see the future?"

"Well, sometimes, yes."

"Well, let me tell you something, Honey, that gift didn't come from no God. That's the Devil's doing. You be right wanting to shuck it."

"I've tried and my God won't take it. So I thought I'd shop around to see if somebody else's God would. What church do you attend?"

"Mount Olive Apostolic Holiness Church, but somebody else's? How many Gods you think they is?"

"Well, just one I guess…" Darcie's theology remained a little vague on that point. The doctrine of the Trinity confused her. She knew it was "One in Three" but she never could work out the details, and then there were the obvious differences in the behavior of the First Assembly God and hers.

"You guess? Girlfriend, you better be more than guessing. There ain't but one God and he the same all over."

"Well, maybe. But the God I was taught isn't in the

habit of spending time on human foolishness." There, she'd said it. The woman, Dolores, stared at her in disbelief.

"No wonder he ain't taken that devilment from you. You don't believe."

"Yes, I do." Did she? "I just thought if we were to pray to the God of the Mount Olive Apostolic um… maybe he would hear me and—"

"Listen to me, Honey, there ain't but one God. If yours seem different it's 'cause you treat him different. Like—you don't expect nothin', you don't get nothin'. That's it."

Darcie mulled over Dolores' words. She thought they made some kind of sense, but then why had the Reverend Franklin Falstoop, D. Min., down at Saint Stephen's, never said so. He, of all the people she knew, seemed absolutely committed to the Doctrine of the Distant Presence. She rocked back on her heels to think. Things had become very confusing since this gift business had started. She wondered how much Dolores, who smelled suspiciously of strong drink, really knew.

"Why are you in here?" she asked.

Dolores rolled over on her side and hiccupped. "D.U.I. and ve-hic-u-lar homicide. What about you, Woman? You a axe murderer or something? You look like that Lizzy Borden I seen on the TV."

"They think I had something to do with a shooting and robbery on the other side of town."

"I knew it. What other side? Oh, you mean like my side, where you rich white folk don't never come."

In fact, for Darcie and the gentle folk she associated with, the other side meant across the Norfolk and Southern railroad tracks, but she didn't say so.

"I'm not rich," she said, instead. "What's vehicular homicide?"

"I done run over somebody. The only reason I'm in here is because I had me a wine or two at Jasper's 'fore I drove home. Then this guy busts out of a alley and step right in front of me. Wham! He's flying like Superman."

"He was drunk?"

"Liquidated. So after a hearing tomorrow, when I'm for sure sober, they'll turn me loose and that's that. Dolores Cathcart be free to go home and figure out how she going to pay the back-rent and keep the Gas and Electric from shutting off her heat. Yes, Lord, big day tomorrow. If my old momma see me now, she drop a calf."

Cathcart? Why did Darcie think she knew that name?

Dolores turned her bloodshot eyes on Darcie. "So why don't you just tell me my fortune while you still got the gift. Then we'll pray it away."

Darcie shook her head. "It's not that way. I mean I don't ask for the visions, they just come."

"You can't see nothing except what come to you?"

"Yeeesss…" Darcie felt one coming. "Oh my," she said. "If we pray right now, I think it will go away. Here, get down on your knees and pray with me. I need the God of the Mount Olive Apostolic Whatever church right now."

"I ain't getting off this bed to pray for nobody."

"Will you if I ask for a vision about you?"

"You said it don't work that way."

"I said it never has, but then I never tried."

Dolores Cathcart rolled off the cot and stood next to Darcie, who had rocked forward on her knees again. She placed her hand on Darcie's shoulder and after a brief pause bellowed, "Almighty Father God…have mercy on this here miserable sinner." Darcie winced. She did not like to think of herself as a sinner, miserable or otherwise.

"She's burdened, Lord. Yes, burdened, burdened, burdened with the Devil's own works. Alleluia and Amen." Darcie did not accept the notion the gift did not come from God and she wondered if he'd be annoyed by Dolores saying otherwise. She certainly did not want to get on his bad side again.

"Yes, Lord, and she needs that burden taken away! Amen and thank you, Jesus."

In the silence that followed, Darcie felt a warm glow that started at the point where Dolores' hand pressed on her shoulder. It spread across her shoulders and down her back. At that moment she received the vision. She did not know why, but she knew it would be her last. She knew, too, that she must pay very close attention to it.

"Oh!" she said.

"S'up?"

"Dolores Cathcart," Darcie intoned.

"Yeah, that's me."

"I see—"

"What? What you see?"

"A package wrapped in brown paper is delivered to your house at 1347 South Main Street. Oh, you're opening the door."

"How you know my address?"

"The mailman leaves and you are in your living room. Nobody else is home."

"Yeah, yeah. What's in the package? Wait, don't tell me. This here is the Devil's work."

"No, no, this is from the God of the Mount Olive Apostolic Holiness Church."

"I thought I tol' you—"

It was at that precise moment that Darcie Starling had her epiphany. The heavens did not open, trumpets did not sound. No angel chorus sang sweet hosannas. She would not have been surprised if they had, but none did. But she finally understood and she knew.

"You're right. Yes, yes, I see now…there is just one God but He needs multiple venues and alternative messengers to do His work." She smiled. She'd found God. It was as if a great weight had been lifted from her shoulders.

"Get on with it, Woman. What about my package?"

"You are opening it. Oh my—"

"What? It's a bomb. I'm gonna die!"

"It's money. Dolores, you're going to be rich."

"Rich? Hold it right there." Dolores scowled. "Mmm, mmm, mmm. You see how it go—boney-assed white woman come in here and bullshit me. You worse than that snotty little brat my Momma took care of back all them years ago. 'You're one of the family,' they'd say, and then give her two dollars a day for ten hours work. And soon's that girl got big enough to find her behind without a map, then it was, 'Goodbye, Amy, we don't need you no more.'"

Amy Cathcart? Was that her name? Then this would be her daughter. Darcie didn't know Amy had a family.

"I am not…deceiving you. I'm never wrong about these things. Like yesterday afternoon. I saw the robbery and shooting that happened this very morning, at dawn, saw it all, clear as day. An armored truck parked across from the Citgo Station and a robber came up behind the guard at the truck's back door while the other one was in the Savings and Loan. The first one was knocked out with a golf club and when he fell, his gun went off and shot the other one coming out of the door. Robber grabbed four big bags of money and ran around the corner and disappeared. I don't remember a witness though. Now that's odd… Well, anyway, tomorrow you will receive some money, a lot of money."

Dolores looked doubtful. Then she smiled. "Can't make no difference either way, but I think I best send Lynel out for cigarettes around the time the mail come. He don't have to know about no money." She helped Darcie to her feet. "You all done with your seeing?"

"All done. That was the last one. Your praying worked. No more visions."

"You sure?"

"I'm sure."

The two women settled into a comfortable silence. Darcie started to mention Amy and then suspected Dolores would either be angry or embarrassed if she did, so she let it drop. Five minutes later, Judge Graybill reappeared.

"I knew it all along, all hoo-haw, Dorothy. I was just in the middle of engaging an attorney for you when the DA came downstairs and said the case is dropped. Seems like their witness, the only one who could have identified you, got drunk in one of those bars down there in Darktown and got himself run over by an equally drunk black woman."

"That would be me," Dolores said, and fixed Judge Horace Graybill with a look that dared him to wander into the area of black lifestyles, which is where he was obviously headed. He harrumphed.

"They will be here in a minute to turn you loose. I told that DA, one of those sob-sister liberal Democrats if I ever saw one, that the whole idea of you, an over-sixty spinster lady with no prospects, robbing an armored truck was ridiculous. And I was right. The witness was a drunk and…well they will be here any minute. They said they were sorry about your house."

The judge took one more look at a baleful Dolores and scurried away down the corridor.

DARCIE SURVEYED THE shambles the police had made of her home and belongings. On any other occasion, she would have been devastated. Perhaps it was the Christmas spirit or just the relief of being out of jail, but she remained calm. Nothing had been broken that could not be replaced.

It had been a near thing. Thank God for Dolores Cathcart. She stepped over a shattered glass bulb, its hook still dangling from the stem. It had been her mother's favorite. She sighed and picked her way into the kitchen. The search team had been a bit more circumspect here. Her silverware had been dumped into the sink but it appeared that what they were looking for would not be found in the kitchen.

She realized she'd eaten nothing since early morning except a bowl of Cheerios. She made a cheese sandwich and poured out the last of the milk. The wall clock whirled and clunked. She'd bought the clock at a yard sale. It was designed to look like a cat, the clock face fitted in its stomach. Its tail tick-tocked back and forth while its oversized eyeballs oscillated in the opposite direction. It reminded her of Cleopatra. The post office would close in less than an hour. She put her half-eaten sandwich aside and went down into the basement.

The police had been very thorough there. The washer

and dryer contents were scattered all over the floor. Her father's golf clubs, the kind with wooden shafts, lay like pick-up sticks in the corner. Cabinet doors hung open, their contents spilled out onto counters and piled high on an old, chipped, porcelain-topped table. She swept these items onto the floor and spread out a large square of brown wrapping paper. She walked back into the un-lighted gloom toward the front of her house. Most of the shelves there had also been cleared except the topmost. She supposed the searcher had been short of stature, or had assumed nothing of interest would be found in a collection of dusty, lidless mason jars.

She pulled over a stepstool and carefully removed the jars, revealing a shallow crawl space. Her father had kept apples and potatoes in that cool dry area. After Ernie Ducotte harvested his potatoes, he would sell Darcie a bag of culls cheap. Darcie bought them when she could and stored them up there, too. She peered in. All four bags were just as she'd left them. She dragged one out and dumped its contents on the wrapping paper.

Eighty-one neat packets each held together by a brown paper tape around its middle. She stacked them like bricks, four lengthwise, five across. She stepped back to admire the etched faces of Jackson, Grant, and Franklin. She stuffed the odd packet in her pocket. She'd need it to buy postage and then she just might stop at the Piggly Wiggly and pick up a steak. It had been a long time since she'd eaten a steak. A steak and a baked potato…and sour cream…and real butter.

She had just enough clear tape to seal the package. She added cording just to be safe. She closed her eyes and called up the vision—the last she would ever have. It was only fair. After all, Dolores' accident had made it possible. God had given her this bounty and he'd insisted she share it.

She addressed the package:

> To: Dolores Cathcart
>   1347 South Main Street.
>   Digby.

She paused, then added,

> From: the Holding Tank

Get 4 FREE REWARDS!

We'll send you 2 FREE Books plus 2 FREE Mystery Gifts.

Harlequin® Intrigue books feature heroes and heroines that confront and survive danger while finding themselves irresistibly drawn to one another.

FREE Value Over **$20**

Get 4 FREE REWARDS!

We'll send you 2 FREE Books plus 2 FREE Mystery Gifts.

Harlequin® Romantic Suspense books feature heart-racing sensuality and the promise of a sweeping romance set against the backdrop of suspense.

FREE
Value Over **$20**

Get 4 FREE REWARDS!

We'll send you 2 FREE Books plus 2 FREE Mystery Gifts.

FREE Value Over **$20**

Both the **Romance** and **Suspense** collections feature compelling novels written by many of today's best-selling authors.

READERSERVICE.COM

Manage your account online!
- Review your order history
- Manage your payments
- Update your address

> ### *We've designed the Reader Service website just for you.*

Enjoy all the features!
- Discover new series available to you, and read excerpts from any series.
- Respond to mailings and special monthly offers.
- Browse the Bonus Bucks catalog and online-only exculsives.
- Share your feedback.

Visit us at:

ReaderService.com

RS16R